A LONG DRUNK AND A BREAKFAST

A Novel

By Alan Wallach

Published by Interlaken Publishing Co.
5 Tenafly Rd. Box 106, Englewood NJ, 07631

Distributed by amazon.com
website:alanwallach.com
email:alanwallach@gmail.com

ISBN 9781703769241

Other Books By The Author
Corviglia, Murder in the Alps
The Kieran Adventure Series
(For young readers, 10 and older)
Book 1 – Kieran and the Weird Window
Book 2 – Kieran and the Visitor From Pimglammam
Book 3 – Kieran and Rajilad's Time Warp
Book 4 – Kieran and the Robots.
Kieran's Adventures (4 books in 1)
Solomon's Dozen (Adult Fiction)
Moffett's Wife
The Super
The Amerada Affair

A LONG DRUNK AND A BREAKFAST

ON TERCEIRA ISLAND

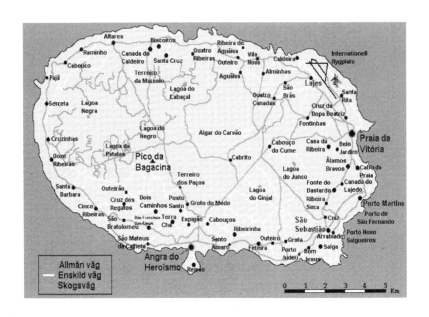

Terceira Island

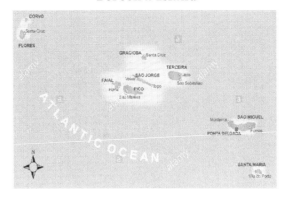

The Azores

May 1958 In The Air

The shaking of the C-118, the military version of a Douglas DC-8, in a fit of turbulence an hour after taking off, together with a loud announcement to get to your seat and fasten seat belts, awakened Captain Sam Golden with a start. He was still woozy, hung over with a terrible headache, and had been dreaming of Nervous Norvous singing *Ape Call*. The words *"A pterodactyl is a flying fool, a mellow-rooney daddy from the old school."* richochetted around his brain. He looked around and became aware gradually, and with considerable surprise, that he was in an airplane. He remembered he was supposed to be on one today, but didn't have the slightest recollection how he got there.

The last thing he remembered was going to the officers club with Marty Redstone. Angry and frustrated that he was bumped off his flight back to the U.S., he took to drowning himself in scotch. He was surprised at Fiona's sudden appearance at his door and very fuzzy about the night that followed. He racked his brain trying to remember without success anything that happened after that.

The stewardess approached him. "I see you're awake, sir . I was instructed to look after you. Can I get you some coffee? Juice?"

"Forgive my asking, where are we going?"

She eyed him with a puzzled look. "You don't know?"

"Nope. I know what I'm hoping, but I don't know."

"McGuire AFB, Captain. Is that OK? In New Jersey?"

"Thanks, couldn't be better. Yes, I would love some coffee."

"Coffee comin' right up, sir."

With the plane heading west, he could see the rising sun through the window because military passenger planes back then had their seats facing the back of the plane. Sam wondered how they got away with that. Perhaps it was safer, but the natural inclination of people was to face forward. The U.S. Air Force had a captive audience and didn't have to worry about selling tickets. Safety was the priority.

Only when he had difficulty lifting his arm to look at his watch did he realize he had a handcuff on his wrist and an attache case on the end of a chain. Added to his scotch-caused amnesia, this confused him even more. So when he saw the sheet of paper taped to the attache case, he quickly peeled it off and read the hand-written note.

Sam,

I know you were really pissed yesterday when you were bumped from your flight back to the States by a courier. We all count the days after FIGMO so I don't really blame you for tying on a big one last night. Unfortunately for you, couriers have priority over 'space-available' travelers and I was not aware that yesterday was your departure day. Otherwise I could have arranged things.

When Marty and I found you sleeping it off in your quarters – your lady friend had obviously left - I arranged to rectify the situation and guarantee you got a seat on today's early morning plane. I made you a courier. What are friends for? Marty and I loaded your semi-limp body onto the plane and checked your bags. You know, you're fucking heavier than you look. When you get to McGuire, and I hope you're awake by then, a courier officer will meet you, remove the handcuffs and give you a receipt. Then you are free to do whatever the fuck you want.

Have a good flight, my friend. Give my regards to the US of A and above all, keep us posted.

Aaron McGee, Captain USAF

Courier Officer

Sam smiled at Aaron's illegible signature. He had the FIGMO sign from his room door in his bag, The acronym for the *Fuck You I Got My Orders* tradition for short-timers with only a month left, was to put a sign on the door that had a calendar on it, crossing off the days, one at a time until 'wheels up.'

He thought about Marty, Jens, Mac, Robbie, Herm, Jeri, Father Campbell, Gordo, the major, and all the others. Jens had already returned to the U.S. to go back to graduate school. Sam and Jens made up their minds they would keep in touch. The nineteen months on the rock flashed through his mind like a fast-forward slapstick movie. They were all real friends. He had good friends at home, from high school and college but he didn't think he would elicit the kind of loyalty from friends in his future life like the ones he had made in the air force. That was the nature of the beast. To paraphrase Frost, 'You had to make friends fast and deep, with miles to fly before you sleep.' You didn't have the time to cultivate them slowly, and they became fast friends in a hurry. Since moving frequently was a military fact of life, you had no idea how long you would keep them. But while they were your friends, they could usually be trusted with intimate information and sometimes with your life.

Now he was on his way back to the States from Lajes Air Force Station on that wind-swept Terceira island in the Azores, 2,390 miles due east of McGuire Air Force Base in central New Jersey, 840 miles due west of Lisbon. One day at the beginning of his tour at Lajes, he asked a new friend, Major Emmet Robbins, whose daily 10:00 a.m. coffee break, he discovered, was really a daily alcoholic nip (or more) with navy Commander Ian Forester, how he managed to endure being without his wife for a year and a half, the normal tour of duty at Lajes.

Robbie laughed, took a swig of his Jack Daniels on ice, then a puff on a filtered cigarette he always kept bitten between his teeth and replied, "Sam, I know I have the option of extending my tour and bringing my wife here. But as you get to know this island, you will understand why I prefer to keep my stay here at Lajes as short as possible. I think of it as a long drunk and a breakfast and then it's time to go home." Sam thought about the wisdom of that and wondered if he were married whether he would have done the same thing or if he was ever capable of an eighteen month drunk. He had then only just arrived, but already he couldn't wait to get off the island.

Sam was a weatherman and even though he had an advanced degree in meteorology, he still considered himself a weatherman, a less pretentious and more realistic title. His new orders reassigned him to McChord, a base in northern California and he was looking forward to it anxiously. As a weatherman, he had an opportunity to travel to the far east to familiarize himself with the military plane routes. His woozy thoughts were interrupted by the stewardess again, and although he knew many of them, this one he didn't recognize.

"Here's your coffee, sir. The two officers who loaded you, or should I say unloaded you," she stifled a laugh, "into your seat asked me to take care of you."

"I appreciate that. How long to McGuire?"

"About four hours, sir, if the headwinds aren't too bad."

"And if they are?" as a weatherman, he didn't have to ask the question.

She responded with a shrug. "It'll take a little longer"

Sam laughed. "Thanks."

His thoughts turned to Fiona, a stewardess from Charleston Air Force Base with whom he had an off and on heavy relationship. Or so he thought. It developed because Lajes is a busy and lonely place for a single guy and she flew through Lajes every couple of weeks. After several months of sporadic dates, their relationship built up to a serious level. But she did some things that gave the relationship wide swings and to finish things, she had been injured on a trip to Rio. The result was that he hadn't seen her or heard from her for several months. She had evidently and deliberately made no attempt to contact him.

Meanwhile much had happened to Sam during her absence. There were other emotional attachments and circumstances that occupied the time and their serious relationship became a memory. She had suddenly turned up unannounced at his door the night right before he was supposed to leave. He was surprised and even cordial, until she told him she had been seriously dating someone at Charleston which was now over. That got him miffed and when she said she wanted to rekindle their relationship, Sam expressed no interest. Still, it didn't stop them from spending a night together that he hardly remembered. He used his drunkenness to excuse his weakness. She, on the other hand gave him the impression that she was using sex to get him re-interested in a relationship. He wondered then if he had misread her.

Somehow, despite the feelings for her before she got hurt, he had the strong sense even then, that he would never see her again. His unreasonable anger at being bumped from his flight contributed to the worst drunk he ever subjected himself to and now he was paying the price with a terrible hangover.

The whole situation, in retrospect, didn't really surprise him. As close as he and Fiona had become, loves in the military, like friends, were also fast, heavy and gone. But not all of them, he hoped. The more recent ones meant much more to him and he sensed they would stay with him.

The stewardess interrupted his thoughts again, asking him if he would like something to eat. He shook his head with a yes. It wasn't the breakfast part of Robbie's wisdom - he had eaten that on the base two days ago. He immediately slipped back into his reverie and anticipated trips to Japan, Taiwan and whatever else the far east had in it's environs.

Flying time was passing too slowly for Sam. Random thoughts were consuming the time. He thought how he had aged, maybe grown up says it better, in the short time in the air force and especially at Lajes.

The situation with Fiona reminded him of Wendy, his serious college girlfriend, with whom he was making post college plans, He realized in retrospect how premature that was when she erupted into his consciousness. The end came when she had stood him up at Cafe Figaro in the village - as Greenwich Village was known to New Yorkers - one Saturday. Her not showing up worried Sam that something happened to her until he found out she was with another guy and had stood him up. He suffered for a long time before he got over it. Almost a year later, she called to coax him into a reconciliation. As much as he had once felt for her, he could only remember the pain she caused him. With Fiona, the situation was somewhat similar except there wasn't any pain, only a little discomfort and mild anger, and that was good.

The drone of the plane's engines put Sam back to sleep and he only awoke when the pilot announced they were getting ready to land. A half hour later, leaving the parked plane, he said goodbye to the stewardess with a smile, thanked her for taking care of him, and was immediately met by a tall, wiry Lieutenant John Archibald who handed him a written order to remove and take custody of his attache case. He gave Sam a receipt to sign and gave him a copy. After the weight of the bag was removed, he rubbed his wrist and looked for the baggage claim. He had two bags, his trusty B-4 and a smaller soft duffle bag. The rest of his personal belongings and his car would come later.

Lajes AFS, 19 Months Earlier, October 1956

Sam had only been to Lajes twice before. Both were on route familiarization flights from Dover AFB in Delaware to Europe and Africa. Weathermen in the air force were supposed to know something about the routes they were making forecasts for. Truth is the flights were just boondoggles, one of the few perks for an air force weatherman. He didn't pay much attention to Lajes then because the stopover was only a couple of hours. On the first flight, he was excited and anxiously looking forward to landing at Orly Field and his first visit to Paris. The other time was a trip to Frankfurt. It hadn't occurred to him then, that he would someday wind up assigned to Lajes permanently. The one consistency was that on both previous trips and this one, the weather was miserably rainy and windy. He hardly noticed it before because the stopover was short.

This time his arrival was very different. He paid attention to everything because he knew he would be here for eighteen months and was apprehensive. He had not heard good things about Lajes. No really bad things either, but the lack of any definitive positive opinion was in itself negative. A former colleague at Dover, recently married, had just received his orders to report to Thule AFB for a one year tour. Thule, in northern Greenland, above the arctic circle was dark all winter with miserable storms, high winds, blowing snow and temperatures as low as 55 below zero. No family was allowed. He begged all the single guys in the weather group to trade tours with him, without any takers. Sam counted his assignment to Lajes a blessing.

Lieutenant Sam Golden had been prematurely promoted to captain because his coolness under pressure impressed the group commander of the base. It wasn't coolness as much as focus, something learned from lab work in college. The incident occurred one morning at about 4 a.m. i.e. 0400 at Dover AFB. The remote weather observation site called the weather station in the terminal and asked why the lights were turned off. They weren't. The entire east coast was suddenly socked in with zero visibility in ice fog, a meteorological phenomenon Sam had never encountered before. Major O'Reilly, the operations officer on duty, told him there were eight planes inbound, all low on fuel. There was no place to land that was without fog and with a runway long enough to accommodate a C-124. A C-124 was a huge four engine cargo plane, sometimes referred to as a three story shithouse, sometimes *Old Shaky*. Sam told everyone in flight operations to leave him alone, closed the door to the weather station, and in ten minutes of intense searching, he was able to locate an airfield in Pennsylvania, about twenty minutes away, that had no fog and a runway long enough. Because its altitude was 400 feet above sea level, it was not fogged in. Colonel Forman himself, whom Sam despised, recommended Sam for promotion.

In the landing pattern at Lajes, he could see the undulating ugly gray scud clouds through the rain. The winds were very strong he judged from the way the low clouds were speeding across the sky. The crosswinds made the plane crab, landing at a angle.

Descending the steps from the plane, he was glad he kept his raincoat available because the rain was blowing hard in his face. He separated himself from the exiting throng of passengers and went right to the weather station in the terminal. He was directed to Major Winegardner's office by one of the airmen in the station. Painted on the door was Detachment 3, 9th Weather Group. Major A.G.Winegardner, Commander.

"Captain Samuel Golden reporting as ordered, sir ," as he put his orders on the major's desk.

"Ah, Golden. Good to see you. At ease. Sit. I was looking forward to your arrival. We're kind of short-handed and we certainly could use another body. What do you know about Lajes weather?"

"Very little, sir . Just what I've read in the forecasts that you issue for planes from Dover. I was here twice before and the weather then was the same as now, miserable."

"Ha! Understated. You'll get the hang of it quick, I'm sure. I'll have Johanssen take you up to the bachelor's officer quarters and get you settled. As soon as you are, get yourself something to eat and come back down here so we can talk. Johanssen," he called out. A captain in shirtsleeves stuck his head in.

"sir?" he asked.

"Jens, please take Golden here to the BOQ. Get him set up and show him what he needs to see." He opened a drawer and pulled a key out. "You got room 42." He tossed the key to Sam who caught it with a swat of his hand.

"Yessir." Golden followed the captain out. "I'm Jens Johanssen." His hand went out.

"Sam Golden," Sam replied, shaking it,

My car is in the parking lot. This is Master Sergeant MacInerny," he pointed. "Mac, this is Sam Golden. Just arrived from Dover."

"Bill MacInerny. Welcome aboard, Captain. I'll cover for you, Jens, while you're out touring," he said sarcastically, but smiling.

"Thanks, Mac," he answered with a return smile. They walked out to the parking lot to a red Chevy. "This is mine. Hop in."

"What about my bags?"

"They'll be in the terminal. We can get them later and keep them in the weather station, take 'em to your quarters after you finish with the old man. You got a car coming?"

"Yeah. but they told me it would be weeks before it gets here."

"If you're lucky."

Sam frowned and asked, "Tell me about MacInerny. I couldn't help but notice he calls you by your first name."

"Bill's an interesting guy. Salt of the earth. He was a lieutenant colonel and was discharged in '54 because of a post-war reduction in force, a so-called RIF. They did that to a lot of guys. Enlisted in '38, I think. Served in the war, got recalled for the Berlin airlift, stayed in until Korea. After fourteen or fifteen years in, and five or six years to retirement, forced out by a congressional budget and a reduction in force.

"I met guys like that at Dover. Seems like a fucking cruel thing to do."

"Sure was. But he re-enlisted like others did, as an enlisted man, got the rank of master sergeant because of his skills and will stay on active duty until he gets his twenty years and retire at the highest rank he attained. Meanwhile, he has to cater to guys like us."

"Doesn't it bother him?"

"Nah. He commands respect because of who he is and what he knows, which is a lot. You did notice he calls me Jens. He'll sir you to death until you're embarrassed." He pulled the Chevvy into a spot in front of the BOQ. When they got out, Jens pointed to the building across the street . "That's the officers' club."

Sam looked. "Very convenient."

"Club is. But until your car comes, walking to the terminal will be OK. It's downhill. But coming back uphill will be a drag especially in this weather, unless you can hop a ride with someone. There is a base bus but its schedule leaves much to be desired. Here it is, room 42." Sam opened the door, walked in and looked around. He punched the mattress on the bed, looked at the view out the window overlooking the green hills in the distance and checked out the shared bathroom. Except for the view, the room was standard issue, like his room at Dover, so Sam felt at home.

"You can introduce yourself to your bathroom partner later. Name's Marty Redstone. I checked. He's a navigator, just arrived yesterday. Working in nav-briefing. I'm sure you both will have a lot to talk about. Just so you know, the BOQ has a houseboy, João. He'll do your laundry and shine your shoes. Just leave the shoes in the hall and hang your clothes on the doorknob and they'll be done. Leave something in the kitty near the front door every once in a while for him. I'm in room 26, around the bend if you need anything. Now let's get you some food." They crossed the street to the officer's club and sat down in the dining room.

"Looks like every other club I've seen. Anything special about this one?" Sam asked.

"Nah. Well, maybe. Bar is there," Jens pointed. "Office is there for cashing checks or whatever. Tax free store there, tax-free booze and slots. That's different."

"Slots?"

"Slot machines. Don't interest me, none. But some guys are addicted. One thing of consequence for crew members is that they can get their shoes shined for a nickel. Trouble is, most of the guys, especially those passing through, give him a quarter which the general rails against, but it's made Fernando, the shoe shine guy, a very rich man."

The waiter came over to them. "May I help you?"

"What'cha want? My treat."

Sam laughed and looked at the waiter. "Eggs over easy and bacon."

"We have only powdered eggs, s*enhor*. You can have scrambled."

"Powdered? No fresh eggs?" Sam echoed.

"Oh, *sim, senhor*. Fresh powdered eggs."

Sam chuckled. "From powdered hens, I suppose."

"One of the faults with this place," Jens shrugged. "Rarely any eggs. Anything we want in the way of food, we have to set up the locals to produce. We want eggs, we have to provide chickens."

Sam looked at the waiter. "OK, scrambled with bacon, toast and coffee."

"And you, *Senhor* Jens?"

"Me, just coffee, Carlos. Not hungry."

On their way back to Jens' car, Sam asked, "Is it always like this, rainy and windy?"

"Oh, no, no. Only about eighty percent of the time. Sun comes out and stays awhile in the summer."

"How do you manage? I mean the weather's gotta get to you."

"Does at first. But then you sort of get used to it. You get busy with hobbies, catching up on your reading. Bart Williams has electric trains running through his room, the most elaborate setup you have ever seen. Fleischmann HO size. He got them at the PX in Frankfurt. Every chance he gets, he goes back to Frankfurt and brings more shit back for his configuration. He can barely walk in his room but it keeps him sane, so he says. A pair of airmen who were here, built a five foot high replica of the duomo of Milan, the cathedral, completely out of matchsticks. Took almost the entire tour and thousands of dollars worth of match sticks. The detail was incredible right down to the religious sculptures outside and the cathedral's floor mosaics. They were really talented guys. Truly a work of both craft and art."

"Sounds maddening."

"Probably was, but kept them busy. Word spread and when the BirdsEye Match Company saw a photo of it, they went bananas and offered the guys a huge chunk of money after they get discharged, to tour with the thing. On the other hand if you have no hobbies or if you have no talent, or you can't find anything to keep you busy, you stay drunk. Lotsa guys do that. You?"

"Me what?"

"Drink."

"I'm not a teetotaler but I'm not what you'd call a drinker. I can take it or leave it."

"Me, too. I suggest you stay that way. Easy to become an alcoholic here. There are a bunch here that have a serious problem. Scares me sometimes."

"Why?"

"I watch them get into a plane to fly when they should be in bed."

"That's nothing new. I've seen that when they leave Dover. One colonel actually showed me how it steadied his hands. Another wise guy told me he just got the rule confused and reversed it - eight drinks, one hour before flying."

Jens smiled. "It's not funny. It gets worse here. Crosswind closes the field often and suddenly."

"What are the crosswind minimums?"

"If the crosswind component is over 35 knots, the field is closed. Since the prevailing wind is from the southwest and the only runway runs southeast to northwest, the problem is continuous, especially in winter."

"Why don't they build another runway?"

"Can't, because of the hills. They've tried pretty much everything. They even planned a short runway that turns into the long runway with a banked turn. Nixed as too dangerous. Crews get grounded by the wind and get stinking. Then the winds suddenly ease up and they get alerted to fly without time to sober up. They're not supposed to drink while they're waiting, but they do. And who can blame them? They never know how long they're going to be grounded. How are they supposed to occupy themselves? No car. No public transportation on the island. There are slots, booze, cards but not necessarily in that order. Then if the winds let up, there's a wild rush to get the planes off the ground before the winds pick up again."

"How much notice do they get?"

"'About an hour."

"Not much time to sober up. Lot of accidents?"

"Strangely enough, no."

Sam laughed quietly as they pulled up to the terminal and Jens parked the car. They got out and went right to Winegardner's office. "Here's Golden, Major, duly set up and fed."

"Thanks Jens. Sit Golden." The major shuffled some papers and looked up at Sam. "Your fitness report from Dover was excellent. I hope you're as good as it seems you are. How did you get promoted to Captain so fast? Very unusual."

Sam laughed. "Just lucky, I guess. Being in the right place at the right time."

Winegardner didn't press the issue. "I'll put you on the shift with MacInerny for a week. That should be enough to wet your feet, then you'll join the regular rotation."

"How does the schedule work here, Major?" Sam asked.

"We work one swing shift - 1600 to midnight, one midnight to 0800, one day shift then one day off."

Sam winced. At least at Dover he had three days of the same shift in a row. "Seems kind of limiting, Major. Not enough time to go anywhere when you're off duty."

"Nowhere to go anyway. 24 hours between shifts. It works well."

Works well, Sam reacted silently and thought. How the fuck do you get your clock working like this?

The major added, "Sergeant MacInerny is on day shift tomorrow so you work with him and get a day off after that. You can get yourself settled then."

"Anything else, sir ?"

"That's it Golden. Looking forward to a good tour from you. My time's up end of the month, so you can break in a new commander."

"Been there, done that, sir." Sam saluted, did an about face and left the office. "I'm on with you Sergeant, tomorrow," he joined MacInerny.

"No sweat, Captain. I'll get you up to snuff fast. By the way, I answer to Mac. What'd you think of the old man?"

"Not much. But don't quote me. Seems a little intense but to be truthful, he seems like a "little" man. My name's Sam." Mac smiled. "What's your opinion?"

"No comment except very glad he's leaving."

"Replacement might be worse, no?"

"Nope. I know the guy well, We flew fighter escort missions over Germany together. Then transport planes in the Berlin airlift in '48. He's a really good guy, good commander. No petty bullshit. Looking forward to it. It'll be a welcome change. Haven't seen him in six years."

"Sounds promising."

Just then, Johanssen walked into the weather station. "Sam, I got your bags in my car. Wanna go up now?"

"That would be great. I can unpack and get ready for my big day tomorrow." Jens and Mac both looked at Sam then at each other. Sam grinned. "Something I missed?"

Jens replied, "I hope you have bigger days than that. Let's go. I'll buy you a free martini. It's almost happy hour."

"Free martinis?"

"Two for a quarter and I'll only drink one."

Right after Sam and Jens left, Major Winegardner burst into the weather station looking around. "Where's Johanssen, Sergeant?" he asked, anxiously.

"Took Golden to the BOQ, sir . What do you need?"

"General Smith is going to Frankfurt tomorrow. I need a forecast for his flight tomorrow."

"There's no weather to speak of, Major."

"I want a written report to send to him."

"Why, Major? There's no weather to report."

"I want to be responsive."

"I can do it in about a half-hour. You don't need Jens."

"I need it now. I don't like to keep the general waiting."

"Major, it's a routine flight, there's no weather to the continent and no weather in Frankfurt. Why the rush? Why a written report? If you want, I'll call him."

"No, I want a written report and I want it now. And I need someone to hand deliver it to headquarters right away."

"Can't do it now, Major. Six flights leaving in the next half-hour need briefings. The general would be upset if they were late getting off. Why don't you just call him? Not much to tell him. A written report would be two sentences at most."Winegardner started pacing nervously. Asshole, Mac thought. Has to kiss the general's ass. "I'd be happy to call him, Major. I'm not afraid of him." Mac was sorry he said that and wished he could take the words back.

"I am not afraid of him," Winegardner retorted, harshly."I just want to demonstrate our efficiency, our responsiveness."

"Major, don't you think a personal phone call makes a better impression than a written report? Call him," then added after a brief silent moment, "sir ."

"Maybe I'll do that. What's the weather for Frankfurt tomorrow?"

"Partly cloudy. Temperature in the fifties. Nice day. No weather en route."

"Thanks, sergeant. Can you make me a copy of the route weather map?" He left quickly.

Mac shook his head. Me they boot out because of a reduction in force and him they leave in. What a fucked up air force, he mumbled under his breath. At that moment, Mac turned and was surprised to see General Smith in the weather station. "Afternoon, General. What can I do for you?"

"I'm going to Frankfurt tomorrow. Mac. How's the weather?"

"Nothing cn route, sir . Weather at Frankfurt partly cloudy. Temp in the fifties. Nice day. Should be a great trip, sir ."

"Thanks, Mac."

"No sweat, General. Have a nice flight."

Winegardner came back into the weather station. "I can't get him on the phone. He's not in his office. I need that report."

"He was just here, Major. I gave him the forecast."

"He was here?" the major said anxiously. "Why didn't you call me?" he added angrily.

"He didn't ask for you, Major. He wanted the weather to Frankfurt and I gave it to him. Two sentences. He was here all of fifteen seconds."

"Damn. What will he think of me now? Non-responsive. If he ever comes in again, you call me. Hear?" He stormed out.

"Yessir." Mac said, sarcastically, coming to attention and saluting the back of the major's head, then went back to his drawing table to finish preparing briefings for the six flights. He's the reason I like working nights, he thought.

The Suez, Hungary and Jeannie

Sam had quickly settled into the Lajes routine. What Sam didn't know then was that his tour of duty at Lajes would be anything but boring and in many ways life changing. There would be humdrum periods, sure, but there would also be enough interest to counterbalance that and make his time pass without resorting to Robbie's drunk solution.

Procedurally, the weather station operated the same way as Dover so that was the easy part. He had even gotten used to what he thought was an asinine shift schedule. The hard part was forecasting the wind speed and direction with a paucity of information.

As he got more comfortable with the weather and work in the station, Sam began to think more about his off-duty time. Watching sitcoms in the TV room of the officers' club started to pale right away. While the world series was on, Sam, the die hard Dodger fan didn't mind the TV room. But now, it was a drag. He needed something or he thought he would go nuts. Either he had to find a project for himself or somehow find a female companion. But where? The thoughts put him to sleep.

The radio which was set to wake him at seven went on suddenly and, sleeping very heavily, he jumped up with a start. The news was on Rescue Radio, a local station broadcasting out of their rooms by a couple of men from the rescue squadron. The bulletin that President Eisenhower sent the sixth fleet to the Suez Canal to make the Israelis leave, chased his grogginess. He listened attentively and heard that the Israeli army had invaded the Sinai peninsula and was within ten miles of the canal. What's going on, he thought? And continued to listen until the report was over. He was upset that the Israelis were being pushed out by the U.S. He took a shower, shave and got dressed in civilian clothes. He had no plans for his day off and was pondering it when Mac called, telling him that the old man wants the whole staff in the weather station at 1000 for a briefing.

Major Gsell had been at Lajes only a short time and Winegardner had left only a few days earlier. The staff was mumbling about the reason for the meeting. Sam was less upset about being called to a meeting on his day off than what he heard earlier about the Israeli army. Being a Jew made him question in his own mind what side we were on. Finally the major came in to talk to the group.

He looked at the group and thanked them for coming. Al Gsell was a quiet southerner. In the short time he was there, he never raised his voice. He told them that President Eisenhower sent the sixth fleet to Suez in Egypt to make the British, French and Israeli forces withdraw. Then he started reading to the assembled group from a summary he got from HQ. "President Nasser of Egypt decided unilaterally to nationalize the Suez Canal, which was owned and run by the British and French." He looked up and ad libbed, "understandably pissing them off." Continuing from his notes, "After failed attempts by Secretary of State Dulles to get the UN to form a commission to run the Suez, the British and French got together with the Israelis who have no love lost for Nasser, considering him a threat to their very existence and with good reason. The three countries together decided to get rid of Nasser militarily. General Moshe Dayan's Israeli army invaded Sinai first, quickly got to within ten miles of the canal and then the British and French invaded. President Eisenhower, fearing an escalation because of a strong Soviet reaction, wanted to calm things down and force the UN back into the mix."

Sam felt a little better that it wasn't just an anti-Israeli action. Meanwhile the whole Lajes installation was on alert until the crisis was over. The major didn't see any reason to increase the staffing. He just told them to keep themselves available in case the situation escalated. He thanked them again for coming in and dismissed the group except for Lt. Leroy Potter, whose shift it was.

The next few days were a little tense for the whole base but things eventually reverted to the boring preoccupation with crosswinds after the announcement of the Eisenhower Doctrine in which congress gave him authority to furnish aid to countries in the middle east. Offers of U.S. aid frequently cajoled small countries with flexing muscles into cooperation. In any case, U.S., U.K. relations, which had been strained as a result of Eisenhower's action, recovered under Prime Minister Harold Macmillan.

"Winegardner is gone," Jens said, out of the blue as he and Sam left the station. "And I can't say I'm sad. In fact, belated as it is, we should celebrate."

"What do you think of Major Gsell?" Sam asked.

"So far so good. No petty bullshit. Mac did tell us he's a good guy. Scuttlebutt has it that the Major doesn't like the schedule. He doesn't know why Winegardner set it up that way and he's planning to change it."

Just then, Captain Bob Billet, a pilot Sam knew from Dover came into the weather station.

"Hey there, Weather-Sam. Long time no see. How you doin'?"

"Not too bad, Bob. How's things on the mainland? This is my colleague Jens Johanssen. Bob Billet." Sam pointed. They shook hands and Sam asked, "Where you flying from these days?"

"I'm flying out of Charleston now. Just got here and doing my duty to debrief you on the weather." He pulled out his navigator's chart and showed Sam where the front was. "Not too bad. Clouds only up to about 18,000. Going to Tripoli tomorrow. Then Riyadh"

"Good weather all the way. A little wind and rain later then front comes through and tomorrow should be great."

"Good to know. Hey, how's your social life on this rock?"

"Here? You fucking kidding me? Virtually non-existent. Been here only a few weeks. Just got my car so I haven't seen too much of the island yet."

"I've got a proposal for you."

"Uh, oh, don't like the sound of that."

Billet laughed. "Really, one of my stewardesses is DNIF.

"What the hell is DNIF?"

"Short for 'duty not involving flying.' She's can't fly. How about keeping her company or something till we get back?"

"What's her problem? Afraid to fly?"

"Wise ass. No, earache, flight surgeon grounded her."

"What's she look like?"

"Very cute, really shouldn't be a chore for you. Name's Jeannie Andrews. From Alabama. Real southern belle."

"Out of Charleston? Isn't there a problem with fraternization with officers?"

"Nah. Not here. At Charleston, sure, officers verboten to date airmen by the CO, but here it's not a problem. Just don't take her to the o-club. There are some guys that have shit for brains and if they saw her would probably report her to her CO."

"I'll try anything for a change, especially if it's female I am already tired of this monk-like existence which has continued from my months at Dover. How do I reach her?"

"Just call the transient barracks and use my name. I'll tell her you're gonna call."

"I get off at four. I'll call her then. It'll be a novelty. Thanks. By the way, if we get along, is there a fee?"

"Shee-it. I'm not a pimp or a matchmaker." Bob laughed. "As aircraft commander, I just like to see that my crew members are taken care of while we're in Saudi-land. Just don't embarrass me."

"OK, I'll do my best to make you proud."

"No need for that. I'm not your mother. See you in a couple of days/"

"Hey weather, tower here, over." came a voice over the intercom.

"What's up?" Sam answered, without the radio protocol.

"When's front coming through?"

"Coupla hours. Should be nice tonight."

"Field gonna close this afternoon? Winds?"

"Not sure. Why?"

"Field closes, I get off early."

"I wouldn't count on it. But then, I don't know everything."

"If you don't know, who does? You're the weather guy."

"Find a guy with arthritic knees and ask him."

After a delay, he answered "OK, I get it. I'll expect the field to stay open. Tower over and out."

Sam looked at the large empty picture frame stuck on the window with the label under it that said "Current Weather" and looked at the gray clouds moving by. They were moving fast so he checked the wind instruments. Southwest at 27 knots. Right across the runway. It'll be close, he thought. 35 knots from that direction and the field is closed. He looked at the latest surface chart. Fucking useless, he thought. No information west of us except ship Echo which was 800 miles away, and an oil tanker report. The only other information I have was Billet's debriefing. Just have to watch it. "Ops, weather," he called on the intercom. "Any inbounds this morning or afternoon?"

"Light day. One at 1120, a connie from Charleston and one at 1345, a 124 from Dover. Why?"

"Field is marginal till front comes through. Can they overfly if necessary? Weather at Santa Maria is OK but I know they hate that."

"I'll check. Get back to you. We got three to leave. Should I rush them out?"

"I wouldn't. Probably better to alert them and if the field is a no-go, wait until front passes. At worst, flights will leave an hour or two late."

"Roger. Ops out."

Sam looked at the instruments again. Winds were still holding at around 25 knots. This was the weatherman's life at Lajes, watching the winds all day long, especially during the winter months. But the weather station was the only place Sam was comfortable. Off duty was boring and Sam, try as he did, couldn't find something satisfying to occupy his off-duty time. He had no idea how his soon his life would change.

The rules say that the operations officer closes or opens the field, but Sam knew realistically that was bullshit. If the weatherman on duty said the wind will exceed 35 knots across the runway, The book says ops has to close the field. And if he said it would be less, the field probably stays open. Sam knew very well that the forecaster on duty, not Ops decided. Sam was fixated on the winds until Lieutenant Buddy Kidder, a tall, lanky Virginian with an accent that indicated he was more southern than that, came at ten to four to relieve him. "It's all yours Buddy my friend. Winds hanging at 240 degrees at between 25 and 30. Lotsa luck. No information to make a good forecast. So keep watching."

"Shit, another one of those days where I smoke a pack of cigarettes and drink myself to the shakes with coffee."

"You're lucky. It's a light day traffic-wise. I think you got only one inbound tonight. Lotsa outbounds but that's not a biggie. Have a nice night."

****

"Jeannie Andrews, please," Sam sat back on his bed holding the phone to his ear.

"Who's calling?"

"Just tell her Sam. She'll know."

Another voice got on the phone and spoke, "Hello, this is Jeannie."

"Hey Jeannie," Sam tried to sound cool. He was definitely nervous about this but his desire for feminine companionship overruled it.

"Bob Billet told me you're stuck here for a few days. Can't fly. Interested in some company?"

"Is this Sam?"

"Yup. Whatd'ya think? Dinner maybe?"

"You kidding? Where? Can't go the the o-club and y'all can't come to the Airmen's club. Mess hall doesn't make for a fun evening, at least not for me."

"I've got a good alternative. I just got my car from the States and haven't been anywhere on the island yet. We can explore together, go to Angra, maybe, and find us a restaurant. You game?"

"You betcha, dahlin'. That's more like it. Sounds great."

Sam's anxiety abated. "When can you be ready?"

"Can you pick me up at the barracks about six?"

"Six it is. I've got a green Ford. Watch for it."

"Will do. See y'all then."

Sam was a little excited, an adventure. He wondered what she looked like. She sounded nice. He walked around to Jens' room and knocked. Door opened and a head appeared. "Hey, Jens, I got a dinner date. Any suggestions about restaurants in Angra?"

Jens laughed. "You really took Billet up on his proposal?"

"Yeah. Do you blame me?"

"What's she look like?"

"I have no fucking clue. But the way I feel, she could be an orangutang, I would take her out."

"Don't blame you at all. Shit, no. In fact if you had refused, I would have volunteered to take out the orangutang. Some guys have all the luck."

"It's not what you know, it's who. Anyway it remains to be seen, but anything is better than my current rut. Just got my car and I've never been to Angra. How do I get there?"

"Easy. Take the main road from the base. No turns. It goes through a pass in the hills and comes right into Angra's main street. Cobblestones. Three blocks to the Beira Mar Hotel. Good restaurant's in the hotel. 'Bout half hour's drive. Food is pretty good and it's cheap. It's the only restaurant I trust. And drink bottled water if you don't drink wine or beer."

"Will he take dollars?"

"You're kidding, right? He'll give you the check in dollars, with a price that rapes you and you'll still think it's a bargain."

"Parking?"

"This isn't Brooklyn, my friend. You'll be able to count the cars on a couple of fingers. Park anywhere. Probably the only place on the island other than the base that has sidewalks."

"Thank, Jens. See you later. Gotta primp, you know."

"Behave yourself. You don't know these southern belles."

Sam laughed. "It won't be hard. I've forgotten everything, it's been a while."

"Like riding a bicycle," he replied smiling. "You'll remember, I have no doubts. Have fun."

"Thanks. I'll try." Sam gave Jens a two finger salute and went back to his room to take a shower and put on some civvies. He was getting excited and a little jumpy. It had been months since he'd been near a woman other than the platonic associations with the marrieds in the officer's club and the one very big nurse, Norma, who was a menace. He was usually death on blind dates but he didn't have the option or the desire to refuse. He hoped she was at least pleasant. Once at Dover, he was so desperate for company, he and his roommate called the nurses quarters at Milford hospital and asked the one who answered to go to dinner and bring a friend. They refused.

Jeannie opened the door to his car and jumped in. "Hi, I'm Jeannie, Jeannie Andrews."

"Sam Golden," he answered. He was impressed. Jeannie had shoulder length dark curly hair and a great body. And she was dressed to kill with a black dress.

"You look fantastic," he said. Where did you get clothes like that? You bring them with you?"

"One never knows in this here air force where one will wind up. So you got to be ready for anything."

"I'm impressed."

The drive to Angra took longer than Sam expected. The road was not like anything he was used to. Well paved, but with cobblestones, pitch black. no lights, and he passed no other cars. Never having been on this road before, he wondered what would happen if he got stuck or had an accident. He quickly pushed the thought out of his mind.

Jeannie was very talkative and didn't often wait for an answer so the trip was pleasant. Ten minutes more and they pulled into the main street of Angra do Heroismo on the south side of the island. Sam parked right in front of the Beira Mar restaurant. "This is it."

"Seems like a nice place. Very different than the rest of the island."

"Rest of the island is agricultural, mostly peasants. This town is at least civilized,"

They were shown to a table near a window by a man Sam took to be the owner. There were a dozen other people in the restaurant who looked like tourists to Sam. He couldn't understand why tourists would even come to Terceira island on vacation. And how would they get there? There were no commercial flights that landed at Terceira. The only flights were military.

The man who seated them overheard them talking and began speaking to them in reasonably understandable English mixed with Portuguese. He handed them menus.

"If you need explain, I help you."

"Tell me," Sam asked. "How did your customers get here? They can't fly in."

"Cruise ships. Tourists cruise around islands. Sometimes a yacht."

Sam made an acknowledging face. Then they both ordered steaks because they could figure that out without help from the waiter/owner. At Jens' suggestion, they ordered a bottle of Mateus Rose, which was familiar to Sam from what was available at the o-club. It didn't take much to make Jeannie giddy, more talkative and very touchy-feely. Sam realized how much he missed it. They talked about life in the air force at Charleston. Sam didn't have to tell her his life story because she hardly stopped talking. When they finished dinner, they had half of their second bottle left so Jeannie put the cork back and took it with them when they left.

"Y'all have your own room?"

"Yeah. Share a bathroom but otherwise, it's all mine."

"Can we go back there and finish the wine? Am I allowed?"

"Why shouldn't you be?"

"Fraternization. Problem with that here?"

"No rules here about fraternization. I can't see a problem. Transient officers stay in a completely different building so no chance you'll be seen by anyone except us locals. And we certainly don't give a shit."

"Such a mouth," she said. "OK let's go. My ear feels better but Captain Billet's probably already left for Tripoli so I've got nothin' to do."

Jeannie stayed giddy as they got to his room. "This is it. My home away from home."

She took off her sweater and sat down. "Where is home?"

"New York, actually Brooklyn. Yours?"

"Small town right outside of Mobile. Chickasaw. So you're a Yankee. Never went out with a Yankee before."

"Never? Not even at Charleston? There must be some Yankees on the base."

"I never run into them."

"That's hard to believe, Do you give a guy a questionnaire before you go out with him."

"No. I just feel more comfortable if the accent is familiar. I guess I'm a little shy."

"Somehow, I don't believe that," he answered. "You don't impress me as the least bit shy. In fact, you seem more outgoing than average."

"Maybe it's you. You're nice." She put her arms around him with the bottle in one of her hands and kissed him. "Let's finish this." She let him go and took a swig of the wine. "Not much left. Too bad."

"I can get more if you'd like. I'll go, o-club across the street."

"Great idea, the night's young. And nothing at the barracks except TV reruns, and a lot of girls."

"OK make yourself comfortable. I'll be right back." Sam left, trotted across to the o-club and bought two bottles of Mateus which at 88 cents apiece he considered a very cheap aphrodisiac. He hurried back to his room where he found Jeannie half-naked reading labels on the vinyl records he had in a stack.

"Fancy clothes just not comfortable. Much as I like to dress up, hope y'all don't mind. I do like your taste in music. You like Elvis? He's heavenly."

"Why should I mind?" He laughed, unable to take his eyes off her. He opened a bottle of wine, took out two glasses and filled them both, handing her one.

She took a gulp and put her arms around him. Looking him in the eyes, she kissed him. "You Yankees should be able to do better than that," she said, "Kiss me proper." Sam obliged and despite how long it had been, he did remember. After a few minutes of increased passion, Sam started getting hard. She must have felt it.

"That's much better. Why don't you take off your clothes and let's play. I want to see what a Yankee can contribute to my education."

"I'm easy," he said. He undressed and she took off what was left of her underwear and jumped into the bed. He joined her and she rolled over on top of him leaning over and kissed him gyrating her butt, smiling. "Y'all like that?" He was already erect but was enjoying it too much to rush. After fifteen or so minutes of kissing, nuzzling and rubbing, she put his erect penis where it goes. It had been a long time for Sam and he had forgotten how good sex felt. It wasn't long before she screamed in pleasure and he moaned for the same reason.

She rolled back onto her back and he kissed her gently. "That was nice. Took my mind right off my earache. Good thing I have a diaphragm, don't you think?" she asked.

"Very good thing. I could make a habit of this, Jeannie. Especially here at Lajes."

"I come through here a couple of times a month and more often than not, we get stuck here. It would be nice to have a friend here. It would make getting grounded here more interesting."

"Certainly more interesting for me too. You have no idea how terrible it is when the weather is like this."

"Would be great. Problem is I can tolerate a Yankee. but I can't abide a Catholic long term. A Yankee and a Catholic is too much for me.

"Catholic? I'm not a Catholic," he answered, looking her in the eyes."

"Really, y'all aren't." She grinned, excitedly, and pulled him toward her.

"No, I'm Jewish."

"A Jew?" she sat up in bed. "You don't believe in our Lord Jesus Christ?"

"You could say that," he fudged. "I'm sure he was a nice guy."

"Why didn't you tell me? That changes everything. Pity, I really like you."

"Sorry I didn't tell you. I ground my horns down last week so no one would know. But how does that change things?"

"I can't get serious about a Jew."

"Why not? No one's asking you to get serious. We're not getting married, you know."

"I don't like to put myself in a position where I might fall for a guy and create problems for myself. I never know how things will work out." She jumped over him and got out of bed. He didn't move, just watched in stunned amazement.

"Dinner and a little love making and you're in a panic. That's crazy."

"Not to me, Sam. I liked y'all right away and was thinkin' ahead. I know me. We shouldn't see each other again."

"Wow. I can't believe this. What would have happened if I lied?" he asked putting his hands behind his head on the pillow.

"I'd have spent the night here and asked you to go out tomorrow. Now, I can't," she whined. "Would you take me back to the barracks? Please," she added.

Sam got up, went to the bathroom. "Let me get dressed. I'll take you back." While he was relieving himself, he couldn't help musing over what had just happened. Bizarre, he mumbled to himself, just fucking bizarre. He put on his clothes and as they walked to the car, he looked at her. "You sure about this? You're a great girl and I don't mind that you're a Christian and a rebel. We could build a relationship. You come through here often, don't you?"

"I told you, A couple of times a month, I would say. But anything more than acquaintance is out of the question."

He stopped the car outside the barracks and before she got out, he said. "I think it's too bad you feel that way, Jeannie. But if you change your mind, you know where to find me."

She got out, looked at him with a funny longing expression.

"Thanks for dinner," she said. "I had a really good time. I'm sorry how it worked out." and walked into the barracks. Sam watched her go and pondered it. Something like that, so bluntly direct, never happened to him before. It was a funny kind of anti-semitism, not based on hate. It was a "stay with your own kind" type, evolved probably from segregation rather than old fashioned European hatred.

Live and learn, he thought. In any case, it was a nice evening until the bizarre ending. How was he going to explain that to Bob when he came back in a few days? He resisted the temptation to go to the o-club and took another glass of wine. He was already a little tipsy, dropped off very fast and slept soundly, especially knowing that tomorrow was his day off.

Marty poked his head into Sam's room and woke him. "Hey, sleep hound, I'm off until 1600. Let's go the flicks."

Same answered groggily, "What's on, today? I'm not really in the mood." He told Marty what happened with Jeannie.

"Weird, I find it hard to believe that she never dated a Yankee at Charleston and never even met a Jew."

"Harry Golden, the famous Jewish writer lived in North Carolina, probably too far north for her to be aware."

"Flick is Strategic Air Command. Jimmy Stewart. I heard good scenery, corny propaganda, but terrible plot."

"Sounds perfect. Let's go. Nothing better to do. What time?"

"Next show is 1000. Get your ass up and let's eat."

He sat up in bed. "OK, Give me twenty to shower and get dressed."

Some days later Bob Billet returned from Riyadh and after Sam gave him a weather briefing for his flight back to Charleston, he told Bob what had happened even before Bob asked. "You know that date you arranged for me with Jeannie?"

"Sure, cute right? How did it go?"

When Sam went into detail about the result, Bob roared with laughter. Being from southern California, he admitted to Sam that southern belles were anathema to him. "You're telling me she never met a Jewish guy?"

"She said she never even dated a Yankee at Charleston."

"Impossible. It's hard to believe in this day and age she never met a Jew, let alone a Yankee. I even know a couple of Alabama Jews. Do you mind if I tell some of the guys what happened?"

"Actually, Bob," his tone turned serious. "I'd rather you didn't. I think that would be malicious and although what I told you is true, I just think it would spread the wrong way, like wild gossip. You know, Jeannie has her prejudices, which I'm sure are not her fault. There was no animus there. She's basically a good person and doesn't deserve what the unintended result might be. So don't. Please. I wasn't offended and I only told you because you arranged the date and I thought you should know."

"Yeah." His smile gradually became a frown. "You're probably right. I will ask her, though, how the date went. I'm really curious what she'll say."

"So am I," Sam frowned. "I'd love to know how she tells it."

"I'll let you know. Meanwhile, keep the faith. See you next trip." He picked up the written briefing and walked out to the flight line. Sam grabbed his coffee cup, took a gulp and turned around, surprised to see Major Gsell standing next to him.

"How's the forecast, Sam? I've been here weeks and the weather has been so lousy, I haven't even been able to get out to the golf course even to look at it, let alone play eighteen holes."

"I know how you feel, Major. I haven't been here much longer, and I haven't seen too much of the island because the weather discourages exploring. The wind only makes you feel like sitting at the bar looking out the window." Sam raised his eyebrows. "I did go to Angra to dinner the other night but the weather had let up for a few hours. The trip wasn't too bad." Pointing to the surface weather map, "Take a look at this. Best I can tell, it won't let up for awhile. You might have to wait a bit before golf season comes. The only positive thing is that the weather data is so scant that it's easy to be wrong. Might just surprise us and clear up."

"OK, I'll keep my fingers crossed. You a golfer?"

"Me? I come from the streets of Brooklyn, Major. Stickball on the street. Basketball and softball in the schoolyard. Tennis was a stretch. Playing golf was too complicated and too expensive for me."

"I can understand that. Lotsa city guys say that. I grew up in suburban Virginia, practically on a golf course so it was easy for me. My first job was caddying. How about coming out to the course with me when the weather clears? Everybody else was very iffy when I asked them."

"Love to. You give me some pointers? I can see it now. Brooklyn boy becomes golf champion."

"That's pushing it just a little, Sam. But you won't have any trouble learning a bit," Gsell said.

"But I don't have any clubs."

"I can help there."

"I'm left handed." He looked at the major with a questioning expression.

"Ah, that may be a problem. Unless you want to learn right handed?"

Sam shook his head. "No way. I tried to bat right handed, switch-hit. "Didn't work."

"OK, let me see what I can do. I might be able to dig something up for you to get started. See you later." He turned and went back to his office.

The next day, not only did the weather get slightly better, traffic activity exploded. Following Khrushchev's Russian incursion into Hungary to put down a revolt against the Imre Nagy communist regime, President Eisenhower declared operation Safe Haven. It involved the transporting of thousands of Hungarian refugees who fled from the revolution to Austria, then to the U.S. as their final destination.

For almost two weeks, Sam and all the operations personnel worked between twelve and fourteen-hour days. This was a joint effort between several military and civilian transport groups so that there was literally no time to breathe. The only respite was meals. Sam decided to eat in the mess hall where the refugees were fed, for curiosity reasons.

One afternoon at lunch, he sat with Ferenz and Gabor, two young Hungarians in their late teens who had just left Budapest, making their way into Austria without even saying goodbye to their families. Had they taken the time to do so, they would have been caught up in the fighting and would not have been able to leave. Their school-learned English was pretty good and Sam found out that although they were technically educated in high school, they were beginning careers as professional gymnasts, which they hoped would allow them to make a living.

They asked Sam about opportunities for education in the U.S. Both wanted to go to college. They were surprised that Sam had free college education at one of the New York City colleges. They had heard that college in the U.S. was expensive. Inasmuch as they had little money between them, New York sounded attractive to them. Sam suggested they could probably get jobs and go to school nights but doubted that they could make any money in gymnastics, except maybe as coaches.

During those two weeks Sam also met some very interesting women, mostly young and traumatized by the Soviet invasion. He spent a dinner with a young woman named Greta and her friends but with fourteen-hour work days, and the transience of the refugees, there was no time to take any social advantage of the situation.

When the last of the refugees was airlifted, things calmed down very suddenly and attention shifted to holiday celebrations. He had never seen so much partying and drinking, much more intense than at a U.S. airbase. Each military unit sponsored a cocktail party. Beginning the week before Christmas, there were two cocktail parties every evening, one from 7 to 9 pm or 1900 to 2100 military time, another from 2100 to 2300. By that time, you were either drunk and continued into the wee hours, or drunk and went to bed. On the weekend, the same thing except that the parties started in the early afternoon and continued with the same result. Sam went to a few parties because there wasn't much else. These parties were the social life of most people on the base.

A strange thing happened one day after work on Saturday. He went to a party but got there late, cold sober. When he saw what was going on with everyone at a different level of tipsy, he was embarrassed to be there. It immediately came to him that if you get drunk with everyone else, you don't realize how ridiculous everyone, including yourself, behaves.

He went into the ballroom anyway just to say hello when a bird colonel, the SAC liaison officer, called out to him, "Hey there, Stormy, go long," and threw a football at him." Fortunately, Sam caught it and threw it back. Just then, the an air police officer approached the colonel and after a few words, the colonel put the ball away and sat down. Sam laughed and wondered if the colonel would remember doing this. Had it been him, he would be in the brig. He left the party and went back to his room and turned on the record that was in the phonograph, the best of Elvis Presley. He vacillated whether to begin reading Dostoyevski's *The Idiot* orNorman Mailer's *Deer Park* a paperback that just arrived from a college friend.

March 1957 Fiona, Martha & Santa Rita

The worst of the winter weather was over, Sam thought. It was still raining a little, but the wind was still offensive. The incessant rain which had its emotional impact on many of those stationed on the island, had let up a bit, at least temporarily. Although the sun occasionally peered out between the fast moving cumulus clouds, the wind was still blowing across the runway. Planes were grounded often for days at a time. Crews were getting drunk or involved in high stakes poker in the officers' club.

The games, usually, had innocuous beginnings with nickel and dime poker being played by local officers. Stranded, bored crew members, some with too much booze under their belts, slowly inserted themselves into the game, increasing the stakes. Little by little, the sober locals were driven out until there were only high stakes players left, making the game a spectator sport for those who dropped out along with other curious poker fans.

Sam was dumbfounded when he saw a tipsy colonel put his house in the pot on a straight flush. The audience almost to a man oohed and aahed. The colonel would not show his cards to anyone and did not even look at them again himself, lest someone see them, so the atmosphere was full of suspense. The tension at the table and in the spectator crowd reached an almost unbearable level to most. In the end, after deafening silence and a "call" the colonel won the pot, but not by much. His opponent in that pot, an equally tipsy major, also had a straight flush but his was ten high. The colonel had a king. Sam found it hard to root for either of the players. Trying to establish any kind of morality on that bet was a real dilemma.

The next evening, one Major Everett Halstead from Dover AFB came into the weather station, introduced himself and immediately began interrogating Sam, asking him for statistics about the winds that Sam didn't have. In fact, he had no idea who might have recorded data like that. Although, when Sam thought about it, having that information would have made a lot of sense to.

"We lose too much flying time, captain. We have to figure a way to overfly Lajes."

That thought didn't make Sam very happy. And it certainly wouldn't make any of the base locals happy. The stewardess traffic stuck here for days was welcome to all. "But you can already do that Major. From Harmon, Newfoundland to Nouasseur, Morocco is not such a stretch."

"True, Captain, but then we have to cut back on the cargo to add more fuel. We don't know if it really improves things. That's why I was looking for those statistics. The goal is to overfly Lajes from Dover or Charleston, with a net gain in cargo movement. It would be a help to find out how many flying days we lose because the field is closed."

"I wish I could help, Major, but as far as I know, there's no one keeping those records. Maybe you could go through the operations log or our weather station log for the past year." Sam knew full well that the major would ignore the suggestion totally. Work was involved. "Trying to forecast won't work because we are not good at it. Not that we're bad forecasters, mind you, we just don't have the information to make good wind forecasts. You know there are just four permanent observing sites in the whole Atlantic."

"That's all?" the major asked surprised. Sam was surprised that the major was surprised.

"And an occasional ship or two. But that's not dependable. Besides, the ships are only surface observations. Doesn't help much with upper wind forecasts for the flights."

The major paced back and forth thinking. "Same problem in the summer?" he asked.

"You know as well as I do, Major, the winds in summer are rarely a problem."

The major continued pacing. "We're still in bad season for winds, no?"

"For another month, if history is consistent."

"Well, I'm going to give it a try next week to see how it works and how much cargo we can move."

"And Charleston flights?" Sam asked, with wishful thinking. "They're not going east via Newfoundland, are they?"

"No. That would be ridiculous. But they will try to stop at Bermuda, refuel and overfly. They do that frequently anyway. Here's how we'll do it. We'll radio here when we're an hour out. If the weather looks bad, we'll overfly. If not, we'll land."

That made absolutely no sense to Sam but he didn't reply. If they had to cut back on cargo for fuel to overfly, why stop? Either they load the plane with cargo and land or load the plane with extra fuel reduce the cargo and overfly. But Sam said nothing, He was beginning to think that the plan was a sham, just so the major could create a project for himself. The results would surely be inconclusive but the analysis was going to be impressive and let him show how smart he was. Sam wasn't about to contradict the major and sabotage what little social life there was. He was content to leave the major thinking he wasn't too bright.

"Thanks, Captain. You've been helpful."

Sam knew he really wasn't, but replied, "Any time Major."

Marty came into the weather station from his haunt in the navigation-briefing office. "I saw that creep Halstead bending your ear. What'd he want?"

"You know him?" Sam asked.

"Yeah, worked with him in ops in Texas some years ago."

"He's got a bug up his ass to overfly Lajes and avoid the crosswind problem."

"That's not good. There goes our fun. Can he do that?"

"I didn't give him any help and his plan is bullshit. I didn't tell him that because I'm sure he's just making work to puff himself up. Ambition, ambition."

Marty laughed,"Doesn't surprise me. Can you get away for some dinner?"

Sam looked at the schedule. "As long as I'm back before 2100, I guess so. I have to analyze the surface map before the briefings. Hey Phipps," he called to the airman intently hovering over a weather map on the desk, "Cover for me until the next briefing. I'll be at the club if there's an emergency."

"No sweat, sir . I've got to finish plotting this surface map before I leave anyway. Lots of ship reports today up north. You back around nine?" Sam nodded.

"I'll drive," Marty said, as they walked to his car. The o-club was more crowded than Sam was used to. It was dinnertime and with his screwed up schedule, he rarely ate dinner at dinnertime. After they had placed their order with the waiter, Marty opened with, "Do you really think they'll overfly?"

"Oh, they'll probably try it for a week but then the weather will get better next month and they'll forget about it until next December."

"Had me a little worried, Sam. I saw on an incoming manifest that there's two stewardesses from Charleston on the flight that just landed."

"So?"

"Double date?"

"What do you know about them? You know I'm a Yankee and a Catholic."

Marty laughed. "Can't all be like Jeannie. Worth a try."

"OK, If you can arrange it. I'll go along. But I get the pretty one, that is, if there is one."

"Deal. I'll look into it. But I got a question for you that's been bothering me. How come your airmen, the weather observers, are never down? Everyone else here is either depressed, drunk, or buried in some hobby or other. Your guys are always in a good mood."

Sam chuckled. "That's the best kept secret on the island. I will make no comment on that."

"Come on, there must be some reason. And it's not that there's a good CO. The last one was terrible and they were happy then, too."

"No comment."

"You're no fun. Gonna keep it to yourself, really?"

"No comment," Sam repeated. "Let's eat. I gotta get back to the weather station. Work to do, you know."

All the way back to the terminal, Marty didn't let up. But Sam continued to stonewall him. He was sworn to secrecy by the chief weather observer, Staff Sergeant Joe Mandino, affectionately known as 'Gordo' because of his girth. It was a secret that had been kept for years and anybody interested, who got close to solving the puzzle, rotated back to the States before they could find out.

The reason, which Gordo told Sam, was that Santa Rita hill where the observation site was, where they launched the rawinsondes, the radar balloons, was the home of some four or five young Azorean girls who were getting rich selling themselves. And if you imagine that Fernando the shoe shine guy became rich at a nickel a shine, you can imagine how those girls were doing given that the services they provided were a bit more expensive..

Sam didn't keep the secret for fun or good morale. He was well aware that discovery would have serious consequences. General Smith, the base commander, nice as he appeared to be, was a prude, and had a hidden bad side. Sam found that to be true of most generals he'd met. And you didn't have to look very hard to find it. If the Santa Rita oasis was discovered, the wrath of the general would not be pleasant. His reaction was even worse if a man checked into sick bay with the clap. Summary court martial was the order of the day with brig time and reduction in rank. The weather guys were very careful. They had a good thing and didn't want to ruin it. Condoms and silence kept them safe.

Sam heard that the general, a divorced and remarried Catholic, was married to Hap Arnold's daughter and divorced her. General Arnold, with four stars, was Chairman of the Joint Chiefs and after the divorce, swore that as long as he was alive, Colonel Smith as he was then, would never get his general's star. Arnold kept his word but died in 1950 and Colonel Smith became Brigadier General Smith shortly thereafter.

Other scuttlebutt about General Smith was that because he was divorced and remarried, he was excommunicated by Captain John Campbell, the Catholic chaplain, who also forbade him from coming to mass.

The general got furious about the excommunication and told Campbell to mind his damn business. The quote attributed to the general was, "Listen Captain," emphasizing Campbell's secular rank, "the chapel on this base belongs to me, and I'll come to mass whenever the hell I want to." Father Campbell suddenly found out that God was not, as he always thought, the last word.

The ringing phone had Marty on the other end. "I met the two stewardesses, both pretty cute and game."

"Pretty one mine, right?"

"Would be your pick but we got a problem. It's an augmented crew so they're continuing on to Wheelus in Tripoli without a stay over."

"That's a bummer," Sam answered. "Story of my life."

"Can't you close the field?"

"You fucking serious? I can't do that. I mean, I could but I won't, "Bad policy."

"Come on, Sam. Just this once."

"No fucking way. Sorry." Just then, Wells came in from Ops. "Gotta go, Marty," Sam hung up.

Wells asked, "How's the wind situation, Sam?"

"Sittin' just below minimums. It's blowing across the runway but hasn't gone above 35."

"You think it'll hold below 35?"

"Can't say, Warren, I'm a good weatherman but nobody's that good. Your guess is as good as mine."

"When will it let up?"

Sam showed Warren the map and pointed. "Best I can tell, front comes through tomorrow afternoon, wind shifts to northwest still strong but we're golden. Until then she's blowin' right across and I can't guarantee anything."

"OK. We can wait until tomorrow. No more inbounds until tomorrow morning. I'm closing her down. Brian Masters can open it next shift if he wants to, but I doubt he will. Thanks, Sam."

As Wells left, Sam thought to himself, Marty will never believe this and will give me credit for it. I don't need that kind of undeserved notoriety. He called Marty's room. "Redstone."

"Hey, field's closed. Make your arrangements."

"You fucking did it. I don't believe it."

"I did not. Wells did it. Don't give me credit I don't deserve and keep it to yourself. I don't need that kind of recognition. It could get me in fucking hot water even though it's not true. The general doesn't believe in coincidences. Wells just decided things were too iffy. No inbounds so he decided not to risk the departures. I have to admit, I didn't fight him, but that was only because I had no basis to object."

"Conflict of interest if there ever was one," Marty stifled a laugh.

"Fuck you."

"Call you later,"

About eleven thirty, Marty picked up the two stewardesses at the barracks and brought them to the BOQ. As arranged, Sam stopped at the club and picked up some vodka and a couple of bottles of Mateus. One of the nice things about a base like Lajes was that it was a twenty-four hour base so almost everything was always open. When he got to his room, Marty introduced him. "Sam, this is Martha and this dark-haired beauty is Fiona. Martha and me seem to have hit it off, so Fiona is yours. Or should I say you're hers."

"Little of both," Sam answered and opened a forty ounce bottle of Smirnoff's. "Vodka OK or wine?"

"Wine for me," Fiona answered.

"You?" looking at Martha.

"If you've got OJ, Vodka and OJ's good for me."

While Sam was preparing the drinks, Marty put on some slow dance music. He took Martha's hand and started dancing.

"You like dancing, too, Fiona?" Sam asked.

"It's OK. But I prefer talking. Where you from?" She took a sip of her wine.

"Brooklyn. You?"

"St. Paul, Minnesota. Twin city of Middla-noplace."

Sam laughed. "Don't like Minneapolis?"

"Nah, prefer St. Paul. Never been to Brooklyn. In fact, never been to New York. What's Brooklyn like?"

Sam took a sip. "Funny, no one ever asked me that before. I don't know what to say. Three million people, very diverse because of immigrant waves at the turn of the century. Mostly congregate in ethnic neighborhoods. Get along reasonably well. I lived in a mixed neighborhood.

"Minnesota is mostly Scandinavian farmers although St. Paul is becoming more diverse. Eastern city folk moving out here."

Suddenly Sam said enthusiastically,"Let's go for a drive. You up for it?"

"Sure. Where can we go around here?"

"We can go to Praia. If the weather isn't too bad, we can walk on the beach."

"Sounds great. All the trips I've made through Lajes, I've never been there. In fact, we hardly ever get to see anything on the island. We don't stay that long. And if we do stay, it's because the weather is so lousy we can't go anywhere anyway without some kind of transport."

The drive to Praia da Vittoria, Bay of Victory in English, took about ten minutes The wind was still blowing but had let up somewhat. Sam thought about Wells closing the station down and resisted feeling guilty. He parked the car in a space facing the ocean. The moon broke through the fast moving clouds off and on. "Button up your jacket and let's go to the beach." They walked along the beach for what seemed like an hour, talking. She liked the travel aspect of the air force. Sam took to Fiona almost instantly. She was easy to talk to and not very pretentious or secretive.

"How old are you?" he asked. "You seem very young."

"Nineteen. Twenty in two months."

"You look young but you sound like you've got your head screwed on right. Whyd'ya join the air force, anyway?"

"You first. Why'd you join?" she asked him.

"I had good reason. ROTC in college kept me out of Korea. Many of my friends and college classmates were yanked out of school during the summer by the draft. They all went through basic training in the army then went to the far east. I lost one friend in Korea. ROTC kept me from being drafted so I got to finish college. When I got my commission at graduation, the fighting was over. I lucked out. Now you?"

"I joined to get away from home."

"Why? Problems at home?"

"Daddy died when I was eleven. My mom remarried not long after that. When I got a little older, he couldn't keep his hands off me."

"Really? How did you deal with it?"

"I couldn't. He's very strong and raped me more than once. I had no choice. Had to leave."

"Couldn't tell your mom? Call the police? Press charges?"

"I suppose I could have. Friends told me to call the police. I was going to, but when I thought about it, I'm sure their marriage would have broken up. Mom needs him. He supports her. This was the best way. Now that I did it, I don't regret it. It's been eye opening, I gotta say, seeing the world."

"Sam looked at his watch. It's getting late. Want to go back to the barracks?"

"I hate the barracks, especially here. I'd just as soon spend the night at your room unless that doesn't interest you."

Sam was surprised at her wish. "I'd love it. I just didn't want to force myself on you. It's not my way." He pulled out of the parking lot and drove back to the base and up the hill to the BOQ. When they got to his room, Marty and Martha were no longer there. Sam assumed they had adjourned to Marty's room.

Fiona went to the bathroom and Sam poured himself some OJ. Fiona came out of the bathroom holding her clothes in her hand except for her undies. Sam stared at her young curvy body, stunned by her lack of modesty as she walked over to the bed, got under the cover and took off her panties. Sam finished his OJ and started to undress himself without saying a word. He felt weird with the situation and looked at Fiona periodically for tacit approval. When he was naked, he turned off the light and got under the cover next to her warm body. She put her arms over him and her head on his chest.

"Do you mind if we don't have sex?" she asked. "I just want to feel a friendly warm body next to mine."

For some reason, that relaxed Sam. No. I don't mind. I told you, it's not my way. Especially since you told me your story. That's the last thing you need."

She turned her back toward him and Sam put his arms around her. He couldn't stop the inevitable erection. She couldn't help but feel it between her butt cheeks but said nothing. In minutes, they were both asleep.

Sam was awakened by the loud telephone ring. "Golden here," he sat up and answered automatically, even though he was groggy.

The sweet voice on the other end said, "Sam, this is Martha. Fiona's not at the barracks so I assume she's with you."

"She's fast asleep."

"Can you tell her we've been alerted for a ten o'clock departure. She's to report to the flight line by nine thirty. I'll meet her there."

"Will do, Martha." Sam looked as his watch. Seven. He tapped Fiona who was not awakened by the phone. "Hey sleepyhead." He spoke in her ear.

She turned around and smiled and put her arms around him. "What's up?"

"You've been alerted. Martha called. You have to report at nine thirty."

She sat up with a start. "What time is it?"

"Seven."

She flopped back down."Plenty of time." She put her arms around him and kissed him gently on the lips and rubbed his belly gently. His dick got hard very fast. She put her hand around it and stroked it gently. "I want you." she said and kissed him again. She continued to stroke him gently as he rubbed her vagina feeling that she was very wet. After minutes of tonguing each other, she got on top of him and inserted him gently and he pushed it the rest of the way in as she moaned. Then suddenly he pushed her off, reached into his night table and got an "in case he got lucky" condom. She kissed his mouth and neck as he put the condom on and reinserted himself. It didn't take very long up and down as both of them wailed in pleasure at almost the same time, her moaning had brought him to climax. She kissed him all over his face and mouth then looked in his eyes. "I'll be back in a few days. I really like you, Sam. You interested in seeing me again?"

"Silly question. You know my number. Call the BOQ and ask for room 42. Or call the weather station."

"I'll do that. How will I know if you're available?"

"If you mean will I be occupied with someone else," Sam laughed. "On this island. I'm lucky I found you and the field was closed."

She jumped up. "Gotta get dressed. You got time to take me back to the barracks to put my uniform on and get my stuff?"

"Sure. Plenty of time. It's my day off."

The night ended sweetly and Sam was interested more than a little. Fiona was pretty, sweet, sexy and easy to be with. He wondered about his feelings and about her. Was it just sex? Was it that he was starved for female companionship? Did he know the whole story about her? He prematurely asked himself if this was something that could be serious with the right chemistry or was it just the military equivalent of a summer romance? Nice as she seemed to be, Sam realized that he was love starved, Nothing more than that. In any case it was a great night and the thought of her coming back in a few days excited him so he stopped trying to make anything more of it and thanked the fates for his good luck. Sam also supposed and chuckled to himself when he thought about it, she was not prejudiced against Yankee Catholics. In fact, it seemed to him that she didn't give two shits about religion.

Several days later, Fiona called Sam at the weather station at about 0500. They arranged to have breakfast in the mess hall when Sam got off work at 0800.

When they finished breakfast, he asked, "How long you staying?"

"Probably until tonight. Expect to leave about 2100."

"Got any plans for the day?"

"Nah, I just need to get a few hours sleep."

"Me too. I worked all night. Wanna nap together?"

She laughed. "That's not exactly what I had in mind."

"I didn't either, but one has to be flexible. Am I wrong?"

"OK. But really, I need some sleep time. Let me get my stuff. Can you pick me up at the barracks in about fifteen minutes?"

"Sure. See you there." They left together, Sam walked left to his car, Fiona right to the barracks.

When they got to Sam's room, Fiona asked if she could use the shower. "Of course," Sam said. "I'll go across to the club. I have to cash a check." Sam passed Robbie's room on the way and since the door was open, he poked his head in. Robbie was having a morning nip with Joan, the woman who runs the airmen's club. She was leaving and gave Sam a pleasant "hi" on her way out. "You amaze me Robbie. I still can't believe that every time I see you, you're always with a different woman. How the fuck do you manage it? You've gotta be worn out, by now," Sam said. To a twenty something like Sam, a fortyish man was old and on his downhill leg.

"Pacing, son. Pacing." Robbie bit his cigarette and when that happened, Sam expected a profound utterance. "First of all, I'm not as old as I look, but let me tell you a story. Sit down a minute." Sam sat and watched Robbie who was always entertaining when he pontificated. "There was a young bull and an old bull on a hill overlooking a herd of cows." Robbie waved at an imaginary herd and took a sip of his drink which purposely increased the drama. "The young bull said, Hey Pop, let's run right down there and fuck us a cow." Another sip for a dramatic pause then, "Whereupon, the old bull said, Son, why don't we just walk down there slowly, taking our time, and fuck 'em all."

Sam laughed raucously and got up. "You're still amazing. Philosophy 101."

"Like I said, Sam. pacing's the answer, pacing."

"Goin' to the club to cash a check. I got company. See you later."

"Seems like you're not doin' too bad yourself."

"It's not the same, believe me." When Sam got back to the room, Fiona was already asleep. Sam took a shower, set his alarm for 1500 and joined her in bed. He, too tired from working the night shift, fell asleep in seconds. When the alarm rang, they both awoke with a start. Sam rolled over to kiss her.

"What time is it? I have to meet someone at four thirty."

"Three. Who you meeting?" Sam asked, surprised.

"He's a passenger, an airman. I promised to have dinner at the mess with him."

"Why would you do that?" Sam asked testily. "I thought we had a date. I asked you if you had plans today. You said no."

"We sort of had a date, but he's a nice guy and I'd like to have dinner with him."

"Sort of?" Sam was angry. "So I was just a passing fad to you? A guy in one of your ports." Sam realized then that he had jumped to conclusions about her and about himself. She was right, but she didn't have to make a date with him when she left.

"That's nasty. I like you a lot Sam but we're not married. In fact, we hardly know each other."

"True but I thought we had a date. You were the one who asked me if I was interested in seeing you again. Or were you just covering your bases. Why would you do that? Besides, wasn't there was something special in the chemistry we have together. You were the one that asked if I was available when you returned. Was I jumping to conclusions about your interest?"

"No. I really like you and I intended to see you. It's just that I'm not ready to restrict myself yet. I'm not Martha. I'll call you next time I come through. We can spend more time together."

"Do that." Sam said bluntly. "Meanwhile, have fun." He thought to himself, on one hand, the sex was great and she was easy to be with. On the other, he worried that he would get too involved and she would cause him pain. He'd been through that once before. "OK, get dressed. I'll drive you to the mess hall." Sam was beginning to seethe but tried to act cool. He understood what Fiona was doing and wondered whether he appreciated her directness or was angered by it. Sometimes the truth is more painful than a little dissembling. When he dropped her off, she kissed him and said she would definitely see him next trip, that is, if he still wanted to.

"Call me, and we'll see," he answered sarcastically and drove away. After reliving the discourse with her, Sam realized he was really jumping in the water at the deep end and had better calm himself down. It was a first date, nice girl, and good sex and that's it.

Jeri, Beginning of a Friendship

Sam went directly to the club to eat and have some wine. He was not in a good mood. Fiona had left him in a grouchy mood and very pissed off. He was also mad for allowing himself to feel so vulnerable. He wanted to throw the feeling off but had difficulty.

The dining room was crowded and Sam sat alone as he usually did. As he gave his order to the waiter, two women he recognized came over to his table. One he knew was Norm Bell's wife. The other one he didn't know asked if he minded if they joined him. Sam reacted instinctively wondering why they asked. He looked around and saw how crowded the dining room was. "Sure, don't mind at all." They introduced themselves. One was Suzanne Bell, very pregnant wife of ops Captain Norm Bell who worked in navigation.

"I recognize you and know your husband pretty well," Sam said. But we've never been introduced. I'm Sam Golden."

"Nice to meet you, Sam. Norm has mentioned you. Weatherman, right?"

Sam smiled. "Right. He didn't blame me for this weather, did he?"

"No," she laughed as she put her purse on the table, "this weather was here long before you arrived and will be here long after you leave."

The other woman introduced herself. "Hi, Sam. I'm, Jeri Buczynski,"

"Oh, I'm sorry. Rude of me not to introduce Jeri," Suzanne said.

Jeri was the wife of Captain Mal Buczynski, the base ophthalmologist. She was a knockout, tall with a lithe body. She looked like a dancer. Jeri asked him, "You always eat alone? I see you here alone a lot, eating alone."

"Surprised you noticed, Jeri. As a weatherman, my work hours are atrocious and rarely seem to coincide with anyone else's. So, company at lunch or dinner is just not usually in the cards. I still gotta eat."

"Well, forgive me for being forward. Next time I see you here alone, I'll join you, that is, if you don't mind, unless you really like eating alone. I can't find any kind of job here so I have time on my hands and it seems that when I'm here, you are too."

"I do like company. I just can't usually arrange it. And feminine company on the island is a crap shoot."

"Good," she stuck out her hand. "It's a deal. If we're both here alone, we eat together. OK?"

"Definitely." Sam's mind was active and her offer did mitigate his anger at Fiona. But he was not being careful, he thought. He had an experience with a married woman in Dover who came on to him very aggressively and it turned out to be a very scary night. Her husband was a navigator and was frequently away on trips but had a reputation as a violent guy. Against his better judgement, impaired by too much scotch, Sam took her up on her invitation to take her home. She literally attacked him and Sam was with her in a compromising position when she thought she heard the door slam.

"My husband," she said jumping up in bed. Sam leapt up and got dressed. The false alarm brought Sam to his senses. "Sorry, I thought it was him coming in the door. Please don't go."

The apology was not effective. He still had the shit scared out of him and his libido with it. In Jeri's case, he hoped this was just a friendly gesture on her part. That would be nice but something more would be a strain.

Suzanne asked, "How do you know my husband?"

"We sort of work together. He tells them how and where to go and I tell them what weather they'll hit. His colleague, Marty Redstone is my roomie."

"So you're the roomie Marty always talks about."

"I suppose so. I'm his only roommate. What does he say about me?"

She laughed, "Only good things." she hesitated.

"Sounds like you're not sure. Should I be worried? Last thing I need is a bad rep. Norm's a nice guy. I see you're carrying around a basketball. Norm never said anything. When are you due?"

"Five weeks, and I hope I can stand it. It's twins and very uncomfortable."

"Stop complaining," Jeri said. "Discomfort now will make you that much happier when they're born."

"What are you expecting?" Sam asked. "There are only three possibilities."

"Norm wants at least one boy."

"Two thirds probability," Sam answered.

"Just his luck I'll have two girls. Wouldn't bother me a bit but he'd be unhappy."

"One third."

Jeri chimed in, "New fathers want boys but when they have girls, they love them to death. Mal is crazy about our daughter."

"How old?" Sam asked.

"Janie's five and in kindergarten. She's on a field trip today. Comes home around five thirty." She looked at her watch. "In fact, I gotta go guys. Let's go Suze if you want a lift. And don't forget, Sam. We eat together."

"OK with me," he replied and stood when they got up. "Take care ladies. It was my pleasure."

Sam watched them leave, sat down, finished his dessert, gulped the last of his wine and went to the TV room. At least the day wass ending better than it started. He forced Fiona out of his thoughts, which seemed to be easier than he anticipated. It was a sign to Sam that maybe he was growing up. That scared kid in Dover was gone.

He wondered just what Jeri's story was. He wasn't sure whether she was being suggestive. He didn't think he was imagining it, but he couldn't figure her out. After mulling things over, he gave up thinking about any of it because he was distracted by Phil Silver's portrayal of Sergeant Bilko.

****

After dropping Suzanne off, Jeri went right home to anticipate Janie's arrival. She took her shoes off as soon as she was in the door and looked in the refrigerator to see what to make for Janie's dinner. She would be home in a few minutes. For her own dinner, she decided to wait for Mal who usually got home about seven. She would try with him again. Lately, he always got home tired, had a quiet dinner hardly talking and fell asleep reading the paper. No matter what she tried, Jeri couldn't get him interested in anything. He seemed depressed but said he wasn't. Their sex life had become almost non-existent. He worked long hours and the only thing that got him excited was the mornings he was off duty and ran out to the golf course. He even neglected Janie.

She made up her mind to try once more. She had already tried everything with one exception. She never directly told him what was bothering her, that she needed attention and that he hadn't shown her any for months. She would just get mad and bury it.

Jeri tried at dinner and he was attentive to her until after they had their chocolate pudding dessert. He apologized but misread her again, not realizing the extent of her anger at him. He thought she was only a little miffed at him, nothing serious, rather than angry and frustrated. He went into the living room and as usual, started reading yesterday's New York Times. In fifteen minutes, he was dozing in his chair, raising her ire once again. She still couldn't get herself to tell him bluntly. She only hinted. She loved him and loved their family but didn't understand him and didn't know what to do. She was becoming more needy as time passed.

Sam interested her and she wondered if she was doing the right thing. She had seen him around, often alone and wondered why. It was mysterious to her. What was he like? She was exaggerating to herself. If Sam knew what she was thinking, he would be curled up in laughter. Him, mysterious?

But he was the reason she convinced Suzanne to try to join him in the dining room. He was very attractive to her and she wanted something, anything, to relieve her frustration, something to think about. Now with Janie in school and the fact that she couldn't find work on the base, she was bored to death. She wondered if she had made a mistake agreeing to come to Lajes instead of toughing out the required eighteen months, seventeen if he didn't take any leave. Having broken the ice with Sam, she would feel him out, to see if he was interested in a relationship, a friendship, anything. It wasn't sex, she told herself. She was very clinical about it, but she had to be.

What if Mal found out, she thought. She didn't want him to. She wasn't doing it as a means to prompt him, to make him jealous. That might rattle things but it was the wrong way and couldn't have a good end. For her, a relationship was survival. But how would she hide it? The base was a potential gossip haven even though most people on the base minded their own business. The base was a proverbial glass house. Almost no one would throw a stone. But the "almost" bothered her. She would see how amenable he was to some kind of relationship, the next time she met him in the club. Suzanne was her best friend on the base and knew about Jeri's problem and wouldn't say anything. At least, she had something to think about or anticipate to overcome her boredom.

Fasching in Frankfurt

Sam had lunch with Jeri twice since that first meeting. It was friendly, casual and non-threatening to him. But she was a very sexy woman and he sensed that all he needed to do was give her encouragement. He came to appreciate her friendship and didn't want to fuck it up with a sexual facet.

After one of the lunches, on the way down to the terminal for his shift, he almost had an accident when his brakes failed going downhill. He swerved to avoid another car and succeeded in turning the car so it stopped with a small skid. He breathed a heavy sigh of relief and parked at the curb where it was level and left it in gear.

There was no way to get the car serviced on the island. The car pool couldn't help because they didn't have the parts for his car and couldn't get them. Sam mentioned his dilemma to Mac, who was once an aircraft mechanic. He told Sam that the Frankfurt PX would most likely have brake pads for his car. If Sam got them, he would help Sam install them.

That sounded like a sensible plan, so he inquired about the next trip the base aircraft was making to Frankfurt and was lucky that it corresponded with his days off, on Major Gsell's new schedule. He arranged to go but Mac cautioned him, "Sam, that's the weekend right before Ash Wednesday. It's called Fasching in Germany and it's fucking nuts. Everyone goes bananas during Fasching. So make sure you get the brake pads first, before you do anything else. Then if you have time go downtown and join in. It's an experience."

"Why so important to get the brakes first?" he asked.

"Fasching does things to people. You might miss the opportunity to get what you need at the PX. Take my advice," he added with a knowing smile.

"OK, OK. I got it."

The way Father Campbell told it to Sam, Fasching was Karneval, the German Mardi Gras. Although the partying was heavy on the days leading up to Ash Wednesday, the season officially begins on November 11 at 11 minutes after 11 a.m.. The significance of the 11 had absolutely nothing to do with the season. It was derived from the Napoleonic invasion which called for *egalität, libertät, fraternität* in German. The acronym of the first letters "elf" is the German eleven. That barely related concept had been blown up completely out of proportion during the previous hundred or so years.

Fasching in Germany is considered to be on a par with Mardi Gras in New Orleans or Carnival in Rio, a celebration to get the lust out of your system before having to suffer the deprivation of lent. And the Germans, particularly the German Catholics, took it very seriously.

The flight to Frankfurt was scheduled two days before payday and Sam was short of cash, as usual. He convinced the cashier at the o-club to cash a check for him but hold it for two days.

The C-124 landed at Rhein-Main airport in the late afternoon on Friday. The weather was cold and raw. Sam rushed to the PX right from the plane and made it just before it closed. He was fortunate in that they still had one set of brakes left for his 1955 Ford. The sales person at the PX convinced Sam to buy brake cylinders as well, just in case. The trip objective was fulfilled faster than he thought. He was glad he took Mac's advice. There were two days to wait for the flight back and he could enjoy them without worrying about the brakes. Since the flight he was on continued on to Chateauroux, France, there was no one in the crew for Sam to go downtown with. It was hard, especially in the air force and especially for someone with his fucked up schedule, to find someone to travel with.

He found Europeans to be friendly and particularly with Americans, so he always seemed to make friends wherever he went. He decided to have dinner in the officer's club, alone as usual. After dinner, he asked the German clerk in the club about Fasching. He told her he had heard it was crazy.

"*Ja*, it is. But you should go downtown and enjoy it. You would have a good time."

"Any suggestions about what to do?" he asked.

"You should go to any beer hall. People are especially friendly during Fasching and Oktoberfest. She winked at him. Try Maier Gustl. It's famous and very *gemütlich*. There is one in Münich and one in Frankfurt. You will definitely have fun."

"Thanks for the suggestion. I'll give it a try."

After dinner, the bus from the airport dropped Sam at the bahnhof in town and he asked someone on the street where Maier Gustl was. It was a long walk but he wanted to see the town. When he finally saw the huge sign Maier Gustl Oberbayern, he was tired of walking and he could hear the welcoming sounds of the band inside.

Sam had never been to Germany, let alone a German beer hall and the inside was noisy and raucous, particularly so because it was Fasching weekend. The atmosphere was friendly, which was intensified by the big family-style tables and the quantity of beer being drunk. People-mixing was required, not a choice. Sam found an empty seat with two young women who surprised him by separating themselves and making him sit between them. They were apparently feeling no pain. Gertrude, whose English was pretty good, was a very pretty zaftig woman with dark brown hair. She told him she was married, but every year she and her husband separate for Fasching. She comes to Frankfurt and he goes to Wiesbaden and each year they switch towns. They stay separated until Ash Wednesday morning when they meet back at their house and go to church together. Maria was single, but came with Gertrude because Trudi, as she called her, was a wild woman and she always had fun when Trudi was around.

Sam was not naturally gregarious and didn't begin to feel comfortable until he finished his first big stein of beer. A stein that size would have normally lasted an entire evening under normal circumstances for Sam. The beer consumption in the hall that night was frightening to him.

The band on the stage, dressed in lederhosen with green suspenders and stupid looking felt hats, looked like a cartoon. In the middle of a continuous stream of old German folk songs that everyone knew and sung, whose melodies were familiar to him even if the lyrics weren't, probably because of their English pop versions. They were especially partial to Colonel Bogey's march from the movie *The Bridge Over the River Kwai* with trombones blaring. They repeated it several times and the volume of the horns made everyone yell at each other instead of talking.

Trudi and Sam made friends very quickly and within an hour after his first beer, Trudi knew Sam's life history and Sam knew hers. Whether he would remember anything the next morning was questionable. The free-flowing pitchers of beer made a good social catalyst. The traditional dancing in a conga line was novel and Sam held onto Trudi's waist as they continued out in a line, into the street, cold as it was, marching around the block being led by a trumpeter, and finally back to the table, singing all the time. He had forgotten to ask Trudi the name of the song.

One thing which was very noticeable was the preponderance of women and Sam mentioned it to Trudi. She told him that most German men her age were killed in the war. She was lucky to find a husband. It takes years, she told him, to regenerate a male population. When they sat down, the band played *Du Kansst Nicht Treu Sein* and everybody joined in, the words being very appropriate for the season. You can't be true, no no, you can't.

Maria had found a friend for herself and at one in the morning, Trudi asked Sam where he was staying. Sam said that he hadn't decided whether to stay in town or go back to the base.

"Come, stay with me. We can get to know each other better," she said with a broad grin.

Sam was full of beer and in no condition to refuse. He didn't feel like going back to the base. Waiting for the infrequent buses at this hour was unpleasant. He paid their check and they walked to the Hotel Baselerhof where Trudi was staying and picked up the key to her room.

The effects of the beer were wearing off both of them and the walk in the cold air gave a kind of gravitas to their mutual libidos. As soon as they got to her room, Trudi put her arms around Sam and kissed him passionately which Sam responded to. Suddenly, she surprised him by grabbing his crotch. An obvious invitation, she offered no resistance as Sam undressed her slowly and sat her naked body down on the bed and then undressed himself. He pushed her onto her back and played between her legs until she moaned and pulled him up on top of her then his face to hers. She rolled herself over on top of him and they never let their lips separate as he entered her wet vagina. She stopped him reached for her purse and took a condom out and gave it to Sam. She put her lips on his and it was the only time in Sam's life that he climaxed twice without separating. Trudi, it seemed to Sam, was in a continuous state of orgasm. From her wailing, he couldn't tell when one ended and another started. They eventually fell asleep in each others arms until Trudi woke him up in the morning by fondling him.

They didn't get out of bed until nine and went down for coffee in the hotel. Sam told her he had to report back to the base, which was a lie. But he was exhausted and suffering a nasty headache, the after effects of too much beer. He couldn't imagine what he would do with Trudi all day. She apparently was fine with that, probably for the same reason. He thought about coming back downtown later and looking for Trudi at the hotel but eventually decided against it. As much fun as the night was, he was almost sure another night like that would not be welcome. But absence of libido didn't last long in a twenty-five year old so he didn't want to burn his bridges before returning to the celibacy of Terceira. And as usual, the crap shoot as to when he would see Fiona again came to his consciousness briefly and even if he did see her, then what? The answer became less important as time passed.

He saw a poster for the Frankfurt Festspielhaus which was featuring pianist Walter Gieseking and conductor Wilhelm Furtwängler doing Beethoven in a Saturday evening concert so he took a cab and bought an orchestra ticket in the third row on the left, the keyboard side. He was excited because Furtwängler, even though he had a reputation for being a Nazi, was musically one of Sam's favorites. He was introduced to Furtwängler's Beethoven by a college colleague.

With time to kill, the rest of the afternoon was spent sightseeing and window shopping. He didn't want to buy anything because he didn't want to have anything to carry. A moot point anyway since, except for a possible souvenir, he didn't see anything he really wanted.

He spent the entire day walking around Frankfurt. He stopped for a late lunch in a small neighborhood restaurant, where the only menu was verbally presented by the waiter. He spent the rest of the afternoon browsing through German newspapers in a cafe, understanding little but with pictures in context he was able to make sense of some of it. About seven, he went right to the Festspielhaus and although he had time to spare until the concert, he went right in and was ushered to his seat.

For Sam, the concert was a marvel. Beethoven's Fifth, oft-heard as it was, was new under Furtwängler's baton especially the explosion from the third to the fourth movement, which was superbly enhanced by the acoustics of the house. He was disappointed with Gieseking's fourth concerto which Sam felt was sloppy, as if he hadn't practiced enough. But overall, the concert was memorable for Sam.

After the concert he went into a nearby pub-like place called the Florida Bar for a beer and wound up sitting and talking to the bartender, a very stunning tall blond woman named Susan. She looked to be about his age. "What's your name?" he asked her.

"Susan, and yours?"

"Sam. Are you from Frankfurt?"

"No. I've only been here a few years. We traveled a lot. My father was in the Wehrmacht."

"Ah, an army brat, as we would say in English."

"You could say that. My father was a general."

"Really. Where did he serve in the war?"

She answered matter of factly, "We spent most of the war in Berlin. My father was on Hitler's general staff."

"Wow. How do you live with that? Is it a problem?"

"Not really. But," she laughed, "it wasn't my choice. It was his. I am not proud of it. In fact I haven't spoken to him for several years. I must say, though, that he was not a war criminal. He was pure soldier, involved in the military defense of Germany. He had nothing to do with the so-called final solution, although Jews are not his favorite people."

Sam didn't want to admit to being a Jew at that point. He felt it would just strain the conversation and perhaps finish the evening for him.

"If he was pure soldier, why are you so angry with him?"

"Hitler was responsible for the destruction of Gemany. My father was therefore complicit."

"Not trying to defend him, but he was a career soldier. What would you have expected him to do? Be a von Stauffenberg and try to assassinate Hitler?"

She laughed. "No. I don't really know what he could have done. I lost both my brother on the eastern front and my childhood boy friend in France in 1945. They were both so young. I was angry with the Nazis and furious at my father in particular. I guess I still am. That kind of anger doesn't dissipate easily."

"You're not really being fair. He was doing his job. He couldn't resign. Hitler would have had him shot, don't you think?"

"Maybe you are right but it's still difficult for me because, although the war has been over for ten years, I think he is still a Nazi at heart. Tell me Sam, the bar will close soon. Do you have any plans?"

"No, just to go back to the base. My plane back to Lajes doesn't leave until the wee hours tomorrow night."

Would you like to go to a private club with me? Bars are forced to close but private clubs are open very late and I hate to go alone."

"I don't know," he hesitated. "I feel kind of funny."

"Why? Come on. We'll have fun. We close in a few minutes and I don't feel like going home yet."

The club was nearby and they walked. She held his arm as if they had known each other a long time. Walking through a hallway into the club, it was very quiet and the sounds were familiar, glasses tinkling, white noise, dim lights. Shortly after they sat down on a red couch and ordered beer, a stand-up comedian came out. After the "*Guten abend, meinen Damen und Herren*" Sam understood almost nothing. Susan had to translate each joke for him which made the evening somewhat weird for Sam.

At three-thirty a.m. they finally stopped dancing and left the club. "I have to work tomorrow. I would like to take you home with me, but it's not a good idea tonight. Will you go back to the base or will you stay in town?"

Sam thought for a minute and decided, "I think I'll go back to the base. Maybe I'll see you tomorrow. I don't go back to Lajes until tomorrow very late."

"I would like that. Let me walk to the bus stop in the bahnhof with you. It's on my way home."

As they walked through the station to the bus stop hand in hand, talking about what Lajes was like, Susan was suddenly stopped by two men in dark suits and hats who asked them both for ID papers. Sam gave his passport and air force ID to one of the men. "Ein Amerikaner," he told his colleague. Susan showed her papers to the other man as Sam watched and after a heated argument in German which Sam didn't understand, one of the men walked her away with him holding her arm.

"Hey, just a minute, what's going on?" Sam asked, raising his voice as he walked toward the departing Susan. The other man put his hand on Sam's shoulder to hold him back.

"Zere is nussing you can do for her. Ze bus vill be here in a moment, You are going to Rhein-Main, no? You should take it," he said, as he walked toward Susan and his colleague.

Sam was stunned. He felt like he was in a Kafka novel. He had a few too many beers and felt as if he didn't react as he should have. He paced back and forth for the few minutes before the bus arrived and all the way to Rhein-Main air base, he continued to speculate on what happened. Nothing he came up with made any sense to him.

He had a room at the transient officers quarters and fell asleep after tossing about for a half hour re-living the experience. He didn't wake up until noon the next day. Groggily walking to the bathroom, he recalled the surrealistic previous evening. His ride back to Lajes was scheduled for two a.m. the next morning so he planned to go back to the Florida bar. His curiosity about what happened was insatiable. He even wondered if Susan would be there. Maybe she was arrested. What did she do? He could not imagine.

Late that afternoon, Sam went downtown sightseeing, to continue trying to get a feel for life in Germany. When he was tired of walking, he sat at a cafe in the early evening, nursing coffee and watching the passing scene through the window. It was too cold to sit outside. He pondered again, his night with Trudi and the concept of mutually agreed-upon separation by a married couple for Fasching.

The incident in the bahnhof dredged up images of a Nazi police state, which he had only seen represented in movies. Suddenly, he didn't know why, but he was uncomfortable and felt out of control, like his roots were pulled up. He became anxious to get back to Lajes which he felt was home. He longed to be home and with the comfort of the familiar work routine which was his anchor. He felt it would stabilize his life and thought. But, he insisted to himself, not before he found out about Susan

He had a snack at a sidewalk würst stand and walked to the Florida bar. As he entered, Susan, behind the bar, saw him and smiled. He sat down on a stool and looked at her.

"I'm so glad you came back, Sam. That was not a pleasant experience for you, I imagine."

"You can say that again. Not only was it unpleasant, but there was the frustration of not knowing what the hell was going on. But I guess it wasn't pleasant for you either, I think. So tell me, my curiosity is killing me, what was that all about?"

"Nothing serious, just annoying and it's happened to me once before. They suspected that you were not German and when they saw your passport it confirmed to them that I was with an American military person. So it was assumed I was a business-woman."

"What's a business-woman? What's that mean?"

She laughed. "Don't be offended. These men that took me are trained well. They can spot a foreigner a mile away."

"And business-woman?"

"It's a literal translation of our German slang for prostitute. So he wanted to see my medical papers."

"Business-woman. That's funny. So what happened. Did he arrest you?"

"Not quite. They took me to the police station because, for a prostitute, which I am not, I have to emphasize that," she smiled. "I didn't have the proper papers. In Germany, we are very careful to see that our business-women are free of disease. I was going to call my boss, which would have been embarrassing, to vouch for me that I wasn't a prostitute. But I didn't have to. The chief at the police station recognized my name von Engelhardt. He asked me if I was related to the general. I told him he was my father so they released me immediately. I think they were afraid of my father who, for people that don't know him, has a reputation for being a very frightening man. Just another incident in the exciting life of a Deutsche fräulein. You want a beer? My treat."

"Sure. I can't tell you what I thought. It was too weird. But besides wanting to see you again, I couldn't go back to the Azores without finding out what happened.

"I'm glad you did. Let me give you my address and phone number. You can write to me if you wish and I would like it if you called me next time. Do you come to Frankfurt often?"

"No, not often, but I can get away from time to time for two or three days. Maybe I will see you again. But I will definitely keep in touch with you." She got a piece of paper and wrote her address and phone number, which he put in his pocket.

Sam reminded her that his flight was in the wee hours so he couldn't stay much longer. He left the bar at about ten when it began to get busy. As he tried to put his money down for the beers, she came around from behind the bar, put her hand behind his head and gave him a gentle peck on the lips. "Please keep in touch, Liebchen. This was a nice time for me. You are a very nice man."

"Nice time for me too," Sam said. "I will write to you." Sam didn't really believe he would keep in touch but promised anyhow.

The plane kept to its schedule and landed at Lajes nine hours later, which was 0900 local time. Sam was greeted by Mac who helped him with his purchases and asked him how his trip was. Sam laughed. "You mean did I get my brakes? Yes."

"I didn't mean that, Sam. How was Fasching?"

Sam smiled. "Exciting to say the least, but I'll talk to you later. It was a trip to remember."

The trip had indeed been eventful for Sam. Not only did he have a wild time with Trudi, he had met a very interesting woman. The thought of Susan stayed with him. The sudden female confusion which he had never experienced before removed any boredom he was experiencing. Would he ever see her again? There was something about her that got him. The Jewish thing bothered him. Maybe he should have told her and found out how she felt right away. He laughed to himself thinking that she didn't wonder if he was a Yankee and a Catholic.

Mac called him at the weather station the next morning. "When do you want to do the brakes? I'm free this afternoon."

"I'm on until 1600. Can you do it then? Will we have enough daylight?"

"Sure, I'll meet you outside the BOQ at about 1630. I have to borrow a brake tool from the motor pool before I come."

"Great, Mac. See you then."

When they removed the front left wheel, Mac said right away. "It's not the brake pads. Look they're still pretty good. But look at this, the brake cylinder is wet. It's leaking." He squeezed it and showed Sam the crack. "I should have looked before you made the trip. Too bad you made the trip for nothing."

"Not for nothing." He smiled. "I got cylinders, too. The guy at the PX insisted I take a set of four so I wouldn't have to come back. He wanted me to buy a master cylinder too, but it was too much money. After a small argument, I took his advice about the wheel cylinders."

Mac grinned. "You did good. Otherwise you would've had to go back to Frankfurt. Let's change this cylinder and look at the other ones."

After they replaced the cylinder, they took off the other wheels. Sam was lucky. It was only one leaky brake cylinder and the first one they looked at was it. "That it?"

"Yup. Looks like just one bad brake cylinder." He took out a can of brake fluid from the bag he brought. "We just gotta put in some fluid, then we'll know for sure. Master cylinder must be empty from the leak. That's why your brakes failed. But keep the pads. You're probably going to need brakes before you leave here. Let's take her for a spin."

Sam wiped his hands with a rag, turned the engine over and felt the brake pedal, which now gave him resistance, and started the car. They drove around testing the brakes and came back to the parking area. He reached out his hand which Mac refused because his was still greasy. "Thanks Mac. I don't know what I would have done."

"No sweat, Sam. But if it wasn't me, one of the guys at the motor pool would have been happy to help. For a couple of bucks they would have done it for you. They just didn't have the parts for your car. See you tomorrow," he got into his car and drove off.."

Golf and the Volcano

Having his dinner at 0830. after the midnight shift had become routine for Sam. He was thinking about the letter he just got from Fiona. They communicated by stewardess couriers delivering letters back and forth. This one was about her return about which he now had mixed feelings.

Herm Slick walked up to the table and sat down with him. "Mind if I join you, Stormy?"

Sam laughed at one of the common weatherman nicknames. "Suit yourself, Herm. Join me in a steak?"

"No thanks, but I will have some breakfast." When the waiter came, he ordered waffles with bacon and coffee.

"Watcha doin' today?" Sam asked, exaggerating his Brooklyn accent.

"Gotta get my flying time in for the month. Planning to take a goonie bird and take a look at Ilha Nova."

"Ilha Nova? What the fuck is that?"

"You, a weatherman, and haven't heard anything about what's going on at Fayal Island?"

"Fayal Island? Only that some pilots reported white plumes arising from the island going up to ten thousand feet. Didn't pay it much attention."

Slick took a gulp of his coffee. "There's an active volcano eruption in the ocean right off the west end of Fayal. Seems to have deposited a little island off the coast. Locals call it *Ilha Nova*, New Island in Portuguese."

"Really, an active volcano? That does interest me."

"Why don'tcha come along? Max and me wouldn't mind company."

"Max Milller? I think he's fucking crazy. You fly with him?"

"Never have. But crazy as he is, he has a rep as a good pilot."

Sam told Herm, "Last time I spoke to him about flying, it was at Dover. He told me he was sure he could flip a C-124 on its back in the air. When I asked him if he ever tried it, he answered, Nah. I'm not sure I could get it back right side up afterwards."

Herm laughed and answered, "Don't believe every story he tells you. He loves to bullshit. But like I said, he has a good rep as a pilot. I can't vouch for his sanity, though," he added, "Come with us. It'll be fun."

"When are you leaving?"

"Meet us at the flight line at 1030 hours. Don't be late if you come. I won't wait."

They finished eating together, paid their respective checks and walked back to the BOQ together. "See you at 1030," Sam said, as he opened the door to his room.

On his way to the flight line, Sam stopped at the weather station and told Jens what he was doing. "That's very interesting." Jens talked very quietly when he was serious, almost in a whisper. "I just heard about Ilha Nova. HQ asked for a forecast because they have to evacuate the whole western part of Fayal. It's being bombarded with chunks of stuff and lava dust and it's covered with ash."

"Wow. Where're they taking them?" Sam asked.

"Word is they're going to the States."

"The States? That's crazy. Where are they going to put them? What are they going to do?"

"Heard they're going to New Bedford. There's a Portuguese enclave that's welcoming them. Jack Kennedy, Massachusetts senator arranged it."

"Wow. How's the weather over Fayal? I'm going with Herm and Max to see it."

"Max? That lunatic. You know he outranks all his flight school classmates?"

"Really? Crazy as he is, how did he manage that?"

"I heard that he rode a horse into the officers' club at Tachikawa air base, Japan, right up to the bar and asked for a beer, while still on horseback. The bartender called the OD immediately who arrested him. The base commander was so pissed off at his arrogance that he got him sent into combat in Korea to punish his ass. So he goes to Korea, gets checked out in F-86 fighters and promptly shoots down six MIGs, escorts his wingman's damaged plane back to the base, gets a silver star and a promotion. I asked him if it was true. He confirmed the story, but as good a pilot as he is, he's off his rocker so pay attention." Jens and Sam looked at the weather map. "Looks good. Got a camera?"

"Yup, just bought the thing, a Kodak Retina IIIc, the latest item in the PX and some Kodachrome, hoping to get some good shots. I wanted the new Leica M3 but couldn't afford it. See you later." Sam walked out to the flight line where Herm and Max were looking over the C-47, the twin engine relic made in 1937 they called a goonie bird because it landed like an albatross, bouncing up and down. It had a relatively large wing span and a tail wheel. If the plane was going too fast during landing when the pilot set it onto its tail, The angle of the wing made the plane begin to take off. It was always several up and down bounces before the plane settled down, just like a goonie bird.

"Hey Sam," Max said. "Good to have you along. We could use a weatherman and I need the company. Herm is a fucking bore."

Herm heard and laughed. "He means I'm sane."

"Is he suggesting I'm crazy enough to be interesting?" Sam answered.

"Who the hell knows. Let's get this bird off the ground. Time's fleeting."

The takeoff was normal after the tower gave them clearance. Herm was the pilot, Max was in the co-pilot's seat. As soon as they got up to two thousand feet, and pointed west, they could see the white plumes going higher than their altitude. "Wow," Herm pointed. "Will you look at that."

"Must be up to about fifteen thou," Max said. Sam looked out the window amazed. In about twenty minutes, they were over Fayal. Sam looked down.

"Shit, look at that," Sam said. The normally green farm land on the western peninsula of the island was covered in brown. The rest of the island, as were all the islands, was a rich green of farm land divided and separated by stone fences, but the farms in that part of Fayal were destroyed. As they got closer, they could see the horseshoe shape bulging out of the ocean.

"Thar she blows, *Ilha Nova*," Herm said

"Never saw anything like it," Sam answered

The plumes were being generated by the water flowing in splashes into the molten-hot center from the open end of the horseshoe and boiling up into the air. All kinds of material was emanating from the center. It frightened Sam, getting too close.

Max was now flying the plane while Herm was taking pictures out of the front window, apparently oblivious to any danger or just ignoring it. Sam was shooting at the brown part of Fayal. When he turned toward the volcano to look, he saw that Max was flying toward the mouth of the eruption. As they got closer, Sam saw white steam boiling up alongside his window from the molten center as the water rushed in, in spurts. Max flew right through it. It was a scary sight. It got even scarier when molten chunks of something started shooting up around them. "Hey Max," Sam shouted. "You're going to get us killed. Don't get so close."

Max answered, "Stop worrying, you only live once. Take your pictures. Don't you want to show people you flew into the mouth of a volcano?" Herm said nothing in response and just kept his camera clicking. Sam was scared but tried to bury his fear and took some pictures. The lava continued shooting up around them and Max took the plane alongside the volcano only about three hundred feet above it.

"Look at that," Max said. Sam could see the black center of the crater and the water flowing into the mouth more vividly than he wanted to. He could feel the heat and was getting more frightened every second as Max took them closer to the crater. "Let's see how close we can get," he added.

Sam, retorted, somewhat panicked, "Max, you're scaring the shit out of me. I am not happy."

"Stop worrying and enjoy it."

Finally, when a piece of molten rock hit the left wing, Herm stopped taking pictures and grabbed the controls. "Enough, you crazy fuck. Sam's right. You're gonna get us killed," Herm said as he banked the plane away from the live crater. Max said nothing. They buzzed the brown end of the island. The houses were so covered that the ground was a homogeneous brown, making the houses hard to see alongside the brown farm land.

On their way back, Sam asked Max. "Weren't you afraid we'd be hit by big rocks or something?"

"It wasn't anti-aircraft fire. They weren't out to get us," Max answered."

"That's your answer? You really are suicidal. You tempt the fates and expect to survive?" Sam asked.

"Have, so far."

"Oh great. I'm pretty big on statistics," Sam said. "I don't want to be in a plane with you when your luck runs out."

Herm laughed, "He makes a good point, you nut. I don't think I'll fly with you again either."

Max got serious and replied, "You guys aren't going to rat me out and get me grounded, are you?"

"No," Herm replied slowly, "but I should. It's nice to know you realize you're fucked in the head."

"I'm not crazy. I just get off on that stuff. I need the rush or I go bananas, 'specially on this island. I miss my F-86 and the MIG sport."

"That's OK. You can risk your own ass. But it's not fair to risk someone else's. You should know that," Herm added, not taking it lightly. Sam said nothing.

"You gonna rat me out?" Looking at Sam.

"Not me. Not my place, but Herm's right. Not fair putting others in your statistical pot."

When they landed, Sam thanked them for the experience and went right over to the PX to get his film processed. He was curious as to what his camera picked up. Back at the BOQ, he dropped off to sleep almost immediately without taking off his clothes. He was awakened a few minutes later by a knock on the door. He groggily got up and answered.

"Hey Sam, I got you some left handed clubs. The weather's great. Let's go golfing," Major Gsell was excited. "I haven't even seen the course yet and I'm anxious."

"Yeah, sure, Major," Sam tried to be convincing that he was OK with it. "Give me ten minutes to change. I'll meet you at your car."

After working until 0800, then chasing a volcano and being scared to death, Sam was drained and not up to it, but didn't want to disappoint the major who was too excited and too nice a guy. Besides, it just wasn't a good idea to refuse your commanding officer. Sam had never been to the golf course either. Not that he never hit a golf ball. In his teen years, he and his pals used to go to the driving range, hit balls for a while then go to the batting cage for a few rounds with a baseball. There were also the few times, he and friends went on their bikes across the Marine Parkway Bridge to Riis Park to play 'pitch and putt' but never played on a real golf course.

But this golf course, as Sam and the major both discovered, wasn't an ordinary course. On the front nine holes, the wind was on your nose usually blowing twenty-five miles per hour. The third hole was on top of a twenty foot rise. You couldn't see the green from the tee. The first time Sam hit the ball, it slammed into the rise and died. He wasn't keeping score so he took a mulligan and tried again. This time, he used an iron to get it up over the rise. It went too high and the wind blew it back almost to the tee. The major laughed and said, "Don't get frustrated. I can see this happening to better golfers than you. Besides who's keeping score?"

"Doesn't make me feel any better, Major."

"You've got a good swing. You just have to keep your right arm out stiff and don't take you eye off the ball to see where it's going. You'll do better next time."

"I think I would do better if it was on my day off rather that after working all night and flying a mission."

"A mission? What mission?"

"I went to see *Ilha Nova* with Herm Slick and Max Miller."

"Really. How was it? I'm going this afternoon with Winchester."

"Very interesting, but with Max, a little scary."

"I've heard about him. Anyway, let's finish the course."

Sam's shots were definitely improving. But when they got to seventeen, which was the mirror of the infamous third hole, dealing with it confused Sam. He looked at the major for a hint. This time the tee was on top of the rise with the heavy wind at his back and the hole was a short 180 yards from the tee, below the rise.

"Use a seven and hit it easy," the major said. Sam pulled the seven iron and tried to hit it easy. He felt the wind at about twenty-five miles per hour, he guessed. His shot was not easy enough. The ball took off and was blown a hundred yards past the hole. The major smiled, looked around at the clouds, evaluated the wind, took his seven iron, hit the ball in the air and the wind took it within five yards of the hole.

Sam was amazed. "Practice, that's all it is. You learn to read the wind like you read the green. Like I said, you'll do better next time."

When they got back to the base, the major offered to buy Sam lunch to thank him for the company. Sam accepted graciously. He would sleep better that afternoon and be ready for his night shift.

Golf From Another Angle

Several days later, Captain Everett Mackenzie, the Canadian liaison officer came into the weather station with three Canadian crew members. It was early morning at the beginning of his shift and Sam was anxious to get to the weather maps. Mackenzie spoke a little louder than was comfortable. He wanted to know how the weather was on the golf course. Sam answered that it wasn't raining, but the wind was terrible. He noticed that they had one golf bag between them with only two clubs in it. "What the fuck kind of golf do they play, anyway with only two clubs for three guys and only one golf bag?"

Mackenzie laughed raucously and reached into the bag while the three golfers watched, pulling out a three wood, a putter, two bottles of Mateus and a forty ounce jug of Gilbey's gin.

Sam reacted, "They don't have to go to the golf course to get shit-faced. Who are they hiding from?" he asked, then looked at the three directly.

"You never been to this golf course?" Mackenzie asked.

"Sure, I have, Ev, with my CO. It's a tough course, wind and all."

"I don't mean that. Didn't you ever notice the stone cabin between holes eight and nine?"

"Noticed, sure, but never paid much attention to it, looked abandoned, like so many other things around here."

Mackenzie laughed again. "You mean you don't know that there are three Azorean chippies plying their trade in that cabin. It's a party for these guys."

"You're shitting me," Sam added, slumping back into the chair he was standing next to.

Mackenzie said, "These guys fake it, although they try to play golf until hole eight and party the rest of the afternoon. Then I come to get them about three hours later."

Sam wondered why they had to fake it. No one really gave a damn. Who were they trying to impress? Then he thought, no women in Canada? I can understand my guys at Santa Rita. They live here. Then he recomposed himself, "Have a good afternoon, guys. See you later at the club." When they left, Sam called Joe Mandino at the weather observation site. "Hey, Gordo. What do you know about the cabin on the golf course?"

Sam heard Gordo laugh. "How'd you find out about that, Cap?"

"I just gave a send off to a Canadian group with a golf bag filled with booze and two golf clubs. They're going out there to party?"

"sir , those girls are a disaster. If you come away with only the clap, you're ahead of the game, if you get my drift."

"How come I never heard about it? Seems strange."

"The reason you never hear about it is that no one stationed here dares to mess around out there, Captain. You've seen the list of forbidden women posted because of disease? Those three are on the top of the list. You know what the general does if someone comes down with the clap."

"Yeah, I know. Sounds nuts to me."

Gordo added, "Canadian crews are really good guys and very serious. I know those particular guys. They're fucking crazy. I don't know how they avoid getting diseased. We were tempted at one time to blow the whistle on it. But we decided if they want to live dangerously, who the fuck are we to stop them? We won't go near the place. No one else who knows about it will either."

"Thanks, Gordo."

"What're you gonna do, Cap?" Gordo added with some apprehension in his voice.

"Not a thing. The secret's safe with me." That eased Gordo's mind. He thanked Sam who told him that if his guys were OK, why should he give a shit. "Peace, Gordo" He hung up. He did wonder at first if he should tell Gsell. He's a golfer and may stumble on it. But he's not the only golfer. If there are others, telling him wouldn't help anything. Better if he doesn't find out from me. Sam was going to try to feel him out but changed his mind. Hear, see and speak no evil.

When Sam finished his shift, he went to the bar at the officer's club and ordered himself a happy hour special, two-for-one martinis. Mackenzie came into the bar, looked around and spotted Sam. He sat on the stool next to him. "Hey, Ev," Sam said, "I got two martinis coming. Take one? On me."

"Sure. Don't want the second one?"

"Negative. I know myself. One martini is a great aperitif. Makes me hungry. After the second one, I don't give a shit if I eat or not and for all practical purposes, the evening becomes a wasted blur."

Mackenzie laughed. "No capacity."

"So I order two because it's the same price but almost always drink only one. By the way, how did your guys do on the golf course? Under par?"

"Sure, ask them yourself when you see them."

"Seriously, is this a habit?"

"Actually, most of the Canadian crews don't indulge in this bullshit. There are a few guys who are a little unhinged like the trio today. They'll eventually sink themselves but I don't want it to be my fault."

"You don't believe in the motto, friends don't let friends get the clap? I asked my guys, who know everything about what's going on. They told me that those girls spread the worst and they stay away. But they asked me not to say anything."

"How come?" Mackenzie answered.

"They don't want the general on the warpath. They said that once he starts, it becomes a major campaign and everyone gets hurt."

"I've heard about him. Anyway, glad to hear you're mum about it."

"I told them that as long as my guys are OK, I couldn't care less. Drink up and let's eat."

"You're on."

The Floating Plane

The next several weeks were ordinary and dull for Sam. He made use of the base library and finally began reading Dostoyevski's *The Idiot*, trying to fulfill the promise he made to himself to read 'the Russians' while he was on the rock. After mentally fighting with the pronunciation of Russian names in his head for a couple of hours, he put the book down and made his way to his car.

At almost four in the afternoon, Sam came into the weather station for the evening shift. Jens was working the day shift with Sergeant MacInerny and seemed agitated. "Hey Sam, we got a problem."

"Saving it for me?"

"I wish. We just got a radio call from a KC-97 in trouble, almost sure it has to ditch in the water about 300 miles southeast of us. Lost two engines, losing altitude, can't reach us or Santa Maria to land and asked about the sea conditions."

"I hope you're not leaving that for me," Sam said. "I barely remember my oceanography professor, let alone the subject matter."

"Negative, negative, not for me either. Fortunately, Mac knows about these things and is making the forecast now. We've got maybe five minutes before the plane hits the drink."

Mac chimed in, "Here it is Jens. You want to call him?"

Jens took the forecast. "Weather to KC-97-432. Come in."

"This is 432. Whatcha got for us?"

"Wind is 220 degrees, fifteen knots. Ocean swells between three and six feet."

"Thanks guys, two engines out. I'm sure I can't make it to Santa Maria airfield. Losing altitude and expect to be in the drink pretty quick. I radioed my position to rescue. Lean on them to get here pronto. Keep your fingers crossed. I think we can survive the impact. But I have no fucking idea how long before she sinks."

"Already leaned," Jens said. "They're on their way but it'll take an hour, hour and a half to get to you. Try to hang on and good luck, guys."

"Thanks, here we go." The transmission stopped. The three of them ran into operations to follow what was happening. There were several people standing around the radio waiting. The tension was mounting, the longer the silence.

"What do you think?" Sam asked Jens very quietly.

"Your guess is as good as mine. Landing in the water is a crapshoot even when the weather is great." They waited through the deafening silence. "Taking too long. Doesn't sound good." Finally, after ten minutes of what seemed like an eternity, they heard.

"432 to Lajes Ops. We're down and damned if we're not floating. Plane didn't break up at all. Ditched like a sea plane, between two waves. Fucking amazing. Were floating gently, bobbing up and down like a boat. Now I gotta worry about getting seasick. Thank Daddy Boeing who built this thing."

"Great, How was the ditching?" Lieutenant Brophy asked.

"Went much smoother than I anticipated. We came down right in a trough like a surfer. And the floating must be the empty fuel tanks. I thought sure we'd sink fast. Bouncing a lot in the waves but it feels stable. I can't see rescue plane yet."

"They'll be there within the hour, hang on." The silence for the next forty-five minutes was loud. Every word uttered sounded like an explosion.

Finally, the silence was broken, "Ops from 432, I see the PBY circling. I guess they're gonna land next to us."

"What's he mean, empty fuel tanks?" Sam asked.

Mac answered, "The plane is a Boeing KC-97. Commercially it's called a Stratocruiser. It's a transport plane. Boeing converted some of them to tankers. They do mid-air refueling. This one just finished a refueling mission of two F-100 fighters being ferried to Aviano. Italy and was returning with empty tanks.

"How many in your crew?" Lieutenant Brophy asked the pilot.

"Seven of us. And for the moment, we're all OK. I can't believe this baby came in so smoothly."

"You ever ditch before?" Brophy said

"Negative. And I never want to do it again. I can't believe we were so lucky. PBY practically next to us already. These guys are great. See you on dry land. 432 over and out."

All of them breathed a sigh of relief in chorus and smiled. Sam said, "Every once in a while, you win one."

"Nice job, Mac," Brophy said. "Baumann said you hit the wave forecast on the nose."

"Thanks, Lieutenant."

As the three of them went back to the weather station, "Baumann is a great pilot. If anyone could have done it, he could," Mac said. "I flew with him on the Schweinfurt raid over Germany in forty four. He's really a natural. See you guys later. I'm already on overtime."

Sam asked Mac, "Did you fly with everyone in the air force over Germany?"

Mac stopped and laughed. "You might think so, but no. Just a few that happened to wind up in our neighborhood."

"No time-and-a-half here," Jens replied with a chuckle. "I'll see you later, my friend. I'm off, too. The weather is all yours."

"Anything I should know before you go?" Sam asked.

"Anything you need is in the logbook. RTFL."

Sam smiled, "Wise ass. Read the logbook," Sam mumbled to himself. "OK, I will." It was a quiet, routine evening. Planes took off on time. The field was open. Sam had finished his map analysis and forecast and had settled into his latest cup of coffee. The doctor told him to cut back on the coffee after he complained of heartburn. Sam heard that one Captain Smith, complained of heart palpitations and was rushed to the hospital. The doctor asked him how heavy a drinker he was. When he answered heavy, the doctor wanted to know what he drank. Seagram's VO and coke was the answer. "Caffeine," the doctor retorted, told him to give up the coke and find another mixer.

Midnight shift was one cup of coffee after another to keep awake. Sam never got used to working those hours. At least with three of the same shifts in a row, as the major arranged it, you can get some sleep. The six days on three days off worked better but midnight shift was always a fight.

The following week was beautiful weather-wise. The wind was negligible. Sam and Marty, making the most of the rare good weather, went on a tourist jaunt and drove around the island, stopping at all the small villages that were mainly on the coast. They stopped at the whaling village of Biscoitos, Serrata on the west coast where they watched a whole hanging pig being smoked and were offered a drink of home-made fire-water which literally burned their throats and gave the villagers a laugh. They had a meal at the Beira Mar in Angra, the only real city on the island. The proprietor recognized Sam from his previous visit with Jeannie. They eventually ended up at the beach in Praia da Vitoria. It was still too cold to swim but they anticipated the coming summer. The next day, Sam was on the four to midnight shift.

The few days following were relatively busy but routine. With good weather, the traffic was heavy but briefings were straightforward. Suddenly, at about 1100 on his last shift, the tranquil atmosphere in the terminal changed dramatically. Warren Wells came barging in from operations, slightly frantic but controlled. He asked Sam what the ocean situation was right now southeast of Santa Maria island and for the next few hours. Sam walked over to the anemometer dial and then the surface weather map without saying anything. Then he looked up and said, "Looks pretty good. The winds are negligible as they have been all week and probably the swells are very small. That's right where Baumann ditched. What's up?"

"That's too bad,' Wells answered.

"Too bad?" Sam frowned. "Why?" Sam asked.

"The KC-97 is still floating. We assumed it would sink eventually. A routine flight around Santa Maria in a goonie spotted it bobbing up and down gently. It didn't sink and somehow the Russians found out about it and intelligence picked up a radio transmission. There's a Russian trawler heading toward it but is still about eight hours away. We can't let them get into the plane. Too much classified material and secret technology."

"A trawler's a fishing boat," Sam replied. "Why is that a problem?"

"Sure, fishing boat." Wells said sarcastically. "That's why it's headed directly for a floating American plane. Right?"

"What're you gonna do?"

"We have to sink it, somehow,"

"Just how do you expect to do that? Hand grenades?"

"The battleship Wisconsin is about seventy miles away, on its way back to Norfolk from training exercises in the Mediterranean. Should be able to reach the plane in a couple of hours. I'll see if I can raise them on the radio."

"A fucking battleship. The Wisconsin, no less. You're kidding me," Sam said incredulously.

"The very one. This is the second Wisconsin. Fought in the Pacific and in the Korean conflict."

"Do you really need a battleship?"

"We don't have much of a choice. It's the closest ship with the weapons to do it and we gotta sink the plane. I thought about sending a navy UDT team with explosives but the Wisconsin sounds like a better, safer bet."

"What about a bomber?"

"Where the fuck am I going to find a bomber with bombs anywhere near here? Unless you want me to nuke it with a SAC B-47. No, thanks. The Wisconsin," leaving the weather station hurriedly.

The Wisconsin is the only possibility? Sam thought for a minute and then he realized there are no significant weapons on the base. Leroy Potter came to the weather station at five of midnight to relieve Sam who was just finishing his long notation in the logbook.

"Anything new?" Leroy asked.

Sam chuckled, went through the routine of the past ten hours and then added that was all written up in the logbook. He suggested Leroy should keep up with the ocean conditions. "The KC-97 is still floating and there's a Russian ship moving toward it. You don't know what ops is going to need." He told Leroy that Wells is trying to contact the battleship Wisconsin on it's way to Norfolk from the Mediterranean.

"Wow. Interesting day."

"Was busy, but boring until Wells broke the news to me. Weather should be good. Full moon tonight. Wait for the battleship. See you tomorrow."

About 0400, the radio in the weather station blared out. "Lajes weather, this is the battleship Wisconsin, over."

Leroy picked up the microphone. "Wisconsin this is Lajes weather. What can I do for you?"

"Are the weather and winds going to remain pretty good around Santa Maria? And for how long?"

"Hang on Wisconsin." Leroy looked at the charts to verify Sam's earlier forecast. "Looks very pleasant and a full moon."

"That's too bad;"

"What? Why?" Leroy was puzzled. "Whatcha looking for?"

"We've been ordered to sink the floating KC-97 tanker but we can't."

"Why not? Not that it's any of my business."

"Never mind, weather. I'll call ops."

Leroy walked into operations to listen. "Lajes ops, this is the Wisconsin."

"Wisconsin, Lajes ops. What's up?"

"We have orders to sink the the floating KC-97 and we would be happy to do so. We've been here a whole day waiting and it's off our starboard bow."

"That's my understanding, Wisconsin," Wells answered."

"Well, we can't."

"You can't what?

"Sink it. At least not now. And we don't relish the idea of starting world war three by blowing a Russian trawler out of the water/"

"What do you mean, you can't sink it? Why not? No ammo? A battleship with no ammo?"

"Oh, we got plenty of ammo. We have another problem. More serious."

"What?"

"International law."

"What the hell are you talking about?"

"Have you ever heard of the right of salvage?"

"Sure. You find it, it's yours. So?"

You won't believe this but there's a fishing boat, about 10 feet long with three guys in it hitched to the plane."

"What do you mean hitched?"

"They managed to get a rope around one of the props and they're trying to tow it."

"How the hell can they do that? They don't have a motor that could pull an 80,000 pound, four engine airplane."

"What motor? There's no fucking motor. It's a rowboat. They take turns rowing."

"Rowing? You're kidding me. A ten foot rowboat and it's trying to tow an 80,000 plus pound, 110 feet long KC-97 by a prop. I can't even picture that without laughing. That's fucking bizarre if you don't mind my saying so. Where are they trying to take it?"

"Beats the shit out of us, ops. But we've been told that international law of the sea, of which we are a participant, says that since the plane was abandoned, these guys essentially own it. Right of salvage. We can't touch them, legally, that is."

"That's a joke. Can't you wait them out? They can't keep this up."

"Sure, we have no choice. We've been watching them for almost a day now and they don't seem to get discouraged. They just keep rowin' along merrily. The plane's not going anywhere but they don't give up."

"Ridiculous. A U.S. battleship waiting on a 10 foot rowboat. It's a local boat, I'm sure you can get them to let go for a c-note, anything. Maybe even a ten dollar bill."

"Easier said than done. We don't have anyone who speaks Portuguese on the ship. Besides, I think you're wrong. They might be whaling peasants, but they're not stupid. They know it's worth more, particularly now that we're sitting here watching them. They just don't know why. Besides, like I said, getting to them is a problem without someone who speaks Portuguese."

At about seven-thirty, General Smith came into ops and recognized Leroy. "What's the weather, Lieutenant?" the general asked, trying to act calm even though Leroy could see he was agitated.

"Pretty good, sir . Almost no wind and some clouds."

The general grabbed the mike at the radio. "Wisconsin, this is General Smith. What's the latest on the fishing boat?"

"Still hanging on, General. We should register these guys in the olympics. The Russian trawler is about a thousand yards away and obviously holding."

"Shit" the general mumbled. "How long can you guys wait around?"

"As far as I know, General, the admiral has all the time needed. We're on our way back from a training mission but we were ordered not to leave until the tanker is sunk. Uh, oh. I just got word that the trawler is moving closer. The fishing boat still won't let go. It's not even moving but they won't let it go."

"Do you think they know anything about the international law of the sea?" the general asked, tongue in cheek.

"I would doubt it, sir . I don't even know if they can read."

"Why aren't they afraid of the Wisconsin?"

"Don't know. You hunt whales around here in a rowboat with hand thrown harpoons, you gotta be fearless, I would think."

"What do you think the Russians are up to?"

"Beats me General. Why don't I get Admiral Crommelin to talk to you directly. I'm sure he has a better idea than I do."

"Do that." Looking at the others the general said, "I know Hank Crommelin."

"Lajes weather, This is Admiral Crommelin."

"Hank, this is Hal Smith. What's happening?"

"Hey Hal. How's the boy? Might have an international incident on our hands. The trawler has launched a small boat which is heading toward the fishing boat."

"What's do you think their game is?"

"I don't know but my guess is they want to buy the plane from the fishermen. I'm sure these fishermen know dollars. But rubles? I don't know. I also think they have the same language problem we do right now."

"Could be nasty. If the Russians wind up owning it."

"No sweat, Hal. I won't let that happen. There is not likely to be a written bill of sale. If they get any closer, I'll stop them. It's one kind of incident if I stop them from getting near the fishing boat. It's quite another if I let them buy the plane and then blow them out of the water."

"Why don't you just sink the damn plane and pay some reparations to the fishermen afterwards? Seems foolish to wait any longer. They would be foolish not to make a deal."

"Might be a good idea, but I'm afraid if I blow it up, it'll sink and drag the boat down with it. Watching the boat, I still can't believe it. They've moved only a few inches in the last two hours but they're still pulling the oars. And I'm sure it's only the current that's moved it. I don't know what they're expecting. They can't have much strength left."

'What are your orders?" General Smith asked.

"Pretty direct, Hal. Sink the plane. I would like to wait until they're ready to give up but the Russian small boat is moving closer to the fisherman. Really shouldn't wait any longer. I'm going to blow a hole in the plane. That will probably scare the fishermen and the Russians both. I'd like to sink the plane slowly and hopefully give them time to unhitch themselves so they're not dragged under by the sinking plane."

Two minutes later the radio blared. "General Smith, this is rescue chopper four. Wisconsin just shot a round right through the plane."

"Is it sinking?"

"No sir. Not yet. But the fishermen are in a panic. They untied the boat from the propeller and are rowing away like crazy. I see the Russian boat turned around, too."

"Chopper four, this is Admiral Crommelin on the Wisconsin. Back off a bit. I don't need any casualties. The fishermen unhitched the boat.

I'm going to wait a bit until they get far enough away. Then we'll destroy it."

A short time later, two explosions followed. The rescue chopper called, "Hey ops, the plane is going down fast. It's already below the surface. Everyone in the weather station began to applaud. The general then grabbed the mike again. "Rescue chopper, this is General Smith."

"General, this is rescue chopper."

"By chance, you got anyone on the chopper speaks Portuguese?"

"Matter of fact, you're in luck, sir . It happens Colonel Noronha came along for the ride." Colonel João Noronha was the commander of the Portuguese detachment at Lajes.

"Thank goodness for small things.," he mumbled. Colonel Noronha was known for the hideously sweet after shave lotion he used. "Ask him if he'd be willing to be lowered to the fishing boat and talk to the fisherman."

"Hal, this is João Noronha. What would you like me to do?"

"Probably the best thing, João, is to get the fishermen's names and find out where they live. Then we can send someone to make a settlement with them. We should pay something, don't you think?"

"Of course," Noronha said. "It's peanuts and it's good public relations."

"I just don't think we should be negotiating in the open sea."

"I doubt the boat is from Terceira. Too far away. I would guess they come from a village on Santa Maria's east coast. I have some dollars, Let me see if I can't settle it right away. They must have seen the plane ditching. If I can't resolve it, I'll find out who they are, Hal. I'll bring the information to you back at the base."

"Great, João . *Muito obrigado*," the general said in his limited Portuguese. "I really appreciate it."

"*Por nada, Senhor*. See you later."

"Smith to Wisconsin."

"Hey Hal. It's done. Plane is gone."

"Good job, Hank. What's the trawler doing?"

"Nothing. Just waiting for their little boat to get back to them. At this point I don't give a shit what they do."

"Can you get away for a bit and meet me in the club for a drink? Long time no see."

"Good idea if you're willing to wait. It'll take me a few hours to get to you."

"Dinner's on me, Hank. Over and out." Good job guys, especially you Lieutenant. What's your name?"

"Potter, sir , Leroy Potter." Leroy was pleased at the recognition but a little surprised since he didn't think he did much. The weather was what it was.

The general shook his hand. "Well, guys, we came out of this weird happenstance smelling great. No personnel losses or injuries, Only loss was a plane. And those KC-97s are being replaced with KC-135 jets anyway. Take care," he said as he quickly left the weather station.

Jens who had been in the weather station but kept out of the action intentionally looked at his watch. "Hey Leroy. I know you love it here now that you're a semi-hero. But..." he pointed to his watch.

Leroy looked at his watch. "Holy shit, I got basketball practice. See ya."

Things quickly settled down in the weather station. In ten minutes, you wouldn't know anything had deviated from the routine. Jens took a look at the weather maps to see what was happening in the skies. Then he looked at the schedule board and made a mental note. Finally he opened the logbook and read where Leroy had meticulously written everything down. He still couldn't believe that an Azorean fishing rowboat was trying to tow a 40 ton airplane. He hoped the rescue chopper took some pictures.

The next morning, the weather station heard Noronha settled with the fishermen for fifty American dollars. He didn't even negotiate for a lesser amount.

The Jewish Thing

Life for Sam and Marty had stabilized. Time was passing pleasantly. Sam's routine was reading Dostoyevski, pick-up basketball and occasionally spending some time playing Robbie's piano when no one was around. He wanted to practice more but hesitated because the repetition of practicing can get annoying to most people. The piano could be heard in several rooms nearby. Another one of his avocations, which he shared with Marty, was to check the manifests of the incoming planes for Fiona and Martha.

On a mid-afternoon Friday, Sam was sitting on the edge of his bed. For some reason he was exhausted from the midnight shift and had fallen asleep without even eating. He hadn't seen Fiona in a while and hadn't received any word lately via their usual channel. Even though their relationship was short, he found himself more wondering about her than missing her. He wasn't sure what it was, sex or did she just fill a void that afflicted many people on the island especially in the rainy, windy, depressing winter. He wasn't sure, but he thought it wasn't more than that. Loneliness can create feelings, he thought.

When he got out of the shower, he noticed that his blue and white lucky boxer shorts were on top of his dresser drawer – a cause for optimism. Sam was not religious but was, for no reason he could fathom, superstitious. Maybe it was a series of coincidences but whenever those shorts came around almost always good things happened. He was meticulous about it and never forced them out of sequence. He was sure that if he did, the spell would be broken. He got to the o-club dining room about four thirty with a ravenous appetite, having skipped his morning dinner. As soon as he sat down, Captain John Campbell, the Catholic chaplain, approached his table. "Open for some company, Sam?"

"Sure, Padre. Have a seat." He was holding a letter in his hand. Sam noticed the letter and nodding at the envelope, "Anything important? Letter from above, maybe?"

"He does indeed work in mysterious ways, Sam, but a letter? Too mysterious. Even an engraved stone tablet with which he has some experience would be weird." Father Campbell laughed at his own comment. He put the envelope in front of Sam with the address facing Sam. "Do you believe this?" he said pointing. "I make a reservation for two at a retreat in Garmisch for Captain Wilhelm and me and I get this answer from the hotel."

Sam looked at the envelope and laughed. I'm Jewish and I think it's a riot."

"What idiot addresses an answer to Father and Mrs. John Campbell? I could understand if I was writing to an Asian or Arab country. But Germany has a very large Catholic population. And a hotel manager has no clue?"

"You sound angry, John. Maybe the hotel manager was Jewish. I understand that the Jewish population in Germany has been increasing since the end of the war. Don't take it so personally."

"I'm not angry and I'm not really offended, just flabbergasted. When I show it to Chaplain Wilhelm, I wonder what his reaction will be. Which brings me to another subject." Sam took a sip of wine. "You know Aaron Rosen, the civilian who works in the quartermaster section?"

"Sure, nice guy. Lotsa kids." Sam added.

"There's no Jewish chaplain here so he runs Jewish services Friday nights at the chapel. It would be nice if you attended tonight."

Sam was surprised. Since his bar mitzvah and especially after his grandfather died several years later, his Jewish practice was limited to going to an occasional passover seder when invited, or an annual Yom Kippur service. No one ever pushed him to do more. "I'm not devout, John. My participation is usually limited to Yom Kippur and an occasional family get together at a funeral. It's been a long time since I've been to a Sabbath service."

"I can't order you to go but it would be nice," he repeated. "Besides, it would help remove your stigma."

Sam reacted with apprehension. "Stigma, what stigma?"

"The stigma of being a Yankee and a Catholic," he added snidely. Campbell was known for his snide sense of humor particularly during his weekly sermons.

"Where did you hear about that, John?" Sam asked testily.

"The grapevine. The word is out."

"But who let it out?"

"I don't really know. In fact, I heard it from someone in the chapel on Sunday but I don't remember who."

"I only told one person, the aircraft commander, and he promised me he wouldn't tell anyone."

Campbell shrugged. "But not to digress, why don't you go, if only to be a part of the Jewish community on the island? You missed a great Passover seder. Chaplain Levitan was here from McGill in Florida and gathered as many Jews as he could find on the base, even two Azorean Jews he found on the island, a brother and sister, both in their eighties. Some thirty people attended. I hear the food was great."

"I wasn't invited."

"If you attended services, you would have been."

Sam's mind was mulling these thoughts over. "What time is the service? Maybe I will go." Sam's food came. "What time is the service?" he asked again.

"1900."

"Not eating?"

"A little early for me. I just wanted to do my chaplaining with you. I'll leave you to eat without being harassed." He got up.

"Thanks, John, and send my regards to the missus." Sam said it with no expression."

"I'll do that. Shalom," he said smiling, as he left the table.

Sam thought about the service. He hadn't been to a synagogue in years. Why did it interest him? He was born and raised a Jew but considered himself an atheist. The old saw that 'there are no atheists in foxholes' made him laugh. He was convinced that even under fire he would be an atheist. Then why the interest, he thought? Maybe it was the nostalgia, the Jewish tradition he grew up with, the memory of his grandfather who was so close to him as a child. His father was probably an atheist, too, but would never admit it. His mother on the other hand was always threatening him with God's punishment as a child, but he always wondered whether she really believed it. In any case, he had nothing to do that evening so he decided to attend the service.

****

There was a certain familiarity that came over him at the service. The prayers which came back to him from his early religious education surprised him. He did not believe the words but the recitation of the prayers was somehow comforting. And when he recited the Kaddish for his grandfather, the mourner's prayer for the dead. the tears welled up in his eyes. He felt like he had satisfied an obligation to a man he loved so much.

****

Marty had not heard from Martha and was getting jumpy. Unlike Sam's flaky relationship with Fiona, Marty and Martha were serious and it seemed as if they found each other. Every time Sam saw them together he wondered, atheist though he was, what divine intervention had set them on the path to meet. He never saw two people on the same wavelength as much as they were.

Marty went down to the terminal and checked the crew manifests of the planes that had landed and the ones coming in to see if he knew any stewardess that would know about Martha. No luck. He would just have to suck it up and wait. He thought about sending her a message but after thinking that a message carried by someone that didn't know her would be a little precarious, he decided against it. They were doing the best they could to stay under the Charleston radar. For the moment, he would just wait.

Hurricane Hunting

"Sam," Major Gsell came out of his office and addressed him directly in his usual quiet manner. "Kindley hurricane hunters are looking for a weatherman for a month or two to fill in for a sick regular. You interested?" He smiled.

Sam knew Kindley AFB in Bermuda. He had been there once as an ROTC cadet. Nice duty, but flying into hurricanes, Sam didn't know. He could sense what it would feel like and got a chill. "They still flying those converted B-29s?"

"Yup. And you get flight pay," the major added.

Sam digested that comment and quickly tried to decide whether an extra $150 a month justified the risk, although Sam was aware that their safety record was superlative. "I don't really know anything about the instruments, procedures..."

"Not a problem," the major interrupted. "They said they'll fill you in. They don't think it's a problem so you shouldn't worry."

Sam didn't answer because his mind was working. "Month or two, you said, Major?"

"Yeah, Sam. They may want to extend you but I won't let them. I need you here."

"OK, I'll go. When do they want me?"

"ASAP, pack a bag and you're off."

Next morning, Sam hitched a ride on a C-124 on its way back to Dover via Bermuda. Six hours later, Major Grant met him at the weather station and arranged for his indoctrination. The major felt that a couple of hours, mostly with the instruments and to go over the standard procedure was all that would be necessary. He'd done it before and everything out very well. It wasn't that big a deal. In fact, the only reason they really needed a meteorologist on board was because the regulations said so. For Sam, it was relatively easy to absorb everything and didn't take much time. He had sent rawinsonde balloons up before. These were almost the same except instead of rising up in a helium balloon, they were dropped from the plane with a parachute and tracked from above.

"Get some sleep," the major said. "We've got a mission early tomorrow. Hurricane Carrie. I'll get someone to show you to your quarters. Be here at 0700."

"Yessir,"Sam said. "See you then."

Sam checked into a room in the transient officers quarters. One thing he noticed immediately was the weather. Compared to the miserable rain and wind at Lajes, the weather was balmy at Kindley and the sunset was gorgeous. Otherwise, the officers club was just another one with different faces in the bar and restaurant. The language of the help in the dining room was English, not Portuguese.

His first trip into a hurricane made him regret that he agreed to do it. Hurricane Carrie was a potential threat to the east coast of the U.S. Entering the storm, he had never been so shaken in an airplane. Contrary to usual flights, which used radar to avoid the lightning and thunder of cumulonimbus clouds, the hurricane hunter pilot aimed at the blackest wall of clouds he had ever seen, plowed into them and through them into the eye, a frightening experience.

Sam got used to the procedure and next few weeks passed by without incident. They flew into hurricane Carrie twice a day, every day, as it headed west toward the east coast. Every day, punch through the black storm wall shaking like riding a car over a test course, into the eye, taking readings of pressure, temperature, wind speed, climb taking more readings at intervals and then drop the instrument package and record the readings. The eye of the storm was a strange contrast. He had heard about it but this was the first time he had seen one first hand. As the dark gray, almost black wall of clouds surrounded them as the plane climbed. Looking up above through the top gunless gun turret, there was a circle of blue sky dotted with fair weather altocumulus but with one difference, an eerie purple tint.

After the first trip, every trip was almost the same. Blast into the center, rattling through the thunderstorms, climb in the eye, then blast out again through the black wall, shaking from the turbulence with lightning all around. The first time unnerved Sam. He had gone through thunderstorms before but this was much worse. He quickly got used to it.

They followed Carrie twice a day for weeks but when she turned northeastward and was deemed to be no longer a threat to the east coast, they stopped chasing her. For the two weeks after that, there was no other hurricane activity and Sam passed time helping out in the weather station.

Major Grant appeared one afternoon, "Sam, it looks like things will be calm for the next month as best we can tell. There doesn't seem to be any genesis activity off the African coast. I think you should probably go back to Lajes."

"That's OK with me," Sam smiled, "I really miss the Lajes weather," he added sarcastically. "After all, how much balmy sunshine can a man take?"

The major laughed. "Tell me, does that mean if I can get Gsell to send you back later on, you'll come back?"

"I'll bite my lip and force myself. Anything for my country and an extra 150 bucks."

"Great. For your information, there are two eastbound planes arriving in the morning stopping at Lajes. So you can take one of those. Check the schedule to see when they're arriving. It was great having you here, Sam. We'll miss you but we can't in good conscience keep you here without any storms to chase."

"Thanks for the opportunity, Major. It really was an experience. And I certainly can use the $150," he added with a grin.

The major grinned back, extended his hand. "Take the evening off and I'll see you in the morning."

Sam saluted and left the terminal just in time to catch the base bus to the club. He thought about going for a swim in the club pool but the weather was too cool, not conducive to summer pleasures. Bermuda was not a tropical island. It was east of South Carolina with seasons appropriate for that latitude but without the cold blasts that often hit the southeast coast in the winter. The winters were mild but not summery.

He had made the most of this two week dead spell. He was able to borrow a car and drove all over the island. He spent almost a whole day in Hamilton, the capital, shopping. After all, he thought, what else should he do with the extra $150 he would get. The thought of returning was mixed. Bad weather, work, but it was home, at least for the time being. After an evening of watching TV in the club, he went back to his quarters, packed his bag and fell asleep. Next morning, early, he called the weather station to check on the flights. The first one to Lajes was arriving at 0700 and leaving at 0900 so he didn't have to rush. At 0800, he walked into the weather station with his bag and waited for the crew to come for their briefing.

When Bob Billet walked in, Sam smiled at him and looked at the crew behind him. He did not recognize the stewardesses and relaxed when he saw neither was Jeannie. "Didn't bring your girlfriend this trip," Billet said, without a grin. "What're you doing here?"

"Chasing hurricanes for fun and profit."

"I can see the fun, but the profit?" he added.

"Hey, don't sneeze at a buck fifty a month. Makes my life. I'm hitching a ride with you back to Lajes if you have space."

"I'm pretty sure I do. If not, you can stay with us in the crew compartment. We leave in a half hour. You can board now, if you want to. Andrea can show you to a seat," he nodded at the red-headed stewardess. "In fact, Andrea, show him to the crew compartment. He can keep us company."

"This way, sir , follow me."

The C-118 cruised at 19,000 feet and Sam relaxed in the seat next to the engineer. Three hours into the flight, Sam looked and saw the black wall of clouds that had become so familiar to him. "Hey Bob, if I didn't know better, I would think that's a hurricane. It sure as shit looks like one. You got any reports of one?"

Bob answered, "The only one that was around was Carrie but once it turned away from the coast, we stopped getting reports."

"That's because they usually turn northeast and evolve into normal storms headed toward Europe. No one's tracking her now. As soon as she turned, we stopped chasing her. I wonder if it's Carrie, weird as it sounds. Maybe she turned due east and maintained her hurricane structure. When we get a little closer, I'll see if I can tell." He asked the navigator . "Show me our position on a map." Sam looked at the map. "Possible, if she turned east."

Sam watched with Bob and his co-pilot as they approached the black clouds which were right on their heading to Lajes. "What do you think, Sam? The radar doesn't show anything more than a scattered thunderhead, which we can avoid with radar. Should we go through it?"

"I can't answer that, Bob. I think it really is the remains of Carrie, but it certainly would be substantially weakened by the colder ocean water. I wouldn't know what to tell you. What would you do if I wasn't here?"

"Well, if the radar images don't scare me, I'd just plow ahead."

"I can't imagine it bothering us much flying into it but I can tell you this, though, if it hits Lajes head on, the winds could do damage to airplanes on the ground. We can deal with 35 or 40 knots. They almost always come from the southwest so the planes are always turned into the wind. But 60 knots from another direction, that could be nasty. Can you get Lajes weather on the radio from here?"

"Worth a try." Bob switched to the weather frequency and the navigator gave him headphones and a mike.

"Lajes weather, this is Golden, over."

"Hey Sam, this is Mac. Heard you were on your way. What's up?"

"Mac, I think the remains of hurricane Carrie is headed directly for the base. It's right in front of us and probably about three hours from the first winds hitting you."

"No shit. You really think so, and it's aimed right at us?"

"Yeah, you know when it turned east we stopped chasing it from Kindley so no one was following its track. Is there an Atlantic storm headed for Europe?"

"None that I can see," Mac answered.

"Then it must be Carrie and it sure looks like it. It's right on our heading. I've been thinking. If it hits the base and if it's a direct hit the winds such as they might be, will be from the south. I have no clue yet how strong they are. But that's not too bad with planes pointing southwest with tail stands But if the eye passes directly over the base or close, fifteen minutes later, the winds, which could be very strong, will suddenly be coming from the north. That could be a disaster."

"You're right if it's true. That means we should turn all the planes around in 15 minutes. Hard to do with tail stands in and no pilots. Let me call Warren and give him a heads up."

Bob chimed in. "Mac, This is Bob Billet. What do you think about flying the planes aerodynamically on the ground?"

Mac answered, "Not weather's call. Sounds like a good idea, though Then they would have the flexibility to aim the noses in whatever direction we have to. Also flying them like that, we don't have to put tail stands in. Without the stands, if they're not being flown, they could get knocked over onto their tails. I'll call ops. Let them decide. It's their job anyway."

"Go, man, go," Sam answered.

"Ops, this is weather," Mac announced. "We think we've got a hurricane approaching the base. We estimate that if it is and hits, we'll get strong south winds, then calm for about fifteen minutes, then strong north winds."

"That could be a nightmare," Wells answered. "We've got to do something."

"Warren, my suggestion is to alert all the crews, man the planes, start the engines and have them wait in the planes with engines running. Then when we see the wind direction and speed, we can decide how to advise the crews to turn."

"Let me see if I can get some flights off early. Then I can alert the crews that are still left," Warren answered.

Bob chimed in, "Warren, we'll be there in about an hour which puts us down ahead of the storm. We can unload the passengers and stay with the plane until we know." He looked at Sam. "The radar response is not too scary, I'll plow right into it. Is that OK with you?"

"Hey, I'm a weatherman, not a pilot. With the thousands of hours of flying time you've got, you know better than I how much the plane can take."

"Pilot to navigator, see if you can get a fix on the wind speed when we hit the black wall."

"Will do."

The crew was quiet from that point on. Everyone looking out the window. "Turbulence expected shortly," Bob announced. "Everybody in their seats and seat belts on." Twenty minutes later, the C-118 hit the black cloud wall at 19,000 feet. Using the radar, Bob steered around the embedded thunder cells and in less than ten minutes the shaking was over and it was calm."

"Done, just like a hurricane hunter," Sam said. "Look up. Wow. The storm still has its hurricane structure." Sam pointed to the patch of blue above them.

"How were the winds, Johnny?" Bob asked the navigator.

"Best I can tell due north at about 60 knots."

Sam replied, "That's at altitude. On the ground probably less. But we don't know for sure. There's very little friction over water."

They anticipated hitting the black wall on the other end exiting the eye. This too, didn't have too much radar return to worry Bob. They hit the wall and it was pretty much the same as the entry except that getting out of seemed to otake longer. No surprise there for Sam who anticipated the east end of the storm would be the heaviest. In an hour, they were touching down and followed the "sigame" truck that led them to a parking berth and pointed them to the south. "Tower to C-118 665. Keep your engines running and stay with the plane. Do you need fuel?"

"No, tower, we're good for a while."

Sam bid Bob goodbye, thanked him for the lift and left with the passengers. He went right to the weather station. Mac was talking to Wells. "What's up guys?"

"Sam, glad to see you. Was it Carrie?" Mac asked.

"Sure as shit looked like it. We went in and out just like I've doing it for weeks. I was surprised that although small, it still had a hurricane structure with a defined eye. The winds were in the vicinity of 60 knots at 19,000 feet. So use your judgement on the surface."

Mac looked at Warren. "Gotta prepare for about 50 knots, especially the north winds on the back end of the storm."

"Then our original plan holds. But I've got a problem, Two crews are not here yet because they're drunk. They apparently are on their way. I sent someone up to pick them up. If they can't hack it, I'll put the co-pilots in command." Just then the two crews came in the station. Warren said to Sam, "There are only six planes to worry about. I was able to get four planes to depart early. These six don't have the duty time and have to stay. This time spent on this will count as duty time and keep them here even longer." Looking at the crews, Warren spotted the drunk pilots and talked to the two co-pilots who fortunately, were both sober. "We have to fly the planes on the ground and then turn them 180 degrees. The tower will advise you." Then he turned to the drunk pilots. "I want to be clear to you two, your co-pilots are temporarily in command. You behave and I protect your asses and say nothing.

The pilots trying their best to behave soberly, agreed and went to their planes. An hour later, the storm hit suddenly and fiercely. The 15 knot winds suddenly jumped to over 50 knots directly from the south as predicted with very heavy rain. The three watched the flight line and could see the six planes, engines racing, pointing south. Mac watched the anemometer hold steady around 50. About 25 minutes later, the winds and the rain stopped as suddenly as they started and it looked like a front had passed.

"That's the eye," Sam said. "You gotta turn them around pointing north right now."

"I second the motion," Mac echoed. Wells called the tower. "Tower, advise planes to turn to heading 360 as quickly as possible." He watched as the planes, revving the engines on one side, started turning. When they were turned, Sam watched the weather vane and anemometer readings. Sure enough, after about fifteen minutes, a wall of rain and wind hit the base from almost due north varying from 40 to 65 knots. They watched the flight line as the planes all held their positions with engines revving. After a half hour, the storm passed and winds jumped back to southwest at 45 knots. If it hadn't been known to be a hurricane, it would have seemed like a frontal passage with fair weather following.

Mac looked at Sam. "Looks like you hit it right on the button Sam. You did good."

Wells chimed in, "I agree, Sam. There's no doubt that the planes would have been knocked over if we hadn't gotten the crews in the planes. I'll tell the general you saved our butts."

"Thanks for that," Sam said. "But we were lucky I was on that plane and saw what I had been flying into twice a day for weeks. What do they say about being in the right place at the right time?"

Mac laughed. "Don't be modest, Sam. If being lucky makes you look good, don't knock it. Take the credit. There will be days when the opposite happens."

"Guess you're right," Then Sam replied, holding out his arms, "Look at me, guys. I'm a hero."

"Don't overdue it, please," Mac insisted.

Word of what happened spread and Sam got a little embarrassed by the attention. Next day things were back to normal except that Sam found General Smith with Major Gsell in his office.

"Nice job, Golden, I told Major Gsell to reward you somehow."

"Thanks, General, but, really, we were lucky."

"Call it what you want. It saved us a mess and *muito dinhiero*. See you later Al." He left abruptly as if he was in a hurry.

"You heard the general, Sam. What can I do for you?"

"I'd be happy with a couple of extra days off."

"I think we can work that out. Let me think about it."

Christmas Trees

Sam was thinking about what to do with the few days off he had become entitled to by a bit of luck. Fiona had just left on her way back to the States. She had come a few days earlier than he expected and their visit was pleasant and sexy. He didn't know when he would see her again. He never did, but wasn't as affected as he once had been. They spent too much time arguing about nothing. His feelings about her were on-again-off-again depending on how she reacted to him. Some days their relationship was warm and tender, but he always felt on edge as if waiting for a shoe to drop. This visit was more temperamentally even.

One dominant characteristic about Lajes was the lack of live communication. It drove Sam nuts. He knew others felt the same way. Telephone service from the island, even the base itself was non-existent If there was any need for instant communication between Lajes and the U.S. or other bases it was by telex which was transmission of typed characters on undersea cable and used only for official business. Letter writing just didn't do it for Sam, but Fiona was quite content with it. She liked writing letters with small talk and passed them on via a stewardess. Sam didn't like small talk and certainly didn't want to create small write, and only did so out of a feeling of obligation. He always had the 'I'll tell you when I see you attitude.'

Considering Sam's state of mind, when Major Gsell asked Sam if he wanted to go to Newfoundland with a group of guys to cutdown Christmas trees for the base - something the Canadian government arranged every year - Sam agreed before asking why. "I'm not that good with an axe. I'm a city boy."

The major laughed. "We don't need your muscles, Sam. The rescue squadron goes every year with a group of musclemen and they always want a weatherman on the flight."

"Why is that?" Sam asked. "Sounds ridiculous. Strong axe wielders, sure, but a weatherman?"

"I haven't the foggiest. Winchester couldn't give me an answer either. Seems they've done it that way for many years and no one wants to change because maybe there was once a reason." The major laughed. "If it ain't broke, don't fix it."

No one knows the reason but everyone is afraid to change what works. A better description is, if no one brings the subject up, don't look for trouble."

"Sounds typical," Sam said dryly. "Maybe just a superstition. That I can accept. Why me, Major?"

"Saves me time. You never refuse." He smiled.

Sam laughed. "So I'm your only patsy. OK, when do they leave?"

"Day after tomorrow. 0700. Meet at the terminal 0630. Jens said he'd cover for you if you don't get back in time."

"Something to look forward to. A Jew on a Christmas tree expedition. Sounds like a Mark Twain novel."

The major laughed. "You have no religious objection, do you?"

"Shit no, Major. Sounds like a secular adventure for me."

"OK, you're on, Sam. See you later."

****

Friday morning, Sam arrived at the terminal promptly at 0630 and found Lieutenant Fernando Hernandez looking over the goonie bird with Lieutenant Wally Pisani. "You the crew? I'm Sam Golden coming along for the ride. " He extended his hand.

"You the weather part? We're the flying part. The navigator and the cutting part are not here yet. Glad to have you aboard, Captain," Hernandez said.

"Sam, please. Sam Golden."

Hernandez smiled. "Ferdie Hernandez, and this is Wally Pisani."

"My pleasure Wally, we gonna leave on time?" Before they could answer, seven muscled airmen wielding axes approached them.

Ferdie looked up. "Ah, the seven dwarfs, the cutting crew. Good to see you guys. Whyn'cha go in the plane and get yourselves comfortable. We leave in about ten minutes."

"Will do, Lieutenant. Let's go gents. This way," the obvious leader of the group said, and the group followed him up the steps of the plane followed by the navigator.

"Heigh ho, heigh ho," Sam said. He must be Doc, Sam thought as he followed them into the plane and strapped himself into one of the seats along the side of the plane. No one spoke but only listened as the plane started its engines and taxied to the runway. A few minutes later, Ferdie announced, "We're off, guys," and repeated, "heigh ho, heigh ho, it's off to work we go," and revved the engines pulling the plane forward.

The flight took six hours and Lieutenant Stu Harris, the navigator got them to Argentia naval base right on the money. They were met by an official who took the axe wielders away in a large van.

The crew and Sam killed almost two hours with small talk and coffee, after which Hernandez and Pisani dozed off. Sam couldn't sleep and he awakened them when the van pulled right up to the airplane. Ferdie saw it through the window and got up. "Hey guys, they're here. Let's get going." When he got to the plane, he asked the axe bearing leader, " Trees loaded?"

"Yessir. Seventy five trees as requested."

"OK, load yourselves on and let's be on our way." Ferdie revved the engines, taxied to the runway and after talking to the control tower, he took off without any wait.

"Hey Skipper," Stu said to the pilot, "Heading 140 degrees."

"Roger that Stu, we're on our way." Sam sat on the wooden box that held Harris' sextant next to him watching what he was doing. The goonie bird was cruising at 7,000 feet, odd numbered altitude for eastbound flights. Sam looked back and could see the huge stack of evergreen trees. Harris opened the glass window above and could see that the sky was overcast. Using the stars was out of the question. The

Long Range Aid to Navigation, LORAN system from Canada faded an hour and a half out of Argentia.

"What do you do with no LORAN or stars to guide you?" Sam asked.

"Dead reckoning and hope the wind forecast I got at Argentia is reasonably accurate. Gotta get me just close enough to Lajes to pick up the radio signals. There's virtually nothing else to guide me. The Atlantic is virtually empty. Sometimes, I try to read the frothy waves below but that's burned me a couple of times. So I don't depend on it."

After four hours, Harris tried to get Lajes on the radio. No answer. After several tries, he called Hernandez. "Hey Ferdie, I can't pick up radio Lajes. Don't know what's wrong."

"Where are we, Stu?"

"We should be a half hour out but I can't raise them."

"You sure you know where we are?" Before getting an answer, Ferdie added, "The sky is clearing. You can probably use your sextant. Stars are out."

"Thanks for the notice, will do. Give me a couple of minutes." Stu took out his star chart, looked at his watch and took readings on three stars with his sextant. Sam watched while he plotted the positions on a map. He wound up with a small triangle of three points and called Ferdie on the radio. "Skipper, I can't believe this but we're about 500 miles north northeast of Lajes. That's why we couldn't pick them up."

"Shit," came the answer. "How'd that happen?"

"Don't know. But the wind forecast I got from Argentia must have been crazy to get us here, I estimate that if we turn south, the head winds will be huge. That's how we got so far north in the first place. In fact, Skip, we'd have to fly a heading of 200 degrees to get home."

"We're that far along. Wow. How long to Lajes from here?" he asked

"Could be as much as three and a half, maybe four hours."

"You're fucking kidding me. I haven't got that much fuel. And I don't relish ditching in the ocean with a load of evergreens that aren't fireproofed."

Sam was listening, getting a little jumpy. His thought was that this was not what he signed on for. He resisted the temptation to ask the question on his mind which was what are we going to do.

"Skipper, I don't relish the idea of ditching at all. Give me a minute." Stu worked over his map with his pencil and dividers and then called. "Hey Skip, if the winds are what they seem to be, should be maybe two and a half hours to Landsend."

"England? That's nuts."

"The numbers don't lie. If we're gonna have heavy head winds flying southwest, it stands to reason we'll have them on our tail flying northeast. I checked them twice. It's the better odds, for sure."

After a long pause, Hernandez said, "OK, but you better be right. As it is, we're gonna look stupid when we finally get back to Lajes. For now, I'm worried about our lives, not a reprimand. Give me a heading, keep watching our position. Meanwhile go back and check the life rafts."

"070 degrees. Sky's clear. I'll keep you posted." Stu looked at Sam. "I need a smoke but with these trees, it's *verboten*."

The lead tree chopper came up to the crew compartment oblivious to the problem. "How long to the base?" he asked. Sam and Stu looked at each other but neither felt like laughing.

Stu answered him, "We're headed for England because we got blown way off course."

He looked at Stu, then at Sam. "England? You're fucking joking, right?"

"Nope," Stu answered," You can do us all a favor and check the life rafts. You know where they are?"

"Yeah, I know. But you're not serious. We gonna ditch?"

Stu said without smiling. "I'm serious. No we're pretty sure we have the fuel to make it. So we don't think we'll need them but better to be prepared. Just make sure they're OK."

"Gotcha. Keep me posted, huh. I didn't plan on risking my life for a bunch of fucking Christmas trees," he said, then added, "sir ."

"None of us did. I'll keep you in the loop," Stu said.

Sam was getting scared. The only redeeming fact for him is that the pilot wasn't Max Miller. But he had never been in a situation like this before and tried to keep relaxed. He went to the back with the axe wielders and sat down in one of the seats.

The tension for the next couple of hours wasn't heavy but it was a little strained. Sam found it difficult to believe how cool the crew was. They did their jobs as if this kind of thing happened often.

Stu commented, "Still on track, Skipper. We did the right thing. The winds on our tail are about 80 knots. If we had turned south we would have wound up in the drink. We should be within range of Landsend very soon."

"Thanks, Stu. I feel a little better. I'll let you know when I get them on the radio."

Fortunately, Stu was right. In just a little over two hours, Ferdie made radio contact with Landsend airport and in two and a half hours, the plane set down on the runway and they all were relieved. Ferdie had a telex sent to Lajes so that they wouldn't send rescue planes out looking for them.

When all official procedures were followed, Ferdie asked the airport dispatcher where there was a good place to eat. It was after 1900 local time and they were all very hungry. Fred said that they were short on crew duty time and had to spend the night. They would leave early in the morning. He looked at his watch. "Say 0730. How's that?" After they all nodded, Ferdie added, "Let's go downtown and eat. Then we gotta get ourselves rooms. I'm fucking exhausted."

They found a Chinese restaurant and then picked the Dolphin Tavern which had rooms enough for all of them. There was little after dinner activity since they were all pretty tired and emotionally drained. They were awakened by the concierge at 0630 and as planned after refueling, got off the ground at 0740, only 10 minutes late. The flight back to Lajes was uneventful except for the chewing out they got from Major Winchester who, after he finished his rant, said. "Glad you guys are back. We gotta get the trees unloaded."

Sam went into the weather station where Leroy was covering for him because of the unexpected delay. "Fun time, Sam? Welcome back."

"Thanks," Sam said. "Flying into hurricane Carrie didn't frighten me like this did. I really thought we were going to ditch. The only thing that surprised me was that the crew didn't seem to be that worried even though they had every reason to be."

"We were worried here when we didn't hear from the plane. The old man was really worried. We couldn't imagine what happened. We thought you had already ditched and that was why we hadn't heard."

Sam laughed, "I can laugh now but I thought about the significance of a Jew dying in the pursuit of Christmas trees."

Leroy laughed raucously. "That irony didn't occur to us. In any case, the major wanted you to call him when you landed. I think he was panicked about losing a golf partner."

"Fuck you," Sam retorted. "I'll call him."

Christmas Season, 1957

This was Sam's second Christmas on the island so he anticipated the maddening sequence of parties. Each organization planned to hold its own cocktail party making the officers' club schedule full.

Fiona was still sleeping and Sam was in no hurry to wake her. Their relationship had grown from lonely intimate to sexually friendly rut. It was a strange feeling for Sam. He speculated occasionally what life would be like married to Fiona, but living in a normal home environment with her was hard to envision. At the ripe age of twenty-five, Sam felt he was already past falling in love. He had become too clinical. He had decided to stop anticipating and take things as they come. *Che sará sará.*

As far as the immediate future, things were up in the air because of his, or anyone's, ability to predict when the field would open. She would be alerted if it suddenly did open, so he wanted her to get some sleep. He left her a note avoiding any romantic adjectives. He considered signing it 'Your Friend Sam' but then thought better of it.

Hey – Didn't want to wake you . I'm working, so call me at the weather station when you get up. So far, the weather looks lousy so we may get another day together.

Sam

Marty and Martha on the other hand, despite their brief relationship, were seriously planning marriage. Apparently the thought didn't bother them. Sam could understand it for them. Their plan was for her to leave the air force and Marty would arrange for her to move from Charleston to Lajes as his wife. He would have to extend his tour of duty at Lajes and find a place to live. The one clinker was that the minute she left the service, she couldn't see him again until he had arranged everything and sent for her, and that could never be rushed. It was all right with him as long as he and Martha were eventually together. They appeared to be very happy. Sam knew they were both adopted as children and they just seemed to go together. Also, Marty was a career officer so the length of his stay on the island wasn't relevant.

For Sam, an air force career had evolved into only a remote possibility. At one point, he was up for it and at Dover, applied to flight school but was turned down because of his meteorology commitment. They had sent him to school for a year to become a meteorologist which carried with it a three-year commitment. He felt that to be a career officer in the air force, advancement would be limited unless one had the pair of wings pinned to his chest. So without wings he wasn't so interested.

He was surprised and flattered when he received an offer of a regular commission from headquarters USAF. Things were beginning to change since the Soviets had sent up sputnik. Suddenly more attention was being paid to our military.

Sam's current status was reserve officer on active duty. Major Gsell told him an offer of a regular commission was a big deal and tried to convince him to stay in the air force and apply for flying school when he finished his weather commitment. Somehow, Sam had decided that he would stay in the air force only if he was absolutely sure it was what he wanted. Any doubt at all would kill the idea.

He pulled up to the weather station, put his head down into the wind and held his hat on against the strong gusts in his face. He gave Leroy a *bom dia* and said, "Looks like the field is closed. That's my educated guess."

"Duh!" Leroy answered. Since he was six foot three and well over two hundred pounds, when a big "Duh" came from him it seemed like Lenny in *Of Mice and Men*. He could picture Lon Chaney talking to Burgess Meredith.

"Any idea when it'll open?"

"Nothing showing to change things, Sam baby. No inbounds so we got no information. We're just watching and waiting."

"OK I got it. Have a good day. What'cha doing today, Leroy?"

"It's Christmas season. You know. I'll look around for who's having a party."

"Everybody."

"See ya." Leroy smiled a big grin and waved.

When the weather was so bad, there was almost nothing to do but routine analysis of charts and forecasts. The only possibility was a call on the radio from an overflying plane because the field was closed. But that wasn't very common. At least not yet. Sam looked out the window and could see the maintenance guys on the flight line with their heads bent into the wind. Sam had seen wind as bad, particularly the east coast hurricanes when he was at NYU, but he never saw such wind for such an extended period. This was the fourth day with winds more than 35 mph from the southwest, right across the runway, with gusts to 50 mph and no letup in sight.

With no flight briefings, no inbounds and very little information to analyze, Sam was getting bored and depressed so Fiona's call was a welcome plus. "Hey Hon, thanks for letting me sleep."

"No point in waking you until I had some idea about the weather."

"I looked outside and saw what was cookin'. Doesn't take a weatherman to know the field is closed. Any news on when it'll open?"

"Nothing I can see. I suspect that the winds will die suddenly and after we watch them stay down for an hour, ops will open the field. But, I haven't got the slightest idea when that'll happen."

"When do you get off?"

"Four. I hate to drive anywhere in this weather. We can eat in the mess hall if you want to have dinner together. Or I can get some takeout at the club and eat in the room. Your choice."

"Rather eat here. Listen to music."

"That's fine with me. Maybe there'll be something going on around the BOQ given the festive atmosphere."

"Great. I did hear an unusual amount of noise coming from down the hall. You might be right. But, for now, shower time, see you later."

"Bye, babe."

As he hung up, Captain Wells barged into the weather station. "Hey Sam. We got an overfly that lost an engine. Afraid to try for Nouasseur. How's the weather in Santa Maria?"

Sam went over to the station board. "Santa Maria weather is good. They're having some winds as well but not as bad as ours and runway 1-9 eliminates the crosswind problem."

"Thanks, Sam. We could use a 1-9 here too. Fat chance with those hills." He practically ran out of the weather station.

Sam marveled at how quiet the terminal was. On a nice day the air traffic was horrendous, making the time pass faster. With the field closed the terminal was like a funeral parlor and the minutes seem like hours. It was compounded because the terminal outside the weather station was a dingy brown. There was no attempt to brighten it. To kill time, he decided to try to do an analysis of the weather pattern using the four points he has. Kindley in Bermuda, Ship Delta, near Greenland, Ship Echo south of a line midway between Lajes and Bermuda. Tough to draw a map of the Atlantic, especially upper winds, with only four points, and two ship surface reports, but worth a try. Using upper winds to infer surface data and the reverse was a puzzle but would kill a couple of hours.

"Weather, this is the tower. Over."

"Yeah Tower, what's up?"

"When's the field going to open?"

"Stop yanking my chain. When I know, you'll be the second to know."

"When do you think?"

Sam only continued the discourse because there was little else to pass the time. "Tomorrow," he answered.

"When?" the tower continued.

"Afternoon," Sam answered, laughing under his breath.

"What time?"

Sam thought to himself. They can't be serious but they are and they know better. I'll play their game. "1524," he answered.

"Your initials, please."

"Sierra Golf. You want me to confirm it in writing?"

"No, sir. Your initials are good enough."

"May I ask what plans you are making based on my prediction?"

"Party time. As long as we got skeleton crew in the tower, we can take turns partying."

"And I thought it was for something trivial. Stupid me. I should have known you guys wouldn't bother me for something that wasn't important."

"Morale, sir . Morale is important."

"I agree, I agree. Have fun." Sam looked out at the flight line. He saw six planes turned into the wind with tail stands on. That made him feel better. He thought about Hurricane Carrie.

He also remembered once at Dover, Colonel Forman was awakened by Ssgt. Bob Bellew, who was a crackerjack weather forecaster on duty, with a warning of thunderstorms and high winds, unusual for February. The colonel didn't believe the forecast, which turned out to be right on the money, preferring instead to listen to John Facenda, the voice of Philadelphia radio weather. Thirteen planes were blown over onto their tails, doing millions of dollars damage. Then the brass led by the very Colonel Forman who ignored the warning, came en masse into the weather station aggressively and very nasty, looking for a way to pin it on the weather. It was usually easy to blame the weather, an act of God. Unfortunately for them, the weather station had all its ducks in a row and the colonel got a severe reprimand. But, in retrospect, Sam thought they were lucky, but the event poisoned his feeling for the colonel. Ordinarily things in a busy weather station are not so well documented and in another circumstance, the colonel would have gotten away with it.

Jens arrived a few minutes before four to relieve Sam. The transfer of information was quick because there was nothing to transfer. Wind and more wind until it stops, a familiar status report at Lajes. When Sam got back to the BOQ, he heard party sounds coming from Robbie's room, which was baptized the "oar house" a feeble attempt at a pun with an oar hanging from the ceiling over the bar in his room. Sam stopped in and saw a small group feeling no pain. Robbie himself was pawing the Red Cross director. He amazed Sam because it seemed that he was going through every female on the base. There were a limited number of women but Robbie seemed to have covered all of them.

"Hey Sam, join us," Robbie waved him in.

"I'll be back but just so you know, I've got company."

"Plentya room. Bring the lady back with you," he added. Sam waved and walked down the hall to his room. Fiona was dressed and reading the back of a record jacket. When she saw him, she put the disk down and put her arms around him. Times like these, he imagined coming home to a permanent relationship that might work. Other times, though, his feelings bugged him.

"Hey, field closed for a while, I think. Party in Robbie's room. You interested in a little celebrating the season?"

"I don't know. I'm a little sad. Times like these, I think of my Mom and Dad. I miss them around Christmas."

Just then Norm Bell phoned. He knew Fiona had arrived and wondered if they wanted to come to his house for dinner and help them decorate the tree. Sam had never decorated a Christmas tree in his life so it didn't mean much to him. But Fiona was excited. Sam could see it in her face. For her it was a piece of home away from home. "Let's go," she said with a big toothy smile on her face. "Please," she begged, unnecessarily.

Sam put the phone back to his ear and told Norm he and Fiona would be there in twenty minutes. Sam asked if they needed anything.

"No. Just bring yourselves. Marty and Martha are here already. Plenty of food and drink. We'll wait for you before we begin."

"No need. We'll be there soon. Feel free to begin without us." Sam had been to Norm's house in Praia once before so he had no trouble finding it. He parked next to Marty's car and even before they knocked, the door opened and Norm handed both of them a glass of wine as they crossed the threshold. For Sam, the evening was warm and homey.

Fiona was immediately in her element. As soon as her coat came off, she and Suzanne were aggressively putting on the decorations and stepping back to admire their handiwork. Sam had never seen Fiona so happy. Sam did not like to be a spectator but in this case, it felt right to him. Eat, drink and spectate. It was three in the morning when they finally left. Both Sam and Fiona had a mild buzz. The effects of the wine had mostly worn off. As soon as they stepped outside and felt the wind, they knew the field must still be closed. Fiona had left Norm's phone number at the barracks in case they were alerted, but heard nothing.

On the way up the hill, they passed Major Winchester's house which had a huge crowd around it.

"I wonder what the hell that's all about."

"I can't imagine," Fiona answered as they heard Major Winchester screaming at the group. Sam stopped the car to see what was happening. A large group of men were standing outside the door of the major's house listening to his tirade.

Sam called out his window. "What's up?"

"Joke on the major, but he's not being a good sport."

"What kind of joke?"

"The Major called a rescue squadron cocktail party at his house from three to five. The Major should know better. If he meant 1500, he should have said 1500. Three is a.m."

Sam looked at his watch and shook his head. "I can understand the Major's not being too happy."

"Ordinarily, we wouldn't pull such a stunt. But it was too tempting as a way to get even. He can't pin it on any one of us. He deserves it. He's such a stickler and prick. Oh, sorry Ma'am," he said, when he saw Fiona.

She laughed, "I've heard the word before."

Sam gunned his engine, "I'll be listening for the scuttlebutt in the morning. Should be interesting. Have fun." They drove to the BOQ and back to Sam's room and fell asleep in each other's arms with their clothes on.

They were awakened shortly after eight by a call from the barracks. Fiona's crew was alerted and she had an hour to get to the flight line. She had her bag and uniform with her so she got dressed quickly and Sam drove her down to the terminal. She hurriedly kissed him and before she rushed off, she looked at him, "Sam, I'll be back in a few days. Leave some time for me."

Sam laughed. "I'll keep my black book closed. Go, my sweet. See you in a few days. Have a good flight." She waved and hurried away clomping her high heels. Sam watched as she entered the terminal. He took off up the hill and decided against going to the club for breakfast. He was a little down. The weather was getting to him. He was also thinking about the situation with Fiona. He had pretty much made up his mind to leave the air force when his time was up, so when he left Lajes in the spring - time had a way of passing quickly - he anticipated that his relationship with Fiona would go the way of all flesh unless he, rather they, made a commitment before he left. In Sam's mind and even more, in his heart, it was just not in the cards.

He went right to his room, took a shower and decided to eat in the mess hall as a change. Sam got into these moods like occasionally. But lately, they came more frequently. He didn't know why. Fiona, the weather, his future! He just didn't feel like talking to anyone. After he ate, he changed into shorts and went to shoot baskets at the gym. There was a pickup game in progress which he eventually joined. He felt better an hour later. Basketball was a great soother. It was a way to forget everything and concentrate on one thing, the game, especially banging other guys around. After a stop at the PX to check out the latest in camera equipment, something he did frequently, he went back to his room, turned on Edith Piaf, plunked himself on the bed and stared at the ceiling for five minutes before he dozed off.

Sam woke with a start about two hours later. He had a bad dream which apparently awakened him but try as he might, he couldn't remember it. He went to the club for breakfast and saw a notice on the bulletin board that they were auditioning for a show to be put on for St. Valentine's day. Six weeks, Sam thought. He wondered who had talent. At Dover, they did a similar thing and Sam was surprised at the unsung talent that was present right at home on the base. The show they put on was as professional as he had seen. Jeri Buczynski, who had become his occasional dining partner sidled up to him looking at the notice and, "You interested, Sam?"

Sam answered still looking at the notice. "Interested in what? Just curious about the local talent. Back in Dover we had some great performers. I wonder about the talent here."

"Interested in a part in the show?"

"Me?" He turned to her, "You kidding, Jeri? The only thing I can do is play the piano and I haven't practiced for over a year, so count me out."

"How's your tap dancing?"

Sam looked at her and frowned. "You can't be serious. I admit I don't have two left feet but I don't have two right ones either. I'm no Fred Astaire."

She laughed, "I'm looking for a tap dancing partner to do a number."

"What number?"

"I'm thinking about Makin' Whoopee," she smiled. "You know it?"

"Sure, I know it. Eddie Cantor made it famous but why me? I'm sure there are others with a little more tendency in that direction."

"But I like you," she said. "I'm sure I can teach you to do a creditable job. Besides it gives me an excuse to spend more time with you."

Sam was a little stunned and apprehensive "You're serious, aren't you?"

"Yup. Ball's in your court. The part's yours if you want it."

"Without even an audition?"

"Nope. No audition. Come on. Should be fun."

"If you're not afraid to have me make a fool of myself, then I shouldn't be. How do you know I can learn it?"

"I've taught left-footed people. I know I can do it. Otherwise I wouldn't offer. I'm not out to make a fool of myself, either."

"OK. I'm in." He was suddenly enthusiastic. "When do we start?" Sam didn't know whether Jeri was coming on to him or not. He was not used to getting this kind of attention from women. But otherwise, why him, he asked himself. She was gorgeous and it certainly wouldn't be unpleasant, however it turned out. That he was sure of.

"Whenever you're available.We've got little over a month, and part-time at that, to make a Fred Astaire out of you. Here's my phone number." She wrote it on a napkin. "Call me when you know your schedule. I know you weather guys have weird hours."

"You sure Mal won't mind your dancing with another guy?"

"I'm sure. He couldn't care less. Too busy at the hospital then golf, golf, golf."

"I'll call you." She walked away giving him a thumbs up. Sam walked into the dining room, saw Jens and sat down. He looked at the phone number automatically memorized it without trying and put the napkin in his shirt pocket.

"Hi." Jens looked up from his sandwich. "How's things with Fiona?"

"OK. She'll be back in a few days. I hope she can stay a while. Always depends on the weather."

"Nice girl. You serious?"

"Frankly Jens, I doubt it. She's a great girl. Smart, easy to be with and sexy. But she's very young and I just don't feel that the relationship is real. It's like a summer romance. When the summer is over, everyone goes back to their regular lives like it never happened."

"I know what you mean. I had what I thought was serious relationship at Kelly AFB. But when I was transferred it was over. It was painful for a while then I moved on. Never see her, never hear from her. Crazy."

"On the other hand, Marty and Martha are deadly serious and are making all kinds of plans. I think for them it might just work."

"Yeah, I feel the same way about them. For some reason, it seems that they belong together."

Sam shook his head. "I guess it's just the military. You're going stateside next month. Staying in?"

"Not absolutely sure but more likely I'll leave than stay. Back to school, probably. But one thing, I don't think I'll go back to Utah. Having been away quite a few years, I realize how narrow my view of the world was."

"Where do you think you'll go?"

"Not decided yet. I've applied to a couple of graduate schools. U Michigan, Duke, NYU. I'll see who accepts me. Also got to find a job. I can't afford going to school without income. The GI bill covers most, but I can't stand being without money."

"I know the feeling, Been there."

"What are your plans? You rotate later in the spring, no?"

"I'll have a few month's left and hope to go to the west coast, to see the far east. And then there's the Fiona thing. I have no clue how that'll work out."

"Between you and me, I wouldn't let that dictate my plans. If it happens, it happens. But don't let it fuck up your life."

"I've been offered a regular commission. Gsell knows I wanted to go to flying school so he's trying to talk me into staying in and applying."

"Regular commission, wow. That's a big deal. Worth thinking about." Jens added.

Sam nodded. "I know but still I don't want to let that be my decision maker either. Graduate school is probably in my plans. too."

"You're thinking straight. It's hard not to let women or commanding officers influence your decision." Jens laughed because he knew how hard it was. "We all gotta keep in mind that this is a lonely place, really. Our view of life gets really colored here, or should I say discolored. But the air force is like a womb, comfortable. But sooner or later we have to fight our way out, get reborn, sort of."

"Great metaphor," Sam smiled then frowned. "A little scary, though, especially for me who came directly from college graduation."

Fiona arrived about three days later, back from Saudi Arabia but the weather was so good that she could only stay three hours. They had an augmented crew with enough allowable crew duty time to leave without rest. They didn't have to stay overnight. Sam was on duty so his time with her involved about ten minutes in the weather station which was too public for anything demonstrable. Her leaving hit Sam harder than he expected. He was bothered that he didn't know when he would see her again and this trip she seemed equally upset at the brevity of their meeting. It was a little unusual, Sam felt. She rarely seemed upset at leaving. It bothered him mostly because he couldn't read her. But he had practically made up his mind after thinking about his future. He was almost sure he would leave the air force and go back to school. As far as making any commitment, he wasn't about go there. He was resigned to his relationship with Fiona disappearing. There wasn't enough there to interfere with his future.

The next day, Major Gsell called a meeting and formalized the new schedule they were working on a trial basis. Similar to what Sam had at Dover which provided the staff with six days working and three days off in a row. Up to now, one day off didn't allow anything except hanging around the base. Now they could take advantage of the flying opportunities and hop a ride to anywhere. The base airplane went to Frankfurt three times a month and Lisbon twice. Also, the traffic through the base was enormous and you could always find a plane with space available going where you wanted to go.

Sam was excited. He wanted to see Frankfurt again and suddenly he thought of Susan. He wondered at why the thought of her gave him a lift. Was it just something new and interesting? The mental vacillation of his fidelity supported the questioning of his possible long term relationship with Fiona. With the new schedule firmed up, it would also be easier to get together with Jeri for his tap dancing lessons. He immediately called the number he had memorized.

"Hello."

"Jeri, Sam. New schedule at the weather station has been made official. When do you want to take me on? As a dance student I mean."

She laughed. "Late morning is good for me when my daughter is in school."

"Tomorrow good? I work at 1600."

"Tomorrow works, about 1030?"

"Where's your house?" After Jeri gave him instructions, Sam went to his desk and looked over his new work schedule. Next month, his three day break coincided with the base flight to Frankfurt. Maybe he would do it. He thought of Susan as an adventure. Maybe because she was German, foreign, a mysterious circumstance for Sam. Somehow, no matter what he felt for Fiona, in the back of his mind he never sensed any emotional commitment from her. He sensed that any feeling she had for him was fleeting and could disappear without any remorse on her part. It nagged at him. He was sure that if he felt differently about her, he wouldn't have a curiosity about Susan or even lately about Jeri. As time passed, he became more convinced rationally, though not completely emotionally, that he and Fiona were not meant to be. She was a manifestation of being on the island.

Sam was lucky, or so he thought. He had to work New Year's Eve. The Christmas season was so crazy and so drunken that he could not even imagine what New Year's Eve would be like. The weather station was busy, but calm. The only problem was that several crews turned up and were considered unfit for flying.

Sam heard Herm Slick with raised voice and stepped into the operations room to see what was going on. "I can't let you fly, Major. I'm sorry. You're not fit to fly. And your copilot is no better."

"I'm perfectly fine, Lieutenant. Perfectly." He held out his hands to show the steadiness. They weren't. "See?"

"Look Major, I don't want you to get in any shit. It is New Year's Eve. I'll do this for you. I'll delay your flight for five hours. I'll write it up as a maintenance problem. Go up to the barracks and get some sleep. You and your co-pilot both. I'll see that you're alerted,," Herm looked at his watch, "at 0200."

The major looked at his watch, then at the co-pilot. Let's catch a few winks, Joe, OK?" he slurred.

"OK with me, Major. Let's go. Is the bus out there, Lieutenant?" the co-pilot asked.

"I'll call him," Herm said. "Should be here in a couple of minutes. Wait for him outside so he sees you."

The major looked at Herm, "Thanks. I owe you one."

"No sweat Major. Just be sure you get some sleep and lay off the booze for the next five hours. 'Cause if you're not fit to fly at 0200,

Captain Wells will catch it and certainly won't let you go. He's much tougher than I am and he won't let you off the hook."

"Will do. Thanks again, see you next time," the major left the terminal.

Sam smiled at Herm. "Tough night?"

"What the fuck am I supposed to do? He's one step from blind drunk. He carries it well but if something happens, I'm dead. Not worth the risk. He was afraid of getting written up. So I gave him an out."

"You're a nice guy. Warren wouldn't have done it."

Herm laughed. "He'd probably have called the air police and made both of them sleep it off in the brig."

Sam raised his cup of coffee. "Happy New Year." whereupon Herm picked up his cup and toasted with Sam. "Couple of hours to go. What're you going to do at midnight?"

"I'd like to go to the club for a beer and then go to bed. But I know damn well that everyone in the club will be different degrees of drunk and acting stupid. How about I get a six pack at the club and we have a new year's beer in my room? It'll keep us out of trouble."

"Good idea. I'll go with you to the club to make sure you don't get sidetracked,"

"Wise move, very wise. See you at midnight."

Frankfurt Redux

Sam now had a reason to take the major up on his reward. With the new schedule, an extra day added to his 3 day break would be great. He asked a crew member destined for Frankfurt to call Susan and tell her he was coming to Frankfurt next Wednesday for a few days and ask if she'll have some time to spend with him. She sent a "certainly" answer back with him the next evening.

Sam awoke suddenly as the base C-54 touched down at Rhein-Main airport. It was mid-morning. Night flights always put him to sleep. When he entered the terminal, he was surprised to see Susan, who had come out to the airport to meet him. She ran up to him and kissed him - another surprise. He dropped his bag and put his arms around her. The feeling was intense. There was something about her.

"What made you come out here? How did you know when my plane was getting in?"

"I was too excited to wait. I called the base and asked. Not so surprisingly, they told me when the Lajes plane was coming in." They walked out to the street. When Sam turned to the bus station, she said. "This way. I borrowed my cousin's Volkswagen. He'll be away for two weeks and I've got the use of it."

Susan was very talkative on the way to her apartment, like a flowing faucet. She didn't wait for comments and for some reason, Sam preferred just to listen to her raspy, sweet voice with the slight German accent. It was enough to be European but not enough to remind him of the stereotyped Nazi that had been continually depicted since the war. "We have three days, you said. What do you want to do with them? I have a car and we can do some traveling. Where would you like to go?"

"Frankly, I hadn't thought about it. I'm open to suggestions. You know better than I do."

"Do you ski?"

"No. I'm a city boy. Haven't had the opportunity."

"Then let's drive to Switzerland, to the Berner Oberland, or better yet, to Luzern."

"Switzerland? That's interesting. Never been there and I love mountains."

"Good, then we go. Luzern is on a huge lake, known familiarly as Lake Luzern but by the Swiss as Vierwaldstättersee. Translated as the "lake of four wooded cantons. There are lake cruises we can take that are pictorially magnificent. They make stops at different towns. And if you're a little adventurous, I'm sure there's still spring skiing. We can go to Mount Pilatus and get you some ski lessons. How does that sound?"

"Sounds fantastic. I would have been content to spend a few days with you in Frankfurt.. But this is terrific."

"OK. Let me pack a bag. We can have something to eat and leave. I want to make mad love to you but I would like to get as far as we can in daylight. Can you wait until we get to Luzern?"

He smiled and turned toward her. "Better wait than a quickie."

"What's a qvickie?" she asked.

"Something I'd rather not have. Quick sex."

"Ah. qvick. *Ja.* I agree. No quickie. Did I say it right?"

"Perfect," Sam answered, with a huge grin.

After they ate the sandwiches she made with bubbly mineral water, they got into the car. "How long is the drive?" he asked.

"Around 4 or 5 hours. If we go along the French border, the ride is shorter. If we go through Zürich, the ride is somewhat longer. Have you ever been to Zürich?"

"No. I'd like to see it."

"Better if we go on the way back to Frankfurt. Is that OK with you?"

"I'm in your hands. Take me wherever. I'm yours."

She laughed and aimed the car at the autobahn. Susan was very talkative during the ride and as usual, Sam was a listener. Finally, she looked at him and said, "I'm doing all the talking. Tell me about yourself, your family. Do you have a brother or sister?"

"Sister, younger. We're pretty close. She worries about me."

"That's nice. I still miss my brother very much."

"Doesn't surprise me. How about your boy friend?"

"Not as much. I don't know why," she answered. "I guess it's because I was so young at the time."

They stopped briefly at the Swiss border, showed their passports and then into Basel for coffee. An hour and a half later they were in Luzern and checked in at the Schweizerhof hotel right opposite the bahnhof. Sam was always surprised that the hotel clerks in Europe never bat an eye when two people with different names checked into a hotel. In the States, Sam imagined that a couple always checked in as Mr. and Mrs. even if they weren't. But in Europe, you had to give your passport to the clerk so even if you wanted to fake it, you couldn't.

Sam looked around the room, taking in the view from the window and then plopped himself on the bed and she next to him. They were tired from the ride, especially Sam who had been traveling since the night before. But despite that, there was no need for a quickie. They had plenty of time and made the most of it. These couple of days for Sam were more fun than he had in a long time. It passed quickly but still seemed to Sam as if he had known Susan forever. There was a certain genuine vibe she emitted. It was different from the feeling he once had toward Fiona. His mind raced and upset him. Would this be the last time he would see Susan? He refused to believe that. But what did the future hold in store?

At dinner on their last day, Susan said, "Liebchen, I have to talk to you. I had a wonderful time and I'm sure you know that I have strong feelings for you even though we hardly know each other. It pains me to think that this is the last we'll ever see each other. I don't want that to happen."

"I feel the same way. Susan, and refuse to believe that this is the idyllic end for us. Do you ever think of coming to live in the US?"

"I think about it often," then she added, "lately. Do you ever think about living in Germany?"

"Yes, I do. But my plans make that difficult. I want to return to school and get an advanced degree and that will take some time before I can earn a living. The only alternative to that is if I decide to push on with meteorology. I did write a letter to the Rossby Institute in Stockholm but that's a long shot. If we do want to be together without waiting several years, I can't come here." A wave of sadness came over the two of them. Then Sam looked up and said, "Susan. Do you trust me?"

"In what sense?"

"To believe what I tell you."

"If I can't believe that, there's nothing for us. You have always been honest with me."

"OK then. I return to the US at the end of April. I will probably go to the west coast. When I get to my destination, I'll write to you and see if we can't arrange something. Is that reasonable?"

"Of course. Is that why you asked me that question?"

"I wouldn't have said it if I didn't believe it. I have difficulty with bullshit. Not that I can't bullshit. I can, but in this case I have no reason to lie. You've never asked me for a commitment. So I have no reason to promise this unless I mean it."

"I believe you and truthfully, I never expected you to make such a promise. I wanted it, oh, did I want it, but I saw too many obstacles so I was resigned to enjoy the time and had already been treating it as a memory. When you live through a war the way we did in Germany, you take what you can get and try to live for the moment."

He smiled and took her hand. "I promise that this is not the end of us. I'm sure of that."

The ride back to Frankfurt was more upbeat than Sam thought possible. Convincing himself he would see Susan again made leaving her bearable. They stopped in Zürich, went into a Coop supermarket and got bread, cheese and a bottle of Dôle wine to enjoy a brief picnic along the lake, on a chilly, sunny day

The four hours back to Frankfurt were quiet but sweet. Sam told her what he wanted to do. He hoped to get a PhD in Math or Physics. He was not sure which, and after that he was not sure whether he would go into the business world or academics. He always had a leaning to be a teacher but wasn't sure he would be happy in academia. He was surprised to discover that Susan had a university degree in psychology but couldn't find a decent job in the field. The bar paid much better so she fell into a rut. Sam suggested that she could go to school as well, and get an advanced degree. Her English is certainly good enough.

"Would I be allowed to work in the US? Won't I need some kind of permit?" she asked.

"Of course. I don't see any reason why not. We have bars in the US too." he laughed.

She frowned at him and said nothing. The look on her face said it all.

"Seriously, there's nothing to stop a company or some government agency from hiring you in your chosen field. Opportunities abound, and you don't need a permit to work, only to stay in the US and I think I can arrange that."

"How can you arrange it?" she asked. "You have influence somewhere?"

He laughed. "Leave it to me."

They made love and fell into a deep sleep in each other's arms. Sam awoke with a start in the morning, then relaxed when he realized he had plenty of time before his flight back to Lajes. Susan got up, went to the kitchen in her robe, made coffee and heated up some pastry. They had a leisurely breakfast after which Sam packed and got ready to leave. "Shall I drive you to Rhein-Main?" she asked. "It's no bother," she anticipated the comment.

"No need. But you can walk with me to the bahnhof to catch a bus. I'll write to you when I get back to Lajes. It will be a while before I see you again. A long drunk and a breakfast."

"What did you say?" she asked.

"I was quoting a friend who answered that when I asked him how he deals with separation. That was his answer. A long drunk and breakfast and it's over."

"Thanks for the philosophy lesson."

"Gotta go," he said picking up his bag. "I don't want to miss my plane." Sam kissed her goodbye and asked her not to wait with him. He wanted to re-enter his Lajes frame of mind, to depart the idyllic aura.

Infiltration

It was a small party for Robbie. His time was up so Sam thought the drunk must be over and this must be the breakfast part. He was going back to Arizona in a few days and was celebrating with a cute nurse that had just arrived a week ago and some other friends. Sam asked Robbie, "What're gonna do with the piano? You're not taking it with you, I assume/"

"Shit, no," he answered. "I bought it here for $88 which has been its price for years. Dollar a key. That's what I'll sell it for."

"I'll take it," Sam said. "Deal?"

"Deal."

"How much time you got left for retirement?" Sam asked him.

"Joined up in 40. Discharged 46. Recalled in 48 for Berlin airlift. Leaves me another five for my 20. I'd like to make Light Colonel before I retire."

"Any reason why you shouldn't?" Sam asked.

"Not really. But you never know who hates you. So until I get the silver leaves, I won't hold my breath. By the way, how's your girlfriend? Seems like a nice kid. Serious?"

"Don't really know, Robbie. The relationship has kinda fizzled. Fiona's a great girl and we most times got along well but somehow, even though I still have some feelings for her, I can't envision the future with her. I don't know what it is. It's a strange feeling."

"Military life's part of the problem. It emphasizes and exaggerates things, sometimes the wrong things."

Sam answered, "I don't think that's it, or at least not all of it."

"I'm married, which might not be so obvious considering my ramblings, so maybe I can't really talk. But from what I've seen, life in the military is usually a bad basis for a marriage. And it's even worse if you meet in the military. I don't know anything for sure and I tend to mind my own business. But if you asked my advice, I'd say enjoy it while you can then turn it off when you leave. Don't let it be a factor in your life."

"And if we love each other. hypothetically, that is?"

Robbie laughed, "Believe me you don't, that is, love each other. Not even close, not yet, at least. You're on a rock, isolated, not a normal social situation. It helps you do your time. Don't make any more of it. Lucky you found her to make the time pass more enjoyably. But that's it."

"You make me feel like I've been using her."

He chuckled. "She's was using you, too. Works both ways, so get off the guilt trip."

"You know Marty Redstone and his stewardess girlfriend, Martha are planning to get married."

"I heard that. I wish him the best."

"That's all you can say about that?" Sam frowned.

"I told you how I feel. 'Nuff said on that subject. Have a drink and join the party. It's not too wild."

Sam laughed. "Marty wants to talk to me. He's in his room waiting."

"Bring him back with you. Party's not nearly over."

"I'll try. But remember, we have a deal about the piano."

Robbie nodded, bit into his cigarette and gave Sam a two finger salute. "See ya later."

When Sam opened Marty's door, he saw Marty sitting on the couch, frozen, with a drink in his hand, staring at a mouse that was sitting quietly on the back of the couch.

"Tell me you see a mouse there, Sam."

"Sure is." Sam reached to catch the mouse and it scooted away.

"Thank God! I thought I was far gone and seeing things from the booze. Been drunk since this afternoon. I finally heard from Martha. She's coming in next week and we think we want to get married."

"Here?"

"Yeah, it's the only way At Charleston where fraternization is not allowed, marriage to an officer would be a disaster. Might get her court martialed. The Charleston CO is a real prick. She plans to get out, but it would be hard to keep it quiet in Charleston. I figure if we get married here, I can file the request to bring her over here. When she goes back, she can resign and get discharged before anyone knows"

"You sure about this."

"No. That's the problem. I really love her, but I'm not sure I want to rush into this.

"Why don'cha wait until she becomes a civilian?"

Marty got up and started pacing. "If I do that, then I'll have to fly back to marry her. She can't come as a civilian visitor. It would cost too much anyway. I would have to fly to Texas on my own hook. When she gets out, she's not staying in Charleston. She's going home."

"How does she feel about it? Marriage I mean?"

"She wants to get married. Really Sam, I think we're soulmates. I never felt this way about anybody. She says she neither."

"Look, Marty. Either way could be wrong. My advice is pick the choice that you think will make you happy. If that's marriage, go balls ahead. If it's wrong, it can be corrected."

"Divorce, you mean?" He made a puzzled face.

"Look at the other side. Your tour is up and you go to God knows where. You can't see her. Maybe you can't even send for her. How would you feel about that?"

Marty sat back down and took another swig from his glass. "Very shitty, very."

"Look, your plan is workable. The only question is do you think the marriage is right? If that's what you both want, do it. You are in control at this point. If you wait, you lose control of the situation and everything would depend on other people's choices, not yours."

"What about you and Fiona?"

"Our situation isn't the same. Not even close." Sam didn't want to go into how he really felt about Fiona. Instead, he said, "I really wonder how things would work for us in civilian life. I'm getting out this year. You're a career guy. It's very different. Besides, I'm not as sure of my feelings as you are. If you're really bothered, why don'tcha talk to Doc Cavanaugh."

"Who's he?"

"Colonel Cavanaugh's the flight surgeon on the base but he's also a shrink. He's a really great guy. Maybe he could help get you to the right decision." Marty got up again and started walking around the room. Sam watched him quietly, letting him think things out. "Robbie's having a party in his room. He's leaving in a few days. I'm going back there. C'mon."

"I'd rather not. I gotta think things out."

"OK. You know where I am if you need me. See ya later."

Marty wandered around the room for at least ten minutes, talking to himself with "If thises then thats." Finally, he blurted out loud, "Fuck it, I'll have to do it. No more vacillating. She wants it as much as I do but if I show doubt, she'll get worried. She looks to me to work things out." He called the chaplain to arrange things. Then he went to Robbie's party and cornered Sam. "I made up my mind. It's a yes. I called the chaplain."

Sam got up, smiled and shook his hand. Congrats," he said. "Hey folks, Marty's getting married. Let's drink a toast." The small group turned to Marty and held up their glasses.

"Hear, hear. Best of luck." Robbie shook Marty's hand."

"Will you be my best man?" Marty asked Sam.

"Of course. Just give me a heads up. Now, I gotta go to a meeting."

"What kind of meeting?"

Sam shrugged, "I have no fucking idea. It's at the air police headquarters and I didn't have a choice. It was a written order, which in itself is strange."

"You haven't been arrested, have you?" Marty asked.

"No such luck. Unfortunately, I'm too well behaved. See you gents later."

Sam had no idea what this meeting was all about. His tendency was to worry that something was wrong. When he got there, he looked around and didn't recognize the other five officers that were in the meeting nor did he know the major who looked like he was ready to address the group.

"Gentlemen. I'm Van Turner. I'm on special assignment here at Lajes. The pentagon feels that security at air bases around the world needs to be tested to see if it's working. You have been selected and organized as three two-man teams." He handed out sheets to the six. "This tells you who your partner is and what your objective is. I will meet with each team separately. Golden and Jefferson first. Follow me." Sam and his partner, whom he had never met, accompanied the major into an empty office. "Sit, please." They both looked at each other and then slowly sat down. "Your objective is simple but not easy to do. I want you to figure a way to blow up hangar four, the SAC hangar, with a bomb."

"What? Sam asked. "Respectfully, you crazy, Major? The Strategic Air Command hangar?"

"My sentiments exactly, Major," Jefferson said.

The major laughed. "I don't mean actually do it. I want you to test security. Your objective is try to plant a box in the hangar which can later be identified as a bomb. Whether or not you succeed will tell us something about how good our security is on the base."

"Why us?" Sam asked. "I for one don't know anything about this kind of activity. I'm a scientist, sort of. I'm not experienced at this cloak and dagger shit, Major."

"But both of you are smart. You, Golden work around the flight line so you may be recognized. That's the idea. Even if they know you, if you have no business in the hangar, they know what they should do. Jefferson, being a negro officer, may evoke a different kind of reaction. We want to know about that as well. You have three days to work out a plan. I will also give you a copy of the security regs so you know how they should behave. You have to know them. Tells you how they'll try to stop you and give you ideas, I hope, about how to get around them. Any questions?"

"Sounds like fun to me," Jefferson said.

"You, Golden?" the major said, looking as Sam.

"I'm not so sure. I don't know shit about this kind of thing Major. Could be fun, sure. But it's not a game and could also get us shot. If what you say about SAC security is true, they won't mess around. They may know we're on the same side but they would be more afraid of General LeMay than shooting us."

"I admit there is a remote possibility things could get out of control. If it comes to that, just surrender yourselves. This is just an exercise. I'm not looking for any casualties. Make a plan and consider enjoying doing it. Be creative, like spies. I'll call you Wednesday to hear your plan and give you a go ahead."

Sam sat for a minute looking at the major then introduced himself to Jefferson. "Sam Golden, weatherman."

Bill Jefferson, navigator. I just got here, expect to work in briefing."

"Bill, let's go to the club for coffee and talk about this."

"Can I get a ride with you? No car yet."

"Of course, let's go."

At the o-club Sam said, "I think the Major is being foolish. We're not spies. He could have and maybe should have gotten pros to infiltrate. If we fail, it says nothing. If a pro fails, that says something. If we succeed, it will quickly point out the problem."

"I think you're right, Sam. But he didn't give us a choice. So let's just do it as best we can."

They talked for about an hour and came up with an idea that their amateur minds thought would work.

On Wednesday, Sam answered the loud ring. "Have you guys got a plan, Golden?" The major asked.

"Yes, we do," Sam answered. "I don't know how good it is but we have one. Where is the bomb?"

"You have to make one."

"Come on Major. You're joking."

"No. That's the easy part. Find a box, put something in it that weighs about ten pounds and leave a note in the box that says: *This is a bomb. The hangar has been blown up.*"

Sam laughed and shook his head in disbelief at the charade, "You got it, Major. You really have a great sense of humor." Sam thought about some spy movie he had seen as a kid with Cagney and Annabella. He began to think of it as a game.

"Yeah, I know," the major answered. But it's really not funny. Anyhow, it's a go. Can you get started today?"

"Gotta ask Jefferson. I can, but I don't know about him. I"ll call you back." He called nav-briefing. "Hey Bill, it's a go for our plan. Can you make it today?"

"Yeah. I'm good. I'm not in the rotation yet."

"OK I'll pick you up at the terminal in fifteen." Sam called the major. "We're good for today."

"OK. Talk to you tomorrow. Unless of course you get captured. Good luck."

"Or shot," Sam added seriously.

Bill was waiting outside the terminal as Sam drove up. "We have to go to the PX first to find a suitable box for our bomb."

"Very funny."

"What would be funny if we really knew how to build a bomb and could really upset General LeMay."

"Sorry, Sam. That's not funny."

"Not a nuke. A run of the mill ordinary explosive." Sam laughed.

"Still not funny."

"OK, no more jokes."

They asked at the PX office if they had a small box for a package to be mailed. The manager gave them a perfect size. Big enough to hold ten pounds but thin enough to put in an briefcase. Then they went off the base and found rocks enough to fill the box. They took the stuff back to Sam's room and wrapped the rocks in a t-shirt to keep them from rolling around and Sam carefully added the note, just as the major asked with an added "GOTCHA" and took off for the terminal.

Sam and Bill drove boldly onto the flight line, something Sam knew he wasn't supposed to do. Parking right alongside the SAC hangar, he and Bill got out and walked in. Sam was carrying a briefcase. The minute they entered, two of the maintenance men, pointed 45's at them. "Identify yourselves."

"Easy, easy," Sam said, putting down the brief case and raising his hands. "I'm Sam Golden, weatherman. You must have seen me around the terminal. Let me show you my ID."

"No, I haven't seen you. And you?" he looked at Bill.

Sam answered. "He's new, just arrived. I'm leaving in two weeks and he's replacing me. Just showing him around. I'm sorry if I got you guys upset. We can leave if you want."

"Both of you sit down there and be quiet." He kept the pistol pointed at them. "Hey Jimmy, call the air police."

"Aw c'mon. I was just showing him around. I'd never seen a B-47 up close ever. I didn't know I wasn't supposed to be here. I don't want any trouble. You should let us go? It's embarrassing. Our CO will have a bird. We'll leave the flight line right away."

"Sorry, sir . Can't do it. You just sit tight until the police come."

"This is ridiculous. I live here. I work here. I give weather forecasts to the pilots. Call one of your pilots, any one. They can vouch for me."

"I'll let the air police do that. You just sit tight, Captain."

"Can I at least use the bathroom?"

"Jimmy, escort the Captain to the head. You sit tight, Lieutenant."

Sam and Jimmy walked to the bathroom. For some reason he never bothered Sam about his brief case. Jimmy kept a gun on Sam all the way but let him go in by himself. Sam looked around and saw a large cabinet. He opened it and put the box that was in his briefcase on the bottom shelf and covered it with a towel. He flushed the urinal and walked out with his brief case still in his hands. "I'm done. Police here yet?"

"They just pulled up. Let's go." They walked over to where one of the policemen was putting handcuffs on Bill.

"Turn around, Captain. Hands behind your back."

"You guys are not really serious," Sam said. "I was just showing my replacement around. This is ridiculous."

"Sorry, sir . Our orders are to arrest first, then let go after verification. What's in the brief case?"

"Just a t-shirt. I delivered some files to headquarters. The t-shirt was in the case to go to the laundry. I had just come from the gym."

"Behind your back, please."

"Seems like a waste of time. How would I have gotten on the base in uniform? We have IDs. Don't you think Bill would have looked a little out of place sneaking onto the base?"

"Hands behind your back, please Captain. I don't want to ask you again."

After they were cuffed, the mechanics put their guns back in their holsters and walked toward the B-47 they were inspecting. Sam and Bill said nothing and got in the back of the police car. At the air police headquarters, they were put in an interrogation room and had their handcuffs removed. In a few minutes, Major Turner walked in and smiled.

"They gotcha, Golden. So the security was good?"

"Not good enough, Major." Sam said and he and Bill both grinned simultaneously.

"What do you mean?" the major asked.

"You got us out of there, saved us for which we thank you."

Bill laughed. "But not before Sam left a box with a bomb in the hangar bathroom."

Sam explained the whole sequence to the major who was amused but angry afterwards. Major Turner answered Sam. "Hangar four is the SAC hangar. When General LeMay gets the report, he will not be amused. You did the job and for that I thank you. You're both free to go."

"I have only one comment, Major," Sam said. "It's even worse than you think. We're just amateurs. How would a pro have done? We weren't a real test."

The major looked at Sam and said nothing.

Bill looked at Sam. "Coffee break?"

"Fine idea." As they were walking away Sam asked, "By the way, how'd you like being a saboteur?"

"Not bad. How's the pay?" Bill answered.

"You don't do that kind of thing for money. It's for a cause."

"Sorry, Sam. I would only do it for the money."

"Greedy," Sam answered as they drove away. "Let's get some dinner and see if we can make a deal with the Russians."

Bill laughed but lost his amusement when he saw Sam's face. "You're not serious?"

"I can't even talk to my father from here if I want to. Where am I going to find a Russian spy to talk to even if I was interested?"

"You had me fooled but I'm too green to realize it," as they walked into the dining room.

Invitation to the Dance

Next morning Sam called Jeri who answered "Buczynski residence."

"Hey hoofer. This is Sam. We still on at 10:30 this morning for my first lesson?"

"Yup. That's great, I was wondering when you'd call. Can you come about eleven? 10:30 is a bit early "

"Perfect. Gives me time to do some errands. See you then." Sam went to the PX to get some razor blades. He took a quick shower and shave and put on civilian clothes. The instructions to get to her house were good and he had no trouble finding it.

Jeri answered the door and Sam was bowled over. She was movie gorgeous and he hoped his staring wasn't obvious. "Well, are you coming in out of the rain." she said. "You are not Gene Kelly and do not dance in the rain, at least not yet." Sam came down from his cloud and stepped across the threshold, "Let me take your raincoat. I didn't realize it was raining. Can I get you some coffee before we start?"

"No, thanks, I'm fine. But that reminds me of an embarrassing moment."

"What?"

"Back in Dover, I was scheduled to give a lecture to 300 pilots and navigators about winter weather. There was a sudden downpour and I got drenched. When I walked onto the stage of the auditorium, I could see all the audience in raincoats. Me, the weatherman was drenched without one. The laughter started slowly but grew to a crescendo."

"That's really funny."

"Didn't seem so at the time."

She led him into the small family room which had no carpet, turned on the record player and dropped the arm on Frank Sinatra singing Making Whoopee. "It's last year's. I learned to dance it to Eddie

Cantor's 1929 recording before Frankie ever sang it. Listen to the rhythm." She tap danced slowly to the rhythm.

"You think I can learn that?" he asked.

She turned off the music. "Sure. We take it one tap at a time. Come on." She reached out and took one of his hands making him stand along side of her. Slowly and meticulously, she broke down the foot taps and made him do it over and over until he got it. "OK, that's one series. Here's the next one." Again, she broke it up slowly into individual toe and heel taps. Sam was surprised that he was actually learning. "You're a natural dancer."

"That never occurred to anyone who knows me, except you. I am a pretty good pianist, though, but dancing?" He shook his head.

After an hour of drilling each tap she wiped her brow and said, "Let's knock it off for the day. I think you'll learn it all in plenty of time. What are you going to do now?"

Sam looked at his watch. "Lunch at the club, I guess."

"How about I meet you there? I'll buy."

Sam laughed. "You don't have to do that. But we can certainly have lunch together." She handed him his raincoat. "Get us a table."

Sam left and on the way to the club, he tried to figure her. She wasn't dressed like she was a dance teacher. Maybe it was vanity he thought. Women have to look their best even for no reason. Half hour later, Jeri came up to the table and sat down.

"Doesn't it bother you that you're having lunch with someone that's not your husband, innocent though it may be?"

"I tell you Sam. The military, and Lajes in particular, is so incestuous. Nobody gives a damn. Nobody wants to know. There is almost no gossip. If there were, General Smith would go nuts. He is a prude and a pain in the ass."

"My relationship with him has only been fleeting in the weather station. He seemed OK. The only thing I've heard about him comes from my airmen who have three or four Azorean women squirreled away." Sam deliberately didn't say where. "They warned me about the general's penchant for summary court-martial for someone who picks up the clap with a local girl"

"I've heard that, too. Although I don't know anyone who's been punished."

Sam smiled coquettishly, "I guess most of the people you know benefit from this incestuous community we live in and don't need to jeopardize themselves."

"You're probably right. You ever mess around with someone in the community?" she asked him. Sam was taken aback but after he got over the surprise question, he sensed she was feeling him out for a proposition.

"Not really. I've dated stewardesses that come in from Charleston and McGuire. It's kept me out of trouble." He didn't mention his relationship with Fiona.

They made small talk and finished their dessert talking about Sam's piano playing. "You'll have to play for me one day. After all, I danced for you."

"Gotta practice. I bought Robbie's piano. I get it in a few days when he leaves. Give me some time and I'll play for you."

"Do you give piano lessons?"

"I worked my way through college that way but it's been a while."

"How about giving my daughter lessons?"

Sam was surprised by the question. "I guess I can arrange it."

"Please do. We can talk about it next dance lesson. When can you make it?" she asked.

Next three days I'm on day shift. But the day after that, Saturday, I work nights. Are you free Saturday?"

"Saturday's no good. Weekends Mal is home so that doesn't work. Can you make Monday?"

"You got it. Same time?"

"Yup. I gotta go now. See you then." Sam watched as she walked away. She didn't slink suggestively, Sam thought. But she didn't have to. She had a majestic sort of sexiness that engulfed her.

Arabian Trouble, Disaster in Turkey

Captain Joe Oldham came into the dining room right after Jeri left and sat down with Sam. "Hows the wind treating you, Stormy? We miss you at Dover."

"Can't complain. Rain bothers me more. You?"

"Pretty good. Going to Agra Friday night. Taj Mahal and all that."

"Really, how long is the trip?"

"Pretty fast. Back here in three days, four days the latest. Tripoli. Sleep eight, then Riyadh to unload for three hours then Agra. Stay over night and return via Tripoli."

"You get to see anything of consequence?"

"Visit the Taj. It's really a wonder. Ever seen it?"

"Only in pictures."

"Come with us. I got room," he insisted.

"I'd love to. If you're serious, let me see if I can get someone to cover for me Saturday. I'm off the three days after that."

Sam talked to Leroy who agreed to cover for him. The only other thing was what happens if he doesn't get back in time. He went to see Major Gsell.

"What's up Sam. Looking for a golf game?"

"No Major, you'll have to fend for yourself. Joe Oldham is going to Agra on Saturday. Three day trip. Leroy is covering for me on Saturday. Oldham says the three days is pretty reliable. But I'm afraid that if anything happens out of the ordinary, I won't make it back in time. What do you think?"

"Take the trip. If you don't make it back, don't sweat it. I'll find someone to cover for you. It's worth while. You ever been on the route to Riyadh?"

"No sir."

"Then the trip is definitely justified." he smiled. *"Vaya con dios."*

"Thanks Major, I appreciate it."

"You owe me a golf game," he said with a straight face.

"Fair enough." He left the major's office and went to call Jeri from the weather station. "Jeri, Sam. Listen, I'm going on a trip Saturday so Monday's out."

"That's too bad. I was looking forward to it. When are you coming back?"

"I should be back Wednesday. I'll call you then and we can work something out. Is that OK?"

"Disappointing, but that's fine. Where're you going?"

"Agra. Never seen the Taj Mahal?"

"Wow, sounds like fun. Have a great trip. Wish I were going with you. We'll talk when you get back."

"Definitely. Bye."

The next morning at 0700, Sam joined the five man crew of the C-124. The leg to Tripoli over Spain and Malta was uneventful. The weather was clear and there wasn't much to see. They had dinner in the Wheelus AFB o-club in Tripoli and without any extra-curricular activity, went to bed.

They were alerted at 0500 and were off the ground for Riyadh by 0700, landing at close to midday. The flight was routine with more good weather en route. When the plane was parked, the crew walked to the terminal. It was extremely hot. At the terminal, the crew presented papers. Sam asked which papers do they need. "I only have a passport."

Oldham said, "They want to see your baptismal certificate to prove you're Christian, unless you're a Muslim."

Sam answered, "I don't have a baptismal certificate. I'm a Jew."

Oldham looked at him "Uh oh, let me see if I can bulldoze you through." He looked at the official. "He is our weatherman. He didn't know he needed to bring his certificate. I can vouch for him."

"I'm sorry Captain, I cannot permit him to enter without it. If I am caught letting him in, I can literally get my arm cut off. I'm sorry," he repeated.

"What am I supposed to do?" Oldham said. "We'll only be here a couple of hours. Can he sit in the terminal?"

"I cannot let him through the door, Captain. He will have to stay in the airplane until you leave."

Oldham, exasperated, said. "It's 110 degrees in the sun. The plane will be even hotter."

"He can wait outside the plane, but he cannot enter the building."

Oldham turned to Sam. "I should have told you, Sam, about the certificate. I'm sorry. Stay with the plane. We'll make it as fast as we can. We just have a small load to drop here. The rest is for Agra. There's drinking water in the plane if you need it. But we have no choice. He's really at risk. He won't even take a bribe because he really will get his arm cut off if he gets caught letting you in."

The official said, "I will get someone to escort you back to the plane, Captain. Wait a moment." He waved for another uniformed person to come over. After a few words in Arabic, the official said, "Follow me, Captain." and led Sam back to the plane. When Sam went up the steps and inside, it was like walking into an oven. It was 110 degrees outside. It must have been 125 degrees at least in the plane. Fortunately, the plane was mostly white. After five minutes, Sam went outside and sat on the tarmac with his back on the landing gear that was shaded by the plane. He waited there barely moving for over two hours. He had never felt a beating sun like this one. He went up into the plane to get some water. For some reason, the plane seemed cooler. Probably because was white. In contrast, the black tarmac was absorbing and intensifying the sun's heat.

When the crew came back, Sam was naked above the waist and lying down in the crew compartment. He looked at Oldham and said, "Joe, you owe me."

"I agree, Sam. I apologize. It was my fault. I didn't think about Riyadh. I also didn't know you were Jewish which as you can imagine doesn't sit well with the Saudis. We have ways with other Jewish crew members to get them past the check. Lucky for you we weren't planning to stay over. Wow, it's hot. Let's get this mother off the ground ASAP," he said to the crew.

Fifteen minutes later, the engines were started and warmed up. The internal fans circulated the hot air in the plane. Oldham got the plane to 7,000 feet as fast as he could. The circulating air got cooler as they ascended. At altitude, with the outside temperature at about freezing, it became comfortable. Sam put his shirt back on and watched through the windshield as they buffeted their way through a line of thunderstorms over the Indian coast. The six hour flight was tedious. Sam wondered how these crew members, who were just well-trained delivery men could make a career of such mundane work. Many pilots realistically called themselves plane drivers with deference to truck drivers. It bored the hell out of him. He wondered if, as he had hoped, he went to flight school and wound up like this. He was sure he would not last if he did.

There was a lot to see in Agra but the pièce-de-resistance as expected was indeed the white marble tomb for Mumbaz Mahal, wife of Shah Jahan. Sam was awed by its magnificence, beauty and majesty. Many had said, in jest, that it was the greatest erection man has ever had for a woman. But after having seen this wonder, Sam thought it was a bad joke. When the Shah died years later, he was buried in the tomb next to his wife as he had pre-arranged.

The crew had dinner at the Taj Mahal restaurant right near the Taj. Sam found a Chinese dish that suited him but Joe insisted that one doesn't go to India and eat Chinese food. So Sam joined in the local dishes they shared. He had never eaten Indian food before and was surprised at how good it was except for some items which were very peppery hot.

They were very tired when they checked into the Hotel Taj Plaza. For Sam it was the end of a grueling day. Staying in the extreme heat drained him and he dropped into a deep sleep almost immediately. Next morning, he was awakened by a hard knock on the door. Groggily, he got up and opened it. It was Joe.

"Sam, we have to pick up a small load at the air base in Adana, Turkey so we're trying to get out of here early. Get your ass dressed and meet us in the lobby."

"Do we have to stay over in Adana?" Sam asked.

"Fortunately, no. We're picking up a pilot and engineer at Adana making us an augmented crew. So we shouldn't be on the ground more than an hour, maybe two. But it's a 12 hour flight."

"Twelve hours. Holy shit. How do you guys do it?"

"We get used to it. So, move it. See you in the lobby."

Sam jumped into the shower with his razor and shaved blind. In ten minutes, he was dressed and in the lobby where the rest of the crew was waiting for him.

Oldham said, "Base bus is coming to pick us up. Should be here any minute." The hotel concierge waved to him that the bus was here.

At the flight line, Lieutenant Aiden Kelly went right into the navigation office to pick up his flight plan while Oldham and engineer Master Sergeant Montini looked over the front of the plane. Co-pilot Lieutenant Roy Kirsten checked the back. "Everything looks good here," Oldham said "Hows the back?"

"Looks good, Skipper," Kirsten replied.

"OK, lets go. "Zurk," Oldham said to Sergeant Harrison Mazurka, the loadmaster, "The hold is empty so you and Golden should stay with us in the crew compartment,"

In fifteen minutes, they were on the runway awaiting the OK to take off. The wait was only a few minutes before Sam felt the engines roar and the pull of the plane. It felt like a different plane since it was empty and many tons lighter.

"Set her at 285 degrees, Skipper." Kelly said on the intercom.

"Roger that. We've got 8,000 feet to ourselves. No traffic."

During the flight, after two hours, Oldham and Kirsten took turns sleeping in two hour turns. Sam was awake for four hours and fell asleep sitting on the bed in the crew compartment. Kelly slept until awakened by Oldham. "Where are we, Aiden?" he asked.

Kelly looked at his watch and flight plan and answered "Should be just over Oman, Skip."

From that point on, with the drone of the engines, Sam had trouble keeping his eyes open until he heard Kelly alert Oldham hours later, "We should be coming up on Adana radio, Skipper."

"We've got two radio beacons to follow. We should hit the first one in fifteen minutes. Buckle up guys for landing. The second one is three minutes later into the landing pattern." There was silence among the whole crew until they heard Oldham, "There's the first one, right on schedule. Nice going Kelly. I don't like these low clouds. We're not visual. Can't see a fucking thing." After a minute Oldham said, "Where the fuck is the second one. I should hear it. I don't like this with these hills around. Still no beacon."

Another minute passed which seemed like an hour to Sam. Kirsten asked nervously, "Where's the second beacon, Skip? I don't like this."

"Beats the shit out of me. Radio stop working?"

"Not that I can tell." Another eternal minute passed without hearing the beacon.

"Something's wrong, Roy. Gotta be" Seconds continued to pass without hearing the second beacon.

"What's happening, Skip? Where's the beacon?" Kelly asked on the intercom.

"I wish the fuck I knew. Maybe we better go around again. I don't like the terrain and visibility is shit."

Suddenly, Kirsten said frantically, "Pull up Skip, there's a hill ahead. Pull up. Pull up," he repeated, louder.

Oldham pulled back on the wheel and increased the power, but it wasn't enough even with an empty plane. Oldham gritted his teeth as the tail just hit the crest of the hill ripping it right off. The front of the plane nosed downward and hit the ground skidding along the crest of the hill. They all held their breath instinctively, waiting and listening as the plane skidded without the landing gear down. They could hear the horrible noise as the ground sheared the bottom off the plane. The fuselage veered to the left as a tree ripped the right wing off. They all let their breath out as the plane finally came to a stop in about 500 yards. The top of the hill was barren except for one tree so the plane didn't hit anything else. The crew compartment which sits high on the plane remained completely intact despite the crash. Oldham had hit his head on the wheel but was still awake. He checked behind him. "How are we back there? Anyone hurt."

Kelly answered, "We're all OK, it seems, except for Zurk who seems to have hurt his arm. Might be broken."

"C-124 to Adana control. Come in," Oldham called.

"Where are you, C-124? We lost your signal on the radar."

"You lost us because we've crashed on a hilltop. Your second beacon is out. Send help."

"C-124, this is Adana control. Which hill are you on? Any casualties?"

"I haven't got the slightest fucking idea which hill. Which one would I be on if your second beacon is out? You figure it out. We passed the first beacon fine. Everyone's alive and there seems to be only one injury. We don't know how bad it is. You better find us and be quick about it." Oldham's anger was building.

"This is Adana control. How many on board? Choppers will be out looking for you in five minutes. Hold tight. Are the lights on the plane still lit?"

"Yes, the lights are on but I don't know the condition of the battery. We're not going any place. There's six of us. Make it fast. Hey Zurk, lucky for you we didn't have a load. Otherwise we'd have lost you."

"You're right on, Skipper. I'm one lucky fuck," he said, while Montini was putting Mazurka's arm in a splint then a sling around Mazurka's neck.

"Probably would have lost me, too," Sam piped in. "I probably would have been keeping Zurk company if we had cargo."

"Didn't think of that," Oldham said. "Lucky you."

Montini said,"Hey, Skipper. You got a black eye, you know."

"Got a mirror? I want to look at my beautiful self."

"Yeah," Kelly answered and pulled a signal mirror out of his carry-on case.

Oldham looked at himself. "Doesn't look too bad. I've had worse in the schoolyard. You think Government Employees Insurance will cover the crash so maybe I can sue somebody?"

Sam interjected, "Who you gonna sue, Joe? The Turks? Good luck. When we get back, I'll help you find a good lawyer."

Oldham forced a laugh. "OK, first things first. Get out the flare gun. When we hear a chopper, we shoot a flare up. I just hope they get close enough to see the lights. How's your arm, Zurk?"

"Hurts Skipper but it's OK. I don't think it's broken. Just a bad bruise."

"Let's go out and take a look Skipper, Kelly chimed in."

Getting out of the crew compartment required jumping down about eight feet to the ground. Although the plane's lights were on, it was still very dark outsice. Kirsten got a flashlight and aimed it outside.

"Left wing is still in tact, Skip. We can let outself down there. Get the ladder? We can get down OK but we have to be able to get back up."

Oldham yelled back. "Get out the ladder, Aiden. We'll have to get back up to use the radio. You wait for the ladder to come down, Zurk. We're lucky the radio still works."

Surveying the situation, Kirsten said, "We are one lucky crew Skipper. We were low on fuel so she didn't blow up. The crew compartment seems to be the only thing that didn't get shredded."

"You're right," Oldham retorted angrily, "It's hard to believe we're alive. But what the fuck happened to the second beacon?" Events happened so fast that the intense fear that overcame Sam when the plane hit didn't last more than thirty seconds and didn't really hit him until after the plane stopped. Despite the near death of the crew, it seemed to Sam little more than the feeling experienced in an auto accident.

One by one they let themselves down. Kelly gave Zurk a hand since he could ouly use one arm. They all huddled under the wing waiting and watching for the chopper. Kelly had the flare gun ready. An hour later, "Where the fuck are they?" Oldham said. "I'm getting really pissed that they still haven't found us. It's getting cold and we're going to have to go back up into the plane soon. Where are they coming from, Istanbul?"

"Maybe from Ankara." Kelly joked.

It was getting colder and a half hour later, the crew was ready to climb back up when they heard the chopper. It must have seen their light and then the flare Kelly shot off. Landing in the clearing next to the crew compartment, the chopper pilot immediately jumped down.

"Sergeant Wilson, sir . You guys OK?"

"Joe Oldham, Sergeant. Very glad to see you. Got room for six of us?"

"Yup, got any gear to take with you?"

"Bags somewhere back there," Oldham said pointing back at the wreckage."

Kelly said, "I'll go up and get what's left of our shit, Joe."

Sam asked, "Would you get my camera bag, Aiden? It's still intact. Besides I want try to to get a couple of shots of this, for posterity. Maybe the chopper's lights will be enough."

"For the insurance company, too," Oldham added, laughing.

Mazurka and Oldham were treated in the hospital. It wasn't until the next day that the Lajes base plane arrived to pick them up. Spending a day at the airport in Adana was an absolute bore. When they got back to Lajes, Major Gsell and Mac greeted Sam with a smile. "Have fun, did you?" Mac said, shaking his hand.

"Ha," Sam answered. "Robbie's motto wasn't quite right. One long drunk and a breakfast? I gotta change that, although I don't recommend adding a crash to it."

"Can you work tomorrow?" Major Gsell asked, then added sarcastically "Or do you need some R and R from your vacation?"

Sam smiled. "I'm good, Major. No sweat. See you in the morning. Right now, I want a drink so I'll take leave of you guys."

Next morning he called Jeri from the weather station. "I heard about it, Sam. Thought I lost my dancing partner, You OK? Didn't hurt your legs, did you?" She added partly joking.

"I'm fine. My golden feet, no pun intended, are OK. It was an experience to say the least. It happened so fast, I didn't get scared until after I let out my breath and we were down and safe. I'll call you as soon as I see what my schedule is. I have to pay back the guys that covered for me."

"Looking forward to it. Glad you're OK."

Sam felt himself dropping into the doldrums from the high adrenalin that pervaded his body from the crash. He took a shower and a shave and wandered into the club dining room where he ran into the crew at a big table. Without asking, he just sat down with them and smiled.

"You send me copies of your photos if they come out. For the insurance company," Oldham said to Sam. "Did they ask you to debrief?"

"No, should they have?"

"Sure. I'm sure they will. So be ready for it. Get out all your notes."

"Right. As we were skidding to a stop, I was taking copious notes as well as interviewing everyone about their feelings."

"Let me know how the pictures come out." Oldham insisted.

Sam replied, "How much do you think they'll pay for a black eye?"

"I'm more concerned about the investigation. They always try to blame it on pilot error. As far as the eye, I'll sue for the emotional pain and suffering, not the eye. My problem," laughing, "is I don't know who to sue. But if only to find out who was responsible for the non-functioning beacon it might be worth a law suit. I hope the investigators find out. Meanwhile, pending the outcome, I'm grounded."

"Do you really think they'll interview me?" Sam asked.

"You bet your ass, they will," Joe answered. "And you better say the right thing."

Sam laughed, "Have no fears. Bad visibility, no beacon. I'll bring my notes."

"Roger that," Joe answered.

Marty and Martha

Marty Redstone was happy yet at the same time, so tense that he wanted a beer. But he had promised Martha that he would lay off until after the wedding. She saw him at his worst and it was hard to believe he had found Martha and she was still with him. There was something about her that hit him hard instantly. Now that they were planning to get married, he was worrying about everything, extending his tour, finding a place to live, getting Martha over, hiding the wedding from her commanding officer, surviving not seeing her after her discharge. The list seemed never ending and he had never been thrust into a situation with so many balls in the air.

But one thing was evident from knowing Marty as Sam found out very early in their relationship. He was incredibly smart. Sam saw it right away the first time he read a note Marty had written. What he lacked in formal education, he taught himself by reading and listening. His command of English was literary. He was at the top of his class in navigation school and got high marks at his first assignment at Kelly AFB. He had only flown several trips when he was tapped by his CO to work in the navigation briefing section. No one could pound out flight plans and wind analyses faster. When Marty joined the group, the wait time for briefings dropped so that there was never a queue waiting for service.

More significantly, Marty was a nice guy and when he and Sam met in the BOQ, the first day they both arrived, their friendship was immediate. It was hard not to like him. By the time Marty's wedding became imminent, Sam predicted that Marty would go far in the air force. He could easily envision Marty as a general fifteen or twenty years hence.

But now, Marty was jumpy. Flying in combat would not bother him like this did. Martha was everything to him and he didn't want to fuck up. She counted on him. That afternoon, he was following leads for living quarters of people who were scheduled to leave in the next six months. He had prepared all the paperwork he would file right after they were married. The chaplain had been arranged. The only thing left was to wait for Martha's arrival. Apprehensive as he was before, he was now excited.

He dialed his phone. "Sam? Marty. Do you think you could take pictures at the wedding?"

"A little difficult getting the ceremony on film if I'm the best man." Then after a thought pause, " I could leave to take the two of you. I could also get someone to take the pictures I'm in. In fact, I know just the person."

"Who?" Marty asked.

"Don't worry your head about it. I'll arrange it."

"Thanks. That's one thing done."

"What else you got to worry about?"

"Right now, I'm looking for quarters to live in. All the paperwork is ready to file to get her over here. I just don't know how long it'll take."

"From what I've heard, the holdup is usually only the living quarters. If you have those arranged, it's supposed to be pretty fast."

"I have to look at a couple in a few minutes. Call you later."

"Good luck,"

The next afternoon, Marty called Sam at the weather station. "Hey Sam. I found a great house for me and Martha. It'll be available in three months, just the right amount of time for me to get her over here." He sounded excited.

"That's great. When is she coming?"

"Next week sometime was last I heard. But I still don't know when."

"Let me know when you find out. I have to find someone to cover for me if I'm on shift."

"You'll be the first to know."

A stewardess appeared at Marty's door after knocking. "Lieutenant, I'm Jackie Birdwell, a friend of Martha's. I have a message for you."

"What's the message? She's coming next week, isn't she?"

"She's very sick and in the hospital. She wanted you to know."

"What's wrong?" he asked anxiously. "How sick is she?"

"They think it's pneumonia but they're not sure yet."

"My God. Thanks, Jackie. I've got to go to headquarters and get some details. You don't mind if I run?"

"Not at all, sir ," she said. Marty frowned at the 'sir'.

He ran out, leaving Jackie standing there, jumped in his car and raced to headquarters. He didn't even stop running to ask, "Hey Jimmy, my fiancee is sick in the hospital in Charleston. Can I find out what's up?"

"She in the base hospital?"

"Yeah," he answered, showing his jumpy lack of patience.

"No sweat. Let me shoot them a telex. What's her name?"

Jimmy typed on the teletype machine as Marty responded, "Airman second class Martha Cantrell."

They waited as Jimmy hit the send button.

"Message sent," Jimmy said. "Now we wait. It might be awhile. They have to call and ask the hospital."

They turned back to the rattle of the typing machine. Jimmy looked at the message. "What's your relationship. Are you a family member?"

Marty thought for a moment and said "No." He was worried that if he said he was her fiancee, she would get into trouble.

Jimmy typed directly into the machine "No, a very close friend."

The answer came back quickly. 'We can only give information to family members.' Jimmy added, "Sorry Marty, not my fault."

"Shit. Thanks for trying." He was becoming frantic. He drove back to his room and called Sam and complained, "What shit is this? She's in the hospital and I can't find out because I'm not family."

"Privacy rules. It's not only military. Did you tell them you're her fiancee?"

"No. I didn't want to get her in trouble."

"Hey. Why don't you call Robbie? He hasn't left yet. He's got a thing going with the red cross lady. Maybe she can do something."

"Great idea. Thanks." His eyes widened as he dialed Robbie at airbase office.

"Major Robbins," came the answer.

"Robbie. Marty Redstone."

"Hey Marty. I didn't get to congratulate you yet."

"Not just yet. I got a problem, Robbie. Martha is very sick in the Charleston hospital and they won't give me any information."

Before he could even ask, Robbie answered, "Let me call Emma, I bet she could find out."

"That's what I was hoping."

"I'll call you back. You in your room?"

"Yeah, Thanks Robbie." Marty paced the floor while he waited. When the phone rang, he picked it up before the first ring was finished, "Redstone."

"Marty, Robbie. Go over to the red cross office and ask for Emma. She says she thinks she can find out for you."

"Thanks, Robbie. I owe you."

"You don't owe me shit. You would have done the same for me. Good luck." Marty rushed to the red cross office where Emma was expecting him.

"I've already made an inquiry. She has pneumonia but it's not viral and it's responding to antibiotics. Her fever's down and she's not in any danger."

"You're a doll, Emma. I can't thank you enough."

She smiled. "I've requested updates if there's any change good or bad. So, I'll let you know if I hear anything."

"Thanks again." He gave her a hug which surprised her and kiss on the cheek and went to the terminal to to tell Sam what happened.

"Lest you think we sit around watching you suffer," Sam said. "Check in with your boss."

"What's up?"

"Just check in."

Marty went next door to Major Kirsch's office in the nav-briefing office. "Hey Major. What's up?"

"Sam told me about your problem and pleaded your case. There's a flight to Charleston late tonight. Gets in tomorrow morning. You want to take it? It's OK as long as you leave Charleston tomorrow night. I can get cover for you for one day. One problem, between you and me. Change into civvies before you go to the hospital. You're her brother."

"Wow, thanks, Major. I really appreciate it." He went to the weather station. "Thanks, Sam," he spoke quietly, as if a weight was lifted from his shoulders.

Sam only smiled and stuck out his hand then gave him a hug.

"Can you get away, Sam? Flight leaves at 2330. Let's have dinner."

"See you later at the club."

The terminal was quiet as Marty, having made up the flight plan for the flight he was to take, waited in nav-briefing office for the crew to check in. Lieutenant Billy Ziegler, the navigator came in and greeted Marty. "Haven't seen you since navigation school," he said. "How do you like it here?"

Without expression, he responded, "You make up your mind to survive and you survive. When's takeoff?"

"'Bout twenty minutes. I heard you were coming with us. Want to sit with us in the crew compartment? You can help a bit."

Marty laughed, "It's been a while since I used a sextant. You gonna let me do it?"

"Why not? Especially since it's probably going to be overcast so you won't see a fucking thing."

"Then you'll be counting on my flight plan and the wind forecast which might get you lost. Pay attention," he added in jest. "You should hope for clear skies."

"Well, maybe we'll get high enough. No, not that kind of high," he added, grinning. They went into the weather station and Jens laid out the weather on their course which at 18,000 feet was overcast for the first third of the trip then clear as a bell the rest of the way into Charleston.

"I guess I might be able to use the sextant," Marty said, as they walked to the plane. The rest of the crew was finishing the pre-flight inspection of the plane and they all walked up the steps of the triple-tailed C-121 Constellation into the crew compartment. The stewardess told the pilot that the passengers were seated and ready to go.

The flight took nine hours and fifteen minutes to touchdown. Marty had gone back to the passenger section and slept for over four hours. He really had no inclination to use a sextant or participate in anything for that matter. His mind was preoccupied with Martha. As soon at he got his bag through customs, he went to the terminal men's room and put on civilian clothes. Billy waited for him and gave him a lift to the base hospital. When he walked into her room, she was wide-eyed and opened her arms to him and grabbed him tight.

"Glad to see me?"

"Am I. How on earth did you arrange it?"

"Actually I didn't. Sam arranged everything with the old man. My problem was finding out how you were. They wouldn't give me information since I wasn't family." He recounted the whole story. Evidently, she was much better.

"I'll be out of here, maybe later today. How long can you stay?"

"Gotta leave today. I have to work tomorrow."

"That's too bad. Let me see if they'll discharge me earlier."

He told her that he found a house, prepared all the paperwork and would file it as soon as they were married. But that was secondary, they were just happy to see each other.

****

Marty's return flight landed at Lajes at 0200. Sam was working the midnight shift when a smiling Marty walked into the weather station.

"Hey," Sam asked. "How is she?"

"She's great. We got her out of the hospital right after I went to see her. Everything's great."

"Never saw you so, I don't know, up."

"That's because I'm a married man."

"What?" Sam was astonished. "Say that again."

Marty continued, "When she got out of the hospital. We went into town, got a marriage license and got married. We'll have some kind of religious thing here when she comes but for now, I can file all the papers."

"What about the fraternization thing?" Sam asked.

"We didn't tell anyone. I found out that filing the papers here for her to come didn't need any details. Her name is now Martha Redstone. That's all they care about. So we have the best of both worlds. She keeps flying so we can see each other and when everything is arranged for her to come, she can resign."

"I'm fucking impressed, you shrewd son of a bitch. Congratulations. Can we say anything here or you just want to fly below the radar?"

"Below the radar. I don't want anyone to know. Even though gossip is rare here, any accidental word to the wrong person could definitely get us into trouble."

"Roger that. My lips are sealed."

"Gotta get something to eat. Haven't had time or the inclination up to now. See you later."

"G'nite Marty. Things are definitely looking up."

Swedish Pastry and German Dessert

"You got five days off? And without taking leave. How'd you manage that?" Mac asked him.

"I covered two days for Jens so he could go to the Frankfurt PX and get a battery for his car. He's paying me back."

"Frankfurt plane goes tomorrow. Why don'tcha go to Copenhagen?"

"Copenhagen? How'm I gonna do that?"

"Easy," Mac answered. "The Scandinavian-Italian express goes from Rome to Stockholm and stops at Frankfurt. Could be a blast. Been many times. Copenhagen is the cat's nuts, especially for a young stud like you."

"Maybe I'll check it out."

"All you have to do is go to the bahnhof. You know the bahnhof, right?" He laughed alluding to Sam's incident with Susan.

Sam frowned."Don't remind me."

"I think the train comes through in the middle of the night some time. They'll know in the Rhein-Main o-club."

Sam listened and let it roll around his mind a little, "I'll think about it. See you later." After mulling it over quite a while, Sam eventually talked himself into going to Denmark as Mac suggested. The decision wasn't easy because he really wanted to see Susan. But he didn't want to give up the opportunity to see Copenhagen before returning to the States.

He always hated the idea of traveling alone, but he had gotten used to it at Dover with his weird work schedule. Nobody ever had the same time off he had. He had come to the conclusion that it he had to travel alone or not go anywhere. The "not go" didn't sit well with him.

The base C-54 landed at Rhein-Main in the late afternoon. Sam went with the crew to dinner at the o-club and went right to the office and asked about the train schedule. The pretty blond German gave him a timetable. "Ze train to Copenhagen shtops at Frankfurt at two sirty in ze morning."

"Are there buses to the bahnhof late tonight?" he asked.

"Every hour at qvarter past."

"It I catch the 0115, that should be OK, right?"

"Ja, zat should be good."

"*Danke*," he said and went to join the crew.

"You work things out?" Dr. Cavanaugh asked him.

"Seems so. I have to catch the 0115 bus to the bahnhof and the train at 0230."

"Need a wake up call?" The doctor asked him. "I've seen guys miss their trains because psychologically they really didn't want to go."

"Nah. No such syndrome with me Doc. I'll get up in time or even better, I won't go to sleep. I can sleep on the train."

Harry Harper, the pilot chimed in after swallowing a gulp of beer, "Buy a second class ticket, even though you can easily afford a first class."

"Why?" Sam asked. "Why shouldn't I treat myself?"

Harry laughed, "You meet people that are more fun in second class. First class people are a drag. First of all, they're usually much older. Then they're richer. Rich people are boring. You go second class, with the people you meet, you'll find out where to stay, where to go for fun. The old farts don't know shit. Besides, the accommodations are not much different. It's usually only the company."

Sam chuckled, "OK, You convinced me. Second class it is."

When they had finished eating, Sam checked in at the transient quarters. He took a shower, shaved and plunked himself on the bed. In a few minutes, dozed off. He awoke with a start. Looking at his watch, he realized he had slept for only an hour. He jumped up, put on his civilian clothes, grabbed his jacket and his packed B-4 bag and decided to catch the next bus. If he was going to fall asleep, it would be in the bahnhof so he wouldn't miss the train. He had made up his mind he was not going to be a Doc Cavanaugh statistic.

Before he left, he called Susan but there was no answer at home. Then he called the Florida Bar. The bartender told him it was her night off. Just as well he thought. If he spoke to her, he might change his mind and stay in Frankfurt.

At 2300, he arrived in the bahnhof waiting room. He bought the recommended second class ticket, went to the newsstand and tried to find something to read, but was thwarted because everything was in German. He was sorry he was traveling light and left his copy of *The Idiot* back at the base. He bought himself a candy bar and sat down on a bench. He watched the passing passengers to occupy himself but soon got bored. He felt himself dozing off and tried to fight it. At about 0130, he dozed off. At a little after two, he was awakened by a German polizei shaking him.

"Dokument, bitte. Sie Kann nicht hier schlafen."

Sam jumped up. He had been sleeping very heavily but when he realized what was happening, he took his passport out of his bag and handed it to the policeman."

"Ah Americaner. Vat are you doing here in ze bahnhof" The policeman handed him back his passport. "You cannot shleep here."

"I'm waiting for the train to Copenhagen. Did I miss it?"

The policeman looked at his watch. "Nein, comes in twenty minutes. Better you vait on ze platform. He pointed to gleis 4. Zat vun."

"Danke," Sam picked up his bag and walked to track 4. Pacing back and forth to avoid the empty bench, he removed the possibility of dropping off to sleep. The train was right on time and he got into a second class car, sitting in a cabin opposite two men who were obviously traveling together. One who was almost bald, offered Sam a cigarette. "Don't smoke, thanks."

"American?"

"Yes, Sam Golden." He stuck out his hand.

"Military? I ask because you are alone. Not usual."

"US Air Force. On my way to Copenhagen. Never been there."

Shaking Sam's hand he said, "Ole Anderssen. This is my colleague Jan Olerud. We are architects returning to Stockholm from a vacation in Rome."

"I have three days to spend in Copenhagen. You guys got any suggestions?"

"Absolutely, you probably should spend a whole day in Tivoli."

"What's Tivoli?" Sam asked.

"I'm surprised you never heard of it. It's an amusement park in the center of town, but it's much more than that. You will see. For hotel, I am not so familiar with them in Copenhagen but I can recommend the Terminus right near the station. A little expensive but not if you have dollars. The place for fun for a person traveling alone like you is probably the Vestergade. No cars. Browse on the street. You see any girls that interest you," he smiled, "follow them into whatever bar they go to."

"It's that easy, is it?" Sam smiled, skeptically.

"It's Copenhagen. I need not say more."

"OK, I'll take your word for it."

Several hours later, the train stopped in Grossenbrode. Ole smiled and got up. "Jan, wake up. Now, we eat," he said in English so Sam understood.

"Where do we go?" Sam asked, a little confused.

"The train goes on the ferry boat now. It goes to Gedser in Denmark. They have the most wonderful smorgasbord. It's worth this trip just for the food," Ole answered. "Are you hungry?"

"Starved," Sam said. "This is a real pleasant surprise. I thought I would have to wait until Copenhagen to eat."

The three exited the train and entered a huge dining room on the ferry. Sam was amazed at the size. The food spread was equally amazing. Looking at the table made Sam salivate. The variety was like nothing Sam had ever seen, even in a gourmet food market. Sam followed Ole on the line, who kept pointing at different items to Sam explaining what each was. Sam's plate was almost overflowing.

"No need to overload your plate. This is an all-you-can-eat spread. You can come back for more." They sat down at a table and continued discussing the food. "You know, smorgasbord is a Swedish phenomenon, not a Danish one. So you get a taste of Sweden without visiting. Although, I think you would probably love Stockholm."

"Next trip." Having wolfed down his whole plate, he got up for seconds. On the line he was behind a beautiful woman, obviously alone, who seemed to Sam a little older than he was. She didn't have the teen age look that women in their early twenties have.

"I heard you talking," she said to Sam. "American?"

"Yes," Sam answered, "Military."

"Where are you stationed?" she asked, as she picked up some gravlax with her fork."

"The Azores. What is that you just took?"

"Gravlax. It's salmon cured with herbs. Delicious."

Sam picked a piece for himself. After filling his plate, the woman said. "I'm Birgit." and extended her hand.

He took it, "Sam," he answered.

"Are you alone?" she asked.

"I'm traveling alone but I'm with two Swedes I met on the train. But I'd be happy to join you, if you don't mind the company."

"I'd like that," she said sweetly.

"Just let me tell them. Where are you sitting?" She pointed to an empty table. "I'll join you in a minute." Sam explained the situation with a smile to his new friends.

Jan answered, "Ah, the fun begins. Let me give you our business card. Should you ever find yourself in Stockholm, we would like to hear from you."

"I certainly will," he said, looking at the card. Sam waved a goodbye at them and carried his tray to join Birgit. She smiled as he sat down. "Tell me about yourself, he said." Sam surprised himself. All through high school and even college, he was shy with women. In Dover, the female situation was so strained that he kept pretty much to himself. Suddenly he found himself comfortable and aggressive.

"You are pretty direct. Aren't you?"

"Sometimes. You seem like the type that doesn't like the indirect approach.? So. Tell me who and what you are."

"I feel like Mimi in La Boheme. You know it?"

"Oh yes," he answered, but your hands are not cold and I want to know anyway," alluding to the first act.

"My name is Birgit Helgesen. I am Swedish. I live and work in the design department of a furniture manufacturer in Malmö. Malmö is in Sweden just across the water from Zeeland, Copenhagen's island. I'm not married. I'm just returning from visiting my friend Ilse in Lübeck. I don't have to return to work until the day after tomorrow." Then after a brief pause, she asked, "And you?"

"Sam Golden. I'm an officer in the U.S. Air Force, a weather forecaster, stationed, as I told you, in the Azores. I'm on a vacation for a few days. I will be discharged at the end of the year and expect to go back to graduate school in mathematics. It was suggested I absolutely must see Copenhagen before I return to the States, so I'm on my way. I, too, am not married. I am from Brooklyn, born and raised there." He took a bite then asked, "Are you a designer?"

"I hope to be. I still have a lot to learn."

"So do we all," he smiled.

"Where will you stay in Copenhagen?" she asked.

"These gentlemen with me suggested I stay at the Terminus right near the station."

"My God, no. I can't imagine why they would suggest that. It's much too stuffy. You should stay at something a little more earthy, more youthful, suitable for someone like you and me, like the Østerport."

"Where is it?"

"Right in town near the Østerport train station. How about I take you there? And if you have any interest in my company, I can show you around Copenhagen this evening. Are you interested in having some company?"

"I'd love it. But I don't want to mess up your plans. What did you have in mind for yourself this evening?"

"I was trying to decide whether to go home to Malmö tonight or spend the night in Copenhagen, have a good meal and browse the city. I haven't done that in a while. Now you've made up my mind for me."

"How come your English is so good? I'm amazed at how fluent you are."

"A necessity. We Scandinavians, like also the Dutch, particularly from a city, know that to communicate with the outside world, we have to speak another language. No one is going to waste their time learning one of the Scandinavian tongues. At one time German was our language of choice. They are our neighbors. Now, we have a distaste of it because of the war, so English has recently replaced German."

"I can understand the Danes. But Sweden was neutral in the war."

"Only in name. Göring was married to a Swede so he convinced Hitler to leave Sweden alone if they remained neutral. There was no love in Sweden for the Germans. So, anybody with an education in

Scandinavia becomes fluent in English. Do you speak another language?"

"Not really. My school French is barely passable. I can understand quite a bit but I would hardly call myself proficient, let alone fluent. I tried to learn a little Portuguese but it's not easy and not really worthwhile since the Azorean accent is frowned upon in Portugal."

The ferry landed and the passengers were asked to return to the train. Sam went with Birgit and when they were settled, he went back to get his bag.

Ole smiled, "Looks like you found a friend, a pretty one at that. These Danish girls are very friendly, aren't they?"

"I wouldn't know, Ole. This one is Swedish."

"Ha. Now I know she's friendly. Have fun and don't forget about our Stockholm invitation."

"I won't. It was great to meet you both." He shook both their hands and left for what he thought would be a more interesting future. Birgit was very interesting and a warm and outgoing person. Europeans surprised him, women in particular. Susan was very engaging and now Birgit. It seemed to Sam that American women were much more guarded and less outgoing with men they didn't know. When they got to the station in Copenhagen and got out, Birgit pointed the Terminus out and reiterated her distaste for its stuffiness.

"There is a train but let's get a cab." she said and waved for one.

Ten minutes later, Sam looked out the window as the cab pulled up to the Østerport train station, right next to the hotel. "Cute," he said as he paid the driver in dollars. When he checked in at the hotel desk, the clerk asked, "For two?"

Birgit answered in Danish and she followed him to his room. "I'll leave my bag in your room while we see the town?"

"What did you tell the clerk?"

"She smiled, "I said I'm not sure yet. Meanwhile, I'll leave my bag in your room.""

"Makes sense. It would be a pain to drag it around with us. Let's go. Where to, first?"

"First, definitely we go to a bank for you to change some money. I saw that you paid the taxi with dollars. That's not a good idea. They charge more in dollars. Then we go to the Langelinie pier to see the little mermaid statue. We can walk."

The weather was pleasant and Sam took everything in. There was something about Copenhagen that made people take to it almost instantly. Birgit told Sam the storied fable by Hans Christian Andersen about the statue.

"What a mermaid in love will do, amazing.

"Andersen was a master story teller. But look at the statue. Isn't she beautiful?"

Sam looked, noticed the mermaid was facing the sea and didn't answer. From there, they went back to the Østerport station to take a train to Tivoli. Tivoli was a wonder tor Sam. There were outdoor shows, amusement rides, restaurants of every ilk. Sam hadn't seen anything like it since Steeplechase in Coney Island. But the feeling was very different. It was a place you passed by right downtown. You could stop in for something to eat or to do. Steeplechase was a destination, a place you went, planning to spend the day. Sam couldn't remember a decent restaurant in Steeplechase. Tivoli was a part of Copenhagen's everyday life. They spent three hours wandering through it, taking rides, watching a circus performance and eating a small meal at a beautiful outdoor cafe.

"I never knew the Danes had such an affinity for food," Sam said.

"It's been said in tourist books about Denmark that when you see two Danes talking, there is a high probability that one was saying to the other 'And then we had...'" Birgit was wonderful company, had a great sense of humor in English, which surprised Sam. Not being fluent in another language, Sam couldn't imagine having a sense of humor in it. "Let's go. I'm tired. I can get a room at the Østerport then we can have breakfast together before I take the ferry to Malmö."

"Good idea. I'm tired as well. It's been a long day, great, but long."

Birgit looked at her watch. "Maybe too late for a train. Let's take a cab. I'll pay this time," she said, waving at a passing taxi.

"Don't be silly." he said, as he opened the door for her. When they got to the hotel, Sam asked her if she wanted to stay with him. "No need for another room," he tried not to seem aggressive.

"I like you Sam and had a very nice evening. But I'm not sure I want to do that."

"Your choice. I just offered as a courtesy," he grinned.

"You are very transparent." She looked at his eyes, lingering a little. "I changed my mind," she said abruptly. "I think I will accept your offer anyway." She took his arm and they went to his room. They took a hot bath together washing each other and then made love before falling into a deep sleep.

The next morning at breakfast, Birgit said, "You know, Sam. I don't ever expect to see you again. I would say if you're ever in Malmö, here is my address and phone number. But that would be expecting too much."

"I know how you feel. It was a beautiful day for me but I can't see a circumstance when I will see you again. We can keep in touch by mail and who knows what life has in store. Will you write, occasionally?"

"Yes, we can be pen-pals," she grinned, sarcastically.

"That's a terrible let down, from intimacy to pen-palitude. The memory of this interlude in my life will remain with me. A letter will only refresh my memory." he said wistfully.

"Mine too. I have to go to make a ferry." She leaned over, kissed his lips very gently. "Bye Sam." She took her bag and he watched while she left the hotel with a brief smiling look back at him. It was a strange, almost clinical goodbye. It gave Sam a shiver.

Birgit liked Sam but tried to be realistic. She wasn't involved with anyone but realistically felt that it was too much to expect any more than she had with him. Better to just end it rather than cling to an unreasonable possibility. All the way across on the ferry, she wondered if she did the right thing being so direct. Too late now, she thought. What's done is done. She did give him her address and phone. One never knows.

Sam wondered how he was going to have a better day than his day with Birgit. He felt today would be a downer. Walking all over town, to Nyhavn, window shopping and eating smørrebrød, the Danish open sandwiches, on the Vesterbrogade. He decided not to return to Tivoli and instead went to the Vestergade as his Swedish friends suggested and followed some people down the stairs to a bar. He was more curious than anything else and was surprised at the familiar American music blaring from the juke box. *The Everly Brothers, Wake Up Little Suzie, Elvis' Blue Suede Shoes*. He sat down at the bar and ordered a beer. He noticed from the English he heard, several American GIs in the bar mixing with and dancing with the local girls. Most of the girls were very young, in or barely out of their teens. But so were the soldiers. Sam felt like an old man at twenty-five.

After a girl, somewhat older, pulled him to dance with her to the strains of *Winchester Cathedral*, she asked him, "What's a cathedral?"

Sam laughed, "You don't know? It's a church."

"A church?" she blurted out and stopped dancing. She called to her friends in Danish obviously explaining the meaning. Then she turned to him, "You spoiled it for me. I liked that song. But, a church," she repeated. "That ruins it. Not very sexy."

Sam sat down at the bar watched the happenings for a while and becoming bored and uncomfortable, he left. He went to the station to check the train schedule back to Frankfurt. He already had his return ticket. The train left in the late afternoon arriving at Frankfurt in the wee hours. It seemed the schedule was built on a planned arrival in Rome in the early evening. To hell with the stations in between. If he caught today's train, he thought, he could spend a day in Frankfurt and maybe see Susan.

Then he fleetingly thought about taking the ferry to Malmö. It might be interesting if only to see Malmö but nixed the idea because he thought it would be too rushed and maybe even weird to see Birgit after the strange goodbye. Then he envisioned that surprising her might be embarrassing. Maybe there was a boy friend she neglected to tell him about, or something like that. He decided to take a leisurely walk back to the hotel, sightseeing as he went, and then he would decide whether to stay the night or catch the train.

By the time Sam reached the hotel, he had made up his mind to take the train to Frankfurt which got there at one in the morning. If it was on time, he could pay Susan a visit. The train ride back was as interesting food-wise as the train to Copenhagen but after the smorgasbord and the setting sun, the ride was dull and Sam was sleepy. When darkness imposed itself, and there was nothing to see across Germany except ugly backyards along the tracks, he fell into a deep sleep and awoke about an hour before the train reached Frankfurt, startled at first that he had missed the stop. He relaxed after he found out from the passengers next to him that they were an hour out of Frankfurt.

The train was a few minutes early and Sam walked to the Florida bar, hoping it was still open. He went in and saw Susan sweeping up. They were obviously ready to close. She openly expressed surprise at seeing him. "Sam. *Himmel*, what are you doing here? We are just closing."

"Just got back from Copenhagen and came to see you. I couldn't come to Frankfurt and not visit."

"I'm really glad you did. Sit. Give me ten minutes and we can get coffee or something to drink. OK?"

"Fine with me." He carried his bag over to a table and sat down watching her. When she finished, she called out to someone and then grabbed Sam's arm and said, "Let's go."

They stopped at a coffee bar in the bahnhof and sat down. "You're not afraid of being with me in the bahnhof?" he asked with a sly grin.

She laughed, "I have proper documentation that will avoid any difficulty. Don't worry. I am not crazy. Tell me about Copenhagen." Sam was reluctant to tell her about Birgit until she added. "I hear the Danish women are lots of fun."

"So are the Swedes." he retorted. "By the way, I called you the other day before I went. No answer at home and it was your day off at the bar."

"I went to the cinema. I saw an Ingrid Bergman film in French. *Elena et Les Hommes*. So you found yourself a companion."

He described the whole trip to her and discovered that she was really interested. Sam at first was a little squeamish until she stopped him at one point and commented, "Don't tell me you didn't sleep with her." At which point Sam relaxed and didn't hold back. She enjoyed his adventure as if living it vicariously. "Sounds like you had a great time."

"Unfortunately, she had to go back to Malmö and I decided after that it would only be downhill from there so I caught the next train, hoping to see you."

"Don't flatter me," she said.

"I'm not. No reason to. You must know I made an effort to see you. Otherwise why come to the bar at one in the morning?"

"When does your plane leave?" She asked him.

"Tomorrow afternoon. About three."

"Tomorrow? Come home with me. I haven't been with a man for months and I need some affection," she said, surprising Sam, who never before received such direct propositions as he had been receiving since leaving the States.

"I can't believe there's no one. Come on, someone as attractive and interesting as you are?"

"Thanks for the compliment, but the war devastated our male population."

"I've heard that. But still..."

She interrupted, "You have no idea of the men that were left for us women. I was a very young teenager when the war was over. Most of my classmates were in the army at the end. They were children and died as soldiers. One of the reasons I hate my father, not even considering the loss, as you know, of my brother. You should see the men that hit on me in the bar every night. You would be ashamed of me if I ever considered any of them." She showed an anger Sam had not seen before, but from what she described it was not misguided. "Come with me." she said, "at least I can offer you a glass of wine. You can't refuse that and I like the company." Sam got up, picked up his bag and she took his arm. He was a little uncomfortable walking through the bahnhof looking over his shoulder. Susan picked up on it. "Don't worry," she laughed, "If they stop us, we'll be OK. I promise."

She had her key ready when they got off the elevator. He followed her in and watched her take off her sweater. "Sit. I'll get us some wine." Sam put his bag down and took off his jacket. The apartment was a tastefully furnished one bedroom and Sam felt comfortable immediately. Susan put two glasses of Liebfraumilch white wine on the coffee table and sat next to him. "Prosit," she said raising her glass for him to touch it. "Let me put on some music. You like pop or classical?"

Before he answered, she put a record of quiet dance music. It was familiar American pop music but created a relaxing mood.

"Tell me about the war," he said. "We in America didn't feel much except rationing and when some of our soldiers didn't come home."

"Are you sure you want to hear it? It was horrible. When the bombings started, the destruction was unimaginable. Then the invading armies, more destruction. There were stories about the Russians in the east with barbaric, vindictive behavior raping and pillaging. My mother and I were lucky being in the west. The allied armies were warriors but were not uncivilized. To this day I have bad dreams. My mother showed no emotion but I could see the hatred in her eyes for my father. We were in Berlin for a while then moved to Stuttgart while my father served the Führer in Berlin. Do we have to talk about this? I try to forget." She leaned over and kissed him. Sam who had not known what to expect after her earlier proposition was not surprised and she added. "Come, let's go to the bedroom. You must have some compassion and make love to me."

Sam got up as she took his hand and led him. They each slowly took their clothes off and Sam commented on her beautiful body. "I was in the BDM, the Bund Deutscher Mädel. This was the girls equivalent of the Hitler-Jugend, the Hitler-Youth. We were kept in very good condition. At the end of the war there were panzer divisions of Hitler-Jugend, teenagers that were all but wiped out." She got into bed first and Sam followed. They made love which was the gentlest, tenderest act he ever encountered. After they both climaxed in a gentle explosion she kissed him, stayed in his arms and said, "That was beautiful, Sam. You have no idea how much that meant to me."

"It was not a chore, believe me."

When Sam awoke about noon, Susan was already up and making breakfast. "Come on, breakfast is on the table," she called from the kitchen. "I left a bathrobe for you on the bed."

Sam put the robe on, went in the kitchen and sat down. Susan put coffee and a croissant down in front of him. Strawberry jam was on the table. For Sam the tragedy was distance. In two days, he had affairs with two wonderful women, both of whom he would love to see again. But distance and circumstance were the obstacles. He sensed he would never see Birgit again. He felt the same about Susan but he felt there was a difference and his mind raced to figure a way around the inevitable result. He couldn't find one.

Maybe he could see her once more before he rotated back to the States. But then what? What it did do was put his feelings toward Fiona into perspective. But the obstacles with Fiona were different. He could see her again if he wanted to. Enough thinking, he told himself.

Live for the moment he tried to convince himself. "I have to go back to the base, Susan." he said.

"Will I ever see you again, Sam? When do you go back to the US?"

"I return the end of April. Do you get any vacation?"

"I get three weeks but I usually don't take it all at once. I would like to take one week in March. The weather is so lousy here, I like to go south, maybe to Italy, al mare," she added.

"If I can get a week, I would like to join you."

"*Wunderbar*," she said. "Do you really think you can? Please don't string me along, as they say in English. I hate vacations alone but I do it anyway because it's better than no vacation. When?"

"I will see what I can arrange and I'll write or have someone call you. I don't have any leave left but I'll try to arrange to take some extra days off. Does that work?"

"That would be wonderful. I will look forward to it. It's something good I can think about." You have my address and phone number, no?"

"Yes, I do." Sam felt he had avoided tragedy if only temporarily. He didn't want it to be a past to be cherished and forgotten. It could also be something in the future. It made going back to Lajes almost bearable. She kissed him goodbye. "Let me hear from you soon, please," she pleaded.

"No question." The goodbye part of this trip was the most painful. With Birgit there was mutual, almost inescapable, resignation early on that they would never see each other again. Birgit was bluntly realistic, but with Susan, there was a cord which didn't have to be completely cut. At least not yet.

The flight back to Lajes gave him time to read. It was better than thinking. Dostoyevski would have to wait. His ride was on a cargo plane bringing supplies back from Germany to the base. Sam was in the crew compartment reading a Time magazine someone had left when the pilot called him to sit in the co-pilot's seat. He was taking a sleep break. "Heard you just had a few days in Copenhagen. How was it?" he asked.

Sam smiled. "It was great and sorely needed. True R and R for me."

"Girls are great, aren't they?" He asked, as if he knew the answer.

"Don't really know, Phil. I met a Swedish girl on the ferry and spent most of the time touring Copenhagen with her. She was a sweetheart. Never had anything much to do with Danish girls. Unfortunately I know I'll never see her again."

"That's the story of our lives," Phil answered. "I hate to tell you how many women I've met away from home that I wanted to see again."

Sam didn't volunteer anything about Susan. It was too personal, too private. But he was happy thinking about seeing Susan again.

Phil got up, "Hold the fort until I take a leak."

"You going to leave me here to fly the plane?"

"George'll handle it. I'll only be a few minutes."

George was the name given to the autopilot, from the *Let George Do It,* Bob Bailey radio drama. So Sam sat there for a few minutes, imagining himself as the pilot and thinking about Susan. It would be a wait but it would keep him in anticipation. For some reason Sam felt like he was more in control of his relationship with Susan than with Fiona.

"Good job," Phil said when he returned.

"Glad I could help," Sam joked. He sat in the co-pilot's seat for another hour before the co-pilot returned from his nap. Sam went back to his magazine.

Sam aimed himself right into the weather station when the plane landed. Jens was working the afternoon to midnight shift. "Hey Sam, welcome back. How did it go?"

"It was great but bitter-sweet. You know, parting is such sweet sorrow. I'll tell you about it later. Right now, I need a shower and a beer so I'm off," waving to Jens.

Jens waved back.

Club Seroza

Next morning, promptly at 1000, Sam called Jeri. "Hey, I'm back. You wanna do this thing? Time's flying and I don't want to make a fool of both of us."

"Sam?"

"Who else? When do you want to meet?"

"How about right now? Are you free for an hour? My house."

"I'm on my way," he answered.

It was a serious hour. Jeri worked him until he was exhausted. "Once more" she said, "then we'll try it together." She put the phonograph arm back to the beginning, They did it over and over until Sam was almost on track. "That's enough for today. You're getting it," she said, "want something to drink?"

"Anything. Water, juice, anything."

She brought him a glass of orange juice, "You're doing great. We'll be ready. When can you come next?"

"I'm working afternoons for the next three days. Any morning is good."

"Let's make it day after tomorrow. Give yourself two hours. I think we can get it done then. After that, just ongoing reinforcement. OK?"

"Gotcha, Boss. I'm drained." He finished his juice.

She laughed. "It'll keep you in shape."

"See you day after tomorrow," he said, as he walked toward the door. Sam was glad that Jeri was all business. He was uncomfortable when he felt she was coming on to him. She was very hot and he was human. The only thing that might have saved him from temptation was that he was just back from a sexually active vacation.

When he returned to her house, two days later, she was still all business and danced him until his feet hurt. Even basketball didn't wear him out like this. But he could see as the session continued that he was not too bad for an amateur, and was certainly getting into physical shape. Enough so that he wouldn't make a fool of himself or both of them.

"Performance is the fourteenth. You're ready to perform. What I want now is for us to get together three or four times on the stage at the club to get the repetition and feeling on stage, which is very different from the house. Pick a time to meet me at the club in the next couple of days. I also need to get my seamstress, Maria, to take your measurements for your costume."

"Costume?"

"Sure. What did you think you were going to wear? Your uniform?"

Sam laughed. "Wouldn't bother me, as long as you wear yours."

"What's mine?" she asked with an eyebrow raised.

"No comment. Seriously, what's the costume?"

"A plaid jacket, a straw hat and a cane. I told you. You have a pair of black slacks, right?"

"You did tell me. I have black slacks. It's part of the officer's standard wardrobe. When do you want to meet next?" Afternoons are better for me the next couple of days," he said. "Mostly working midnight shift."

"Let's do Thursday, about 3 OK? I'll have Maria come."

" You mean 1500, right?" he chuckled. "That works. See you then."

She commented, "You know, you really picked it up fast. I knew I could teach you, but I didn't know you would absorb it that fast."

"I'm an athlete. I'm sure that helped. If only you could teach me some basketball moves," he quipped. "Anyway, thanks for the encouragement. I'll see you Thursday. Bye Jeri."

"Ciao."

Sam had stopped thinking about Fiona completely since he hadn't seen or heard from her for several weeks. But there was more than that. He just didn't know what. Was Fiona just something he talked into himself because he needed companionship and there wasn't any on the island? Susan elicited a different reaction. He knew it wasn't the same thing because he had just spent a terrific time in Copenhagen and Frankfurt. By rights, he should have been satisfied hormonally. But he still wanted to see Susan and made an effort to see her. He hadn't worked out getting a week off yet but would go see the major that afternoon.

Jeri called him to meet her at the club to try on their matching costumes, Up until then, Sam didn't feel stupid. But when he put the costume on, he felt like an idiot. Jeri told him that was one of the reasons she wanted him practicing on the stage. She wanted it in costume. The last time would be a dress rehearsal.

The 14th came and the show went off without a hitch. Before he and Jeri danced *Makin Whoopee*, Marty and Brophy did a *Won't You Be My Little Bumblebee* number dressed as bumblebees and with Frances Gsell, the major's wife, as a flower. And then Aaron Rosen with his handlebar mustache, dressed in a one piece tank-top striped bathing suit, did a turn of the century number Sam had never heard before, *I Love To Go Swimmin' With Women* which brought the house down. After the show, there was a party, a show biz tradition, and Jeri came on strong. Sam was surprised at her change from deadly serious to warm and friendly.

"Mal missed the show. He was on temporary duty at McGuire. Why don't we go somewhere?"

"You think that's a good idea? Where could we go and stay out of trouble? Your house? Child. My quarters? Anyone can see us and you know this is fertile gossip."

"Up to now I've been all business but now that it's over, I really want more of you, Sam. Mal's away two more days. Can you come over tomorrow morning?"

"Why me, Jeri? You're a knockout. You could have any one of the horny guys on the base."

"Most of them are shallow one-dimensional creeps. You're different."

"That's serious talk and you're a married woman," he said.

"I know. But my husband has stopped paying attention and I need the excitement. Now that the show's over, it's a downer with little to look forward to. Am I so hard to take?"

"You know that's not true. And I'm human. I had a thing with a married woman at Dover and it left a very bad taste in my mouth."

"This is different. I promise. I just need an interlude. You're stuck on this island. I can be your friend. Maybe with benefits, we'll see. We can help each other survive this crummy Atlantic rock."

They both noticed that people were watching them. "Listen Jeri, if you want to talk some more, this is not the place. Leave now and meet me at the beach in Praia in a half hour."

"OK. I'll go home and tell the baby sitter I'll be a little late. See you then."

Sam went over and exchanged congratulations with Aaron, then gave Marty a hug. "Great bumbling," he said.

"You were great," Marty said. "A real surprise. I didn't know you could dance."

"Neither did I. I didn't know you could sing. I'm going to bed," Sam lied. "It's been a long day. See you in the morning." Sam left and headed for the beach. When he got there, Jeri, was waiting in her car. He pulled up alongside her and she got out and into his car. Leaned over and kissed his cheek.

"Can I talk to you frankly, Sam? I think I can but I want to be sure."

"If you mean am I discreet, I'm not a talker. Never have been."

"I love my husband and I'm sure he loves me but we have problems I won't talk about. It's enough to say I want and think I need a temporary relationship outside of my marriage. Otherwise, my marriage will fail. And I don't want that."

"A couple to things you should know," he said. "First, I am in a relationship which I would like to intensify and it's going to take some work. Finally, I'll only be here until end of April."

"I'll take what I can get for now. Will another relationship stop you from having a friend, probably with benefits. I can't go running around like a single woman sitting at the o-club bar waiting to be hit on. I got married very early, had a child. Never really lived a free life. I'm not about to start it now."

"You know, Jeri. There were many moments in the last month or so that I thought about jumping your bones and agonized over it. I came to a rational conclusion when I came back from vacation, it was better not to get involved."

"I'm not asleep. I sensed your interest otherwise I never would be talking to you now."

"I'm might be willing to go along with you, Jeri. That would be easy. You are all woman in every sense, and I've lived with feminine scarcity for a long time. In Dover where there were 6,000 guys on the base and a town with a population of barely 4,000. there were a half dozen local girls the proper age making the rounds of the officer corps on the base. I refused to get in line. I went out with the Dairy Queen girl for something to do. Here on this rock for many months, it's been even worse. A friend would be great. No apologies, no excuses, just friends. But for both our sakes, absolute discretion is paramount."

"I agree. Otherwise it would be a disaster. One of the reasons I thought I could get away with it is because I think you can handle it. Am I wrong?"

He kissed her gently. "OK, we have a deal," he said. "We barely know each other. Agreed? Now that the show is over we have no excuses. I saw the piano in your house. Do you really want piano lessons for your daughter? It's a good excuse."

"That would be great. I was hoping you would ask. We can discuss it on the phone."

"OK. Go home now and take care of your baby sitter. I've gotta get some sleep."

"Talk to you tomorrow?" she asked.

"Yup." She kissed him on the cheek, got into her car and he watched her drive off. He asked himself whether he was making a mistake or not as he drove back to the BOQ. A friend with benefits, he repeated to himself. What a concept.

Friendship and Frankfurt, Spring 1958

Marty and Martha's religious ceremony happened at the end of March. Martha was fully recovered from her pneumonia and came over, still in the air force, to marry Marty. The wedding was a quiet one at the Bell house. Chaplain Wilhelm was in on it and agreed to keep mum. They didn't want to jeopardize things by having someone from Charleston find out. Norm had arranged for the food and drink. As Marty had planned, the day after he returned from the quickie Charleston ceremony, he had already filed the papers to bring Martha over as his wife.

Suzanne Bell gave birth to twin boys two weeks later and Sam, who conveniently had the same blood type, agreed to give Suzanne some blood. Norm joked that the Jewish blood would definitely improve the twin's prospects.

Sam saw Jeri as frequently as decorum would allow and she apparently was much happier for it. Suzanne knew about it, being Jeri's best friend, but told no one, not even Norm. Jeri's daughter serendipitously turned out to be a very good piano student which surprised Jeri. It didn't surprise Sam who saw immediately that she had the temperament to take to it and practice diligently. Those kind of students always keep a teacher interested. And it became a reasonable justification for him to see Jeri.

Since Sam bought Robbie's piano, the $88 relic, he found himself practicing every day. He was happier doing that with his spare time than reading the Russians. He never did finish *The Idiot* and somehow thought that he never would.

Sam answered the phone, "Golden."

"Sam, Al Gsell. You got a few minutes to come to the office? I want a favor from you."

"No problem, Major. Be there in a half hour. That OK?"

"Time enough, thanks. See you then."

He wondered what that was all about. He had gotten his orders to report to McChord AFB May 1st. On April 1st, he would be officially FIGMO and would start counting the days. He greeted Leroy and knocked on the Major Gsell's door.

"Come on in, Sam"

"Hey, Major. You called? What's up?"

He laughed. "Happy huh? FIGMO?"

Sam grinned. "Soon, soon. Had to happen eventually, right?"

"Would you be upset if it got delayed a bit?"

"What do you mean? What'd I do wrong?"

"Nothing. Nothing at all. I've got a proposal for you. How much leave you got left?"

"Actually, none. Used it all. I'm trying to drum up 5 or 6 days for a trip to Italy. Not even enough time to spend a few days with my family before reporting to McChord."

"Here's my proposal. Stay the month of May to train yours and Jens replacements and I'll get you two weeks leave. One you can take here sometime before May 1. The other before you report to McChord."

Sam plopped down into the chair. "You're kidding."

"Dead serious." Sam immediately thought about Susan.

"Can I leave the base? Go to Frankfurt?"

"Anything you want. It's your week."

"You got yourself a deal, Major. FIGMO will have to wait a month. Anything else?"

"Nope. I got what I want."

Sam left and called Jeri. "Hey Jeri, my friend. Just so you know, our goodbyes got a one month reprieve."

"What do you mean?" Sam explained the deal the major offered. "So now, except for a week in Frankfurt, I wouldn't be leaving the base until the end of May."

"Fantastic," she answered. "Another month of piano lessons for my daughter."

"You're a scream," he said.

"You believed all my bullshit about friendship with benefits? It was all a ploy to get piano lessons for Janie. Worth the price I had to pay."

"I hate being taken advantage of," he answered with a slight sarcastic tone.

"She's not home yet. Won't be home for another hour. But you're free to come early and wait."

"No thanks. Besides, smart ass, her piano lesson is not until tomorrow. You're very sneaky. I'll call you tomorrow morning to arrange a lesson if that's all right with you."

"That's fine. Talk to you tomorrow," she added snidely,"friend," which made Sam laugh. Even her sarcasm didn't have a personal edginess.

Sam called the air base squadron to check the Frankfurt flight schedule for the base aircraft for April. Then he wrote a letter to Susan telling her that he could come April 15th for six days. Was she available to spend some time with him. He went to the post office to mail it and then to the gym to shoot baskets and hopefully find a pickup game.

After an hour of half court basketball, a shower and shave, he went right to the weather station to work the four to midnight shift. Leroy greeted him.

"Anything I should know?" Sam asked.

"The field is open. Winds seem to be holding. The only thing of significance besides normal flights is there's a guy named Bill Malden flying a Piper Apache to Newfoundland."

"Really. That's a stretch for an Apache, isn't it?

"It's pushing it," Leroy said. "But he seems more worried about navigation than fuel. He asked if he could follow our C-124 flight at 1930 to Harmon. For navigation purposes."

"Follow a C-124. That's crazy."

"No it's not. I asked the C-124 pilot if it was OK with him. He didn't see any reason to object. He just asked what happens if the Piper loses him."

"I told him I asked Mr. Malden the same thing. He said it's no problem if he can keep up with it for a few hours. After that he can manage the rest of fthe way."

"I would think he would prefer a daytime flight."

"I asked him that too. He claims following the plane's lights is easier and that it's easier to lose a plane in the daylight. Other than that, should be a routine night. Oh, I forgot to add. There's a bulletin that there's a burst of sunspot activity generating electromagnetic waves that might fuck up communications."

"Won't that affect Malden's flight?"

"I told him about it. It didn't seem to faze him."

"How's the weather en route? He needs visual at about 8,000 feet, no?"

"Looks fine at least for the first 3 or 4 hours."

"Thanks, Leroy. Go. I'll see you tomorrow." Sam looked over the weather and wind charts. He understood now why Malden wanted to go this evening. The winds were favorable and could shorten the flight by almost an hour from the usual. Sam was preparing briefings for his next two departures when there was a radio call on the weather frequency.

"Casablanca weather, Casablanca weather, come, in please." Three times the call was repeated. Shit, Sam thought, Casablanca is over a thousand miles from here. Way, way out of range. On a whim, he answered the call

"This is Lajes weather, who's calling Casablanca?"

"This is Panam Flight 14 due in at Casablanca in fifteen minutes. Looking for weather report for the field."

Sam looked at the weather map and the plot for Casablanca. "Panam 14. I don't know how in hell you're talking to me but the weather in Casablanca is clear. Winds are 240 degrees, 10 knots. Looks good."

"Thanks Lajes. I can't believe I can't raise Casablanca but got you."

"Must be the solar electromagnetic bombardment I just got an alert about. Messes up communications. I hope you can reach Casablanca control when you get closer. Otherwise, you're in for a wild time."

"Right you are. And you can't help me with Casablanca traffic information, if I need it?"

"You're right about that, Panam. Good luck. Over and out. Hey, Gordo. You got the 700 millibar chart plotted yet?"

"Ten minutes, Cap. I hear you're FIGMO."

"Got extended a month till end of May. When are you leaving?"

"December and my wife's anxious to get back to the States."

Sam answered, "I can't say I blame her. I don't care where I go when my time's up. Just get me off this island. I don't understand some of the people that homestead here, stay for years."

"It's not my cup of tea but I can understand people who do it. They have a reason, usually. Family. Some women, like nurses, looking for a place where there are good odds to find a husband. Cheap living. I can see it."

"I guess you're probably right. I can accept your logic but it's hard for me to understand it."

Gordo answered, "Me neither, Cap. But I see it. Here's the 700. Do your thing,"

"Thanks." Sam sat down at the drafting light table where the map was laid on top of the previous map to see through. "Wow," he said.

"What's up? You look disturbed, Cap," Gordo asked.

"This guy Malden."

"You mean the guy in the Apache?"

"Yeah, him. The winds have changed. He's not getting the tail winds he though he'd get. He's following a 124. Let me see if I can get him on the radio with this sunspot shit that's going on. Piper Apache, this is Lajes weather. Come in."

There was no response until the fourth try. "Apache here, come in Lajes."

"Apache. I just got latest 700 millibar wind analysis done. Your tail winds have dropped off considerably."

"How much, Lajes?"

"As best I can tell, your 50 knot tailwinds for the first three hours are about 10 knots."

"Wow. I think I'm still OK as long as I don't get serious headwinds or get lost. I'm still visual on the 124. So far, so good, over."

"I just wanted to give you a heads up, Mr. Malden."

"Much appreciated. I'll contact you when I land via relay from Harmon. If you don't hear from me, send out a rescue party. As soon as I'm in range of Harmon. I'll contact them."

"Roger, Apache. Lajes weather out. You heard him. If he doesn't get lost, he's OK. Nice guy. I hope he makes it all right."

"Yeah," Gordo said. "He impressed me. He's cool and with a big pair to fly an Apache that distance."

Just then, a crew checked in for debriefing at the weather station. When Sam finished, the stewardess asked Sam quietly, "Are you the officer dating Fiona Mandrel?"

"I'm not sure I should admit that to a Charleston crew. I was, but haven't seen her for some time."

"She hurt herself in Rio. Fell down the steps of the plane in hundred degree weather."

"Really. How bad it she?"

"Hurt her back and broke an arm. She's in the hospital in Rio. She asked me to tell you."

"How long's she gonna be in Rio?"

"Dunno, Captain. The back injury is keeping her there."

"What's your name?"

"Millie. Millie Gerbig."

"Thanks, Millie. I appreciate the news even it it's not good."

"No sweat, sir ," she answered. "I could get a message to her. Anything you want to tell her?"

Sam smiled. "Just tell he to get well quick. Anything else you don't want to hear."

Millie laughed, "Got it, Captain, will do."

Sam was upset at the news but surprised that he wasn't as upset as he thought he should be. He was also surprised that she wanted him to know. He still had some feeling for her but it had cooled considerably given the circumstances and that he hadn't seen her for quite a while. He also felt no guilt that he was planning his trip to see Susan anxiously, but forgave himself as he rationalized that he didn't really owe Fiona anything. She had already indicated by her behavior that she didn't think she owed him any particular loyalty.

Gordo overheard the conversation and when they left, he asked Sam, "Captain, you datin' Fiona Mandrel?"

"Was for a while. Why?"

"I know her from Charleston. Nice kid."

"I agree but I haven't seen her for a while. She hasn't flown through. I just heard she hurt herself in Rio."

"Serious?"

"You mean her injury or our relationship?"

"Relationship. Just curious."

"I thought it was for a while. But not right now. Her visits are very sporadic. I haven't seen her in quite a while. She's probably seeing someone in Charleston. Anyway, I'd rather not say any more."

"Gotcha, Cap. Maps are finished so I'll be leaving, unless there's something else."

"Nah. Take off. See you tomorrow."

The rest of the shift was busy and flew by quickly. When Mac came in to relieve him at midnight, he couldn't believe the time had passed so fast. He told Mac about Malden in the Piper.

"I remember him. He did the same thing about six months ago. Guy's a little crazy to risk it. Followed another plane then as well."

"Anyway, I told him the winds weren't as good as when he left. He said as long as he didn't get lost, he was OK."

"He won't. He's a very good navigator."

"Then why is he following a 124?"

"Lazy. Why do it when someone else is doing it for you?"

Sam laughed, "Have a good one. I'm leaving."

"G'nite Sam. See'ya later."

The King and I

The sun was out and the day was balmy. He met Leroy who was leaving the BOQ at the same time. "Where you going?? Leroy asked Sam.

"The club for breakfast."

"Dining room closed. I'm going to the mess hall. Come on."

"Why is it closed?" Sam asked. "That's strange."

"Word is that King Saud of Saudi Arabia has stopped here on his way to the States. Treatment for his eyes. They have to clean and arrange the whole dining room to conform to islamic dietary laws."

Sam responded angrily. "Why do we kiss his fucking ass? That anti-semitic prick. Because of him I had to wait in 120 degree heat on the tarmac at Riyadh airfield for two hours."

"I didn't know that. Why?" Leroy asked.

"I'm a Jew. I didn't have baptismal papers to show at the terminal so they wouldn't let me in the air-conditioned terminal. Where is he staying?"

"I heard a few rooms at the BOQ. They moved a few guys in the end rooms out temporarily to house him and his entourage."

"I wish I could do something to inconvenience the mother-fucker without getting myself in trouble. I would even accept a reprimand as long as it didn't get me a dishonorable."

"Like what?" Leroy asked. "What can you do? They'll arrest your ass. Hey look. Here comes his limo now."

"Can we go into the club?" Sam asked.

"Yeah. Only the dining room is closed."

"Let's go. I wanna see this prick." Sam said.

"OK, OK." They went in the front door of the club. The limo went around to the side door. When they got inside, there was a small crowd waiting to see him enter the dining room. Several minutes later, his huge entourage came down the hall to the dining room. There were plain clothes American bodyguards, Saudi bodyguards in arab dress. The king was right in the center, a very dark skinned man with thick glasses and an arrogant look on his face, staring back at the crowd watching him, as if expecting everyone to kneel. He was decked out in a pure white outfit with white headdress fitted with gold band.

"I hate that guy. I really wish I could do something. When is he leaving?"

"Tonight, I think."

"So after he eats, it's back to his rooms, I assume. What else can he do?" Sam speculated.

"Probably right."

"Let's go eat. When we come back, I'll see what mischief I can drum up."

All during the meal, Sam was preoccupied with the king. When they got back to the BOQ, Sam smiled when he realized that the king's quarters were across the hall from his. They had four rooms. Sam didn't know which room the king was in but felt he could make enough sound to annoy him. He went through his records and found his record of Israeli music which had a wonderful version of Hatikvah, the Israeli national anthem, sung by Al Jolson.

He listened in the hall and could hear the din being made by the king's bodyguards so Sam assumed the king was actually in his room. He put the record on, carefully put the phonograph stylus on Al Jolson and when it started, opened the door to his room, turned up the volume and laid himself down on the bed with his hands behind his head. Before the song was finished two air policemen were looking over him on his bed.

"You have to turn down the music, Captain and close your door."

Sam got up instantly. "Why is that?" he asked.

"sir , we got a call from the Saudi entourage across the hall that the music was bothering them. Would you turn it down please."

Sam turned down the volume and closed his door. "It was intended to bother that anti-semitic, arab prick."

One of the policemen laughed. "I can imagine, Captain. But I'm afraid that the king is our guest and we are disturbing him."

Sam repeated his story. "Because of that miserable bastard, I had to sit in 120 degree sun on the tarmac at Dhahran airfield for two hours. I was certainly inconvenienced. It's just payback time."

"We hear you, sir . But you can't do that. So please, this is only a warning. If you continue, we will arrest you."

"Can I knock on his door and tell him to go fuck himself? I'll do it quietly."

Both the police laughed. "Sorry, we can't let you do that either. You know that, sir . So please don't make things difficult. We have no love lost for the man either. You have no idea the hoops we've had to jump through yesterday on short notice."

Sam turned off the record player completely. "OK, OK, I get it. I'll behave."

"Thanks, Captain. Don't turn us into bad guys," one said, as they were leaving.

Sam smiled as he waved goodbye to them. Just then, Leroy came into his room. "Police just leaving, I see. Happy now?"

"I would assassinate the mother if I knew I could get away with it."

"What good would that do?" Leroy asked. "There are 60 or 70 princes, just as bad. waiting to jump into his spot. I hear his half-brother Faisal, next in line, is really evil."

"Yeah, I heard that, too. I just couldn't do nothing." he answered sadly.

"Let it go, Sam. He'll be gone tonight and be only a memory. You can spend your energy hoping they fuck up his eyes at the hospital in the States. That'll give you something to do. Meanwhile, let's go to the gym and shoot around."

Vacation in Italy

Sam got the letter from Susan he was anticipating. She confirmed that they were meeting in Frankfurt on April 15th, the day the base plane was scheduled. They would have six days together. The plan was to go to Rapallo, enjoy and be tourists in the mild weather and return to Frankfurt.

Sam was a combination of excited and apprehensive. He really liked Susan and the chemistry was very intense, but he knew so little about her. His feeling was that she was genuine – that what he saw was what he was getting. But he was wrong about Fiona, so his confidence was a little under par. He wondered whether this whole week together was a bad idea, too much and too premature. Maybe after a day or so they would just be tolerating each other. He thought about maybe after a week with her, they wouldn't even be talking to each other. That was certainly possible.

His relationship with Fiona which started out so warmly progressed rapidly to weird. Maybe he had read more into their relationship than there really was. Considering the lonely Lajes syndrome, it wasn't surprising. He thought clinically, not emotionally. Her responses had given him every indication that she requited his feelings. That's what puzzled him. Had he read it wrong? In any case, it was moot. She hadn't flown through for over a month and lately there weren't even any letters. Now with her injury and message, he knew he wouldn't see her for a while. That she sent him a message puzzled him more than anything else. There had been for Sam, a drought of companionship for a while. Then came a mild deluge with Copenhagen and Birgit, Frankfurt with Susan and lately his friend Jeri whose only fault for Sam, and a big one, was that she was married.

****

Susan was a combination of excited and puzzled at her own feelings. She had not shown any interest in any man for a long time but Sam, as little as she knew about him, got her excited again about the possibility of loving. Not that she loved Sam, she knew she didn't.

But somehow he had removed the wall she had put up since the war. She realized she could finally feel again, whether it was Sam or someone else.

She looked at herself in the mirror before she left to meet Sam at the bahnhof. For the first time in a long time, she actually cared about her appearance. She wanted Sam's interest for some unexplained reason.

The plane landed at Rhein-Main in the evening and they met at the bahnhof at midnight. She had bought the train tickets. His anticipation had been uncomfortable. He had jumped into the unknown. But when he was with her, he was glad to see her. She was more stunning a woman than he remembered with a new hair do, blond shoulder length and with a genuine ear-to-ear smile. When he first met her, her hair was tied back in a businesslike pony tail. But now, it was as if she cared and seemed happy to see him.

They slept most of the train ride to Milan which arrived in mid-morning. Before their train to Rapallo, they treated themselves to a pastry and cappuccino at the Stazione Centrale. The connecting train arrived at Rapallo in the afternoon and they checked in at the Hotel Astoria where Susan had made reservations.

The week was idyllic at first, but instead of getting annoyed at each other, as they each admitted to their respective selves, the relationship grew more serious as they got to know each other. She was completely open about her life, her past and her family. Sam was equally honest but when he courageously told her he was a Jew, she laughed raucously.

"What's so funny? Does it matter to you?"

She answered, "I am not laughing at you. For me, that you are a Jew matters not at all. I laugh because if our relationship ever became permanent, it would be the ultimate irony for my father. He does not like Jews, which is why der Führer loved him so much. Does it matter to you that I am a Catholic?"

"No. Unless you are a practicing Catholic and insist on my being the same."

"*Himmel, nein.* I haven't been to a church in well over five years. You?"

"My family is Jewish, not practicing but identifies strongly. I go to major events occasionally mostly for traditional and nostalgic reasons."

The week flew by. They went to Portofino and Santa Margherita and seemed to appreciate the same things. When they were packing, she started crying. Sam was surprised because gentle as she was, she seemed so in control. "What's wrong?" he asked her, wiping a tear off her cheek.

"I have not felt this way in a long time. I was only thirteen when my teenage love was killed on the Russian front and it took me a long time to recover. I would never let myself get so deep into a relationship. Young as I was, the pain of the loss was terrible. I can't imagine another."

"So why cry now?" he asked.

"I really don't want to lose you and I feel that it's inevitable given our separate lives, different cultures and especially the distance. I am trying to savor this week."

"I've thought about the same thing, Susan, but maybe we can persist. If we both feel the same way, it's worth a try?"

"Do you really feel the same way?" She looked at him.

He put his arms around her hugging her tightly. "Let's see what we can arrange. These days what with being in the air force, the concept of distance seems much smaller. I return to the States end of May and will probably go to northern California. Why don't you think about making a trip this summer."

"Really?" She smiled and kissed him. "I'll see. You are serious, aren't you?"

"Oh yeah," he said. "Not something to joke about." They finished packing and got a cab to the station. They waited an hour for the train to Milano. The connection was almost perfect. The train to Frankfurt arrived five minutes after they arrived at Stazione Centrale. They just made it. The ride back to Frankfurt was bitter-sweet. Both their thoughts were warm, tender and sad. They didn't know what the future had in store for them. They fell asleep almost immediately and were awakened by a uniformed German.

"Deutsche Passkontrol. Dokument, bitte."

They responded but couldn't fall back to sleep so they made small talk the rest of the way. They had discussed the serious aspects of their relationship already and didn't want to rehash the conclusions.

All during the flight back to Lajes, Sam basked in the memory of the previous week. Just as a curiosity, he was puzzled that he still hadn't heard anything from Fiona except Millie's relay. He was not at all upset. Between his feelings for Susan, his friend Jeri and not seeing or hearing anything for a long time, his interest in her had all but disappeared.

Later that week, he got another letter from Susan reminding him of his promise not to let distance keep them apart. He really liked Jeri but tried to repress any deep feelings because he knew it would only be a problem. He would take the companionship with benefits selfishly and enjoy it while he could. His warm feeling for her made the relationship not only easy to take but desirable. She had really become a good friend and confidante. Janie took to Sam as well.

As he pulled up at Jeri's house, he saw their car parked outside and continued on. He stopped at the gym to work out, then called her. She answered, "Hi Sam. Janie'll be home at two thirty. Piano lesson then. If it's OK?"

"Got it. See you later." Sam went back to the club for coffee and to cash a check, then back to the BOQ. His planned morning was preempted by an obvious necessity so he decided to hit the piano for a while, then catch a nap before the piano lesson. Just as well, he thought. He didn't get to sleep until after 0100 anyway. Piano lesson at 1430 then to work at 1600.

When he pulled up to Jeri's house, he saw Mal's car in the driveway. This was the first time he was surprised like this. Up to now, Jeri always had things carefully controlled. It's not that they saw each other that often, They didn't, but there was never a conflict. He wondered why Mal was home. He got to the house, and as planned he gave Janie her lesson and Mal was impressed. "How much is my wife paying you?"

"We haven't agreed on a price, yet. I really do it for something to do. One has to keep busy on this fucking island. But she insists on paying me something so I told her we'd arrange a settlement before I leave. I'm rotating end of May. You know Janie's got some talent."

"I had no idea."

"You wouldn't unless she takes lessons or she's a genius and teaches herself." Noticing Mal's arm in a sling, he said, "What happened?"

"Wrenched my shoulder trying to move a huge x-ray machine. Doc said I should keep it immobilized a day or two. Pisses me off. Fucks up my golf. You play?"

"Rarely. Major Gsell drags me out to the course every once and a while. Usually after working all night. He's my CO so I go. But I'm a city boy. Golf is not my thing."

"So am I, but I love it. So much so, that Jeri gets pissed off at me."

Schmuck, Sam thought. He messes up his relationship with Jeri for golf? He could understand if he'd been married for years, if his wife had let herself go and he couldn't get it up. But none of those things was true, even though Mal hadn't hit thirty yet, Sam couldn't vouch for the getting it up part. "Anyway, say goodbye to Jeri for me. I'll see Janie next week. I hope the shoulder feels better."

"Thanks, Sam. Take care."

Sam felt a little better. First because he was sure Mal knew nothing about his friendship with Jeri and also because he saw Jeri's problem. Mal's a good guy but as a husband, he selfishly is a golf fanatic. Sam made up his mind that before he left, he would insist Jeri tell things to him straight.

Next morning, he called Jeri. "Hey, how's tricks?"

"Sorry about yesterday. I was surprised."

"Nothing to feel sorry about. Want to meet me for coffee at the club?"

"That would be nice. When?"

"Now."

"Give me half hour to make myself beautiful."

"No need. Come as you are."

"I don't think you'd want that, at least not in the club."

Sam chuckled, "OK, see you in a while." Sam was reading the newspaper when Jeri came up to his table and sat down. "You succeeded," he said.

"At what?"

"Making yourself beautiful. She frowned and ordered coffee. "Tell me, does Mal know how angry you are at him?"

"I'm not angry at him."

"Don't bullshit me. You wouldn't be so hungry for friendship if you weren't. Isn't just a little of our friendship revenge? Just a little?" He made a "little"sign with two fingers. He is a nice guy but he thinks you're a little pissed off about his golf but not really angry."

She didn't say anything. Then after a pregnant pause, she said, "I guess I am."

"Why don't you tell him what's bothering you? Tell him directly."

"I tried once but he didn't get it. He didn't take me seriously."

"Try again. He's your husband."

"Frankly, I will. I intended to, I really did. But what I have with you, I don't want to give up."

"You're going to have to. I'm leaving in a month and unless something unusual happens, we will be relegated to an occasional note or phone call."

"I know that and when you leave, I'll do it. I'm not going to find a friendship like we have. It was a gift and I'm not going to turn my back on it. As long as I have it, I'm going to savor it."

"I wonder. It's certainly made my life more bearable on this island. But maybe if we weren't such good friends, you would have to face the music."

"Tell you what. Let's enjoy the short time we will have together and then I promise I'll tell him how I feel."

"Promise?"

"Promise, cross my heart. You know, I got married at eighteen. He was the only guy I ever slept with."

"Why did you get married? Actually, I should probably ask him why he married an eighteen year old."

"We were in love and would have waited until he finished medical school and I finished college but I was pregnant with Janie. I never lived alone. I went from my parents' house right to marriage. I think, in the back of my mind, I felt I missed something."

"So you want to live a bachelor's life without giving up your marriage?" He raised an eyebrow.

"Sounds terrible when you say it like that."

"Just trying to be realistic. Sorry."

"Let me be realistic for a change. Mal's going to Santa Maria tonight. Surgery in the morning. Can you come over for a visit tomorrow?"

Sam smiled. "You know, Jeri. I wonder what would have happened if you weren't married. Between us, I mean."

"I've thought about it myself but it's not a good idea. It's an interlude and I try to put it in perspective."

"I just think about it from time to time. Idle speculation."

She got up. "Nuff said about that. See you in the morning?"

He shook his head and she left abruptly. Sam watched her leave, continued to think, nursed his coffee and went back to yesterday's NY Times brought over by a crew the night before.

Next morning, Sam decided not to park in Jeri's driveway. The lack of discretion was beginning to bother him. She let him in, closed the door and kissed him. "What's that all about?"

"Sam. I have strong feelings for you and I know it's going to be over very soon. But before it is, I want you to know it. Up to now, it's been friendly with sex. But it's more than that to me. She put her arms around him and hugged him tightly. He cupped her head in his hands and kissed her gently.

"I'm not going to fight you on that. I have the same feelings," Sam said. He picked her up and carried her into the bedroom. "I want to remember you. I want to cherish this period in my idle moments regardless of where my life goes." He slowly undressed her and carried her to the bed. He undressed himself, got in beside her and began to kiss her all over. The passion built slowly and inexorably. Sam had come to a serious realization that a man, at least he, could be in love with more than one woman. How that would affect his life, he had not the slightest idea. But this epiphany was undeniable.

****

Susan was happy. The vacation in Italy was wonderful and Sam seemed like he was really considering things between them on more than an ending-soon basis, she began to let her feelings overcome her. Things were different for her. She wanted to believe Sam, that he would keep up their relationship but despite his promises, doubt often crept into her head. When she entered her apartment, the phone was ringing.

She put her packages down. "Hallo."

"Susan, it's Papa."

"This is really a surprise." She felt her throat tense up. "It has been a long time. How are you?"

"Fine, thanks. And you?"

"I'm fine. Why the sudden call?"

"To see how you are and what you are doing. Are you still working at the bar or have you found something more suitable?"

"No. Still at the bar. It pays well."

"If you come to Berlin, I'm sure I can find something closer to your talents and education."

"No way, Papa. I'm fine here in Frankfurt."

"Any love prospects in your life?"

"Nothing that would interest you."

"I have heard you just got back from a vacation in Italy. How was it?"

"How would you know that, Papa?" she perked up. "You keeping tabs on me?"

"You might say that, You are my daughter. I have my sources."

"Stay out of my life. And stop spying on me. I am none of your business," she answered with her voice raised.

She hung up on him. Several seconds later, the phone rang again. She picked it up. "Leave me alone," she said.

"Susan. I have heard that you were on vacation with an American, a military person. Is that true?"

"Yes, it's true. What of it?"

"I have also heard that the relationship is serious and he is a Jew. Is that also true?"

She could not figure who knew so much about her and Sam. She told no one. "Yes, if you must know. It is."

"You know I cannot tolerate that, Susan. Much as I would like to see you married, I cannot permit you to marry a Jew."

"What do you mean you cannot permit me. My choice is my own. I don't need your permission and it's not about you. I have nothing against Jews. And he is a wonderful man."

"I cannot permit it."

"Once a Nazi, always a Nazi. Right Papa?"

"I will not permit it. It will be an embarrassment to me."

"It's not about you. It's my life and what you think does not matter to me. I am not your concern and you certainly are not mine. You are responsible for Eric's death, my only love, for Karl's death, He was my brother and it destroyed Mama. And I haven't even said anything about being complicit in the destruction of Germany, serving that madman."

"I was only a soldier doing my duty."

"That's what Sam said, defending you. Yes, you were a soldier, a vicious, anti-semitic, Nazi soldier. I cannot forgive the damage you have done. You were fortunate you were not tried for war crimes at Nürnberg. But you still have to live with what you did, but without me. Goodbye Papa. And please don't call me again." She slammed the phone down.

The phone rang again. Susan did not answer it. She was angry and at the same time melancholic and she couldn't control the tears that welled up. She began to pace and scour her activities the last weeks to see if she could identify the person spying on her. Her boss? She never told him about her vacation with Sam. Who knew about Sam being a Jew? That took more than casual keeping track of her. But who? It was a stone wall. She began to worry for Sam's safety. She would put nothing past her father. He could be vicious.

****

Sam wanted to see Susan again before he left for the States, both to reinforce his own feelings and perhaps allay Susan's fears. He worked out another three day getaway to Frankfurt in early May. He was looking forward eagerly to surprising her. But when he boarded the C-54 he could feel the winds picking up. Shit, he thought, just my luck the field will close. He sat down and looked out the window and the scud rolling by above him. Just as the plane got to the end of the runway ready to take off, the pilot announced. "Sorry, people, operations just closed the field. The flight is delayed. I ask you to remain in the terminal until we know whether it will reopen. As soon as I know, I will announce it.

Sam went to the cantina and got himself a cold drink. As soon as he sat down, it was announced that the flight was cancelled and rescheduled as soon as the field opened again. Disappointed, Sam drove back to the o-club and camped himself in the TV room.

Fiona and FIGMO

From the moment the flight to Frankfurt was cancelled, Sam buried himself in working as much as possible. He was tough on the new arrivals whose training he had agreed to undertake. He covered for anyone wanting some time off and obliged the major as often as he asked for company at the golf course. In between, he practiced his piano seriously and made a daily notation which became an occasional letter to Susan.

On a rainy afternoon, Jeri met Sam in the dining room of the officers club.

"Open for company?" she asked standing over him.

"Sure," he signaled her to sit with an open extended palm.

"We still friends?" She asked him looking at him. He could see the discomfort she was feeling.

"Of course, Jeri. I apologize for not calling. I'm not the greatest of company these days. I didn't think I wanted to subject you to my blues."

"You're only going to be here a few weeks more. Do you want to end our friendship like this? Besides, Janie asks for you and wants her piano lesson. I'm not making it up."

Sam smiled. He told Jeri about Susan and what had transpired. He was still apprehensive that he wouldn't see her again even though he had made a commitment. "I thought at one time I loved Fiona and that's pretty much finished. I just think this whole environment is a false reality, that I can't take anything seriously. The up-and-down feelings and second thoughts are making me miserable. And not to treat it lightly, I have very strong feelings for you. I've never been so fucked up."

"Look, I understand full well what you are going through. I think about our friendship and that it's a factor in saving my marriage, believe it or not. I know what I have to do as far as Mal is concerned, but I don't want to think about it until you leave. I don't think that's wrong. We all have to do what's necessary to survive. Otherwise we die."

He looked at her and for a long time, said nothing. Finally he sat back and said, "You're probably right. It's just hard. I'm not a prick at heart, Jeri. I can't mitigate my problems at the expense of someone else."

"Look Sam, maybe it's selfish of me. But we have something special and it has a finite duration. I don't want to give it up until I have to. Come tomorrow afternoon for lunch then you can give Janie a piano lesson." She smiled and added, "I'm being transparent on purpose. Besides, you aren't going to find your reality until you get the fuck out of here. This island is poison. As long as you're in the forest, you can't possibly see the trees."

"He had never heard her use the word. "OK," Sam said. "1300 OK?" he added in military time.

"I'll save my thanks for tomorrow. I really think we can help each other get through this. You're FIGMO but not ready yet for the breakfast," alluding to Robbie's philosophy.

"I am ready for the drunk part, though. I really miss him," Sam said. "He always had a word of wisdom when I needed it. I wonder how he's doing."

"I'm sure he's fine," she said. "He's been through this kind of thing several, if not many times, so he knows how it turns out. We, unfortunately, don't have his experience so we are not confident about walking off into the sunset singing *Smile*."

The next few weeks were better for Sam and Jeri. They made the most of their benefits and were philosophical about his leaving. But they did agree to keep in touch, one way or another. He gave her his parents address and said, "I can always get a message there, even if I'm not there." As Sam discovered, parting is sweet sorrow only if you can agree that it's not really the end.

The day arrived and Sam had checked the last day on his FIGMO calendar hanging on his door. He had packed everything up and was ready to leave. He had said his goodbyes and had his metaphorical breakfast. When he got to the terminal, the stewardess approached him, "Captain, I'm sorry but we have a full flight and a courier needs a ride to McGuire. He has priority and the captain told me that we're going to have to bump you. Maybe there's a later flight you can take."

Sam checked the schedule. There was only one flight and it was fully booked. "Shit," he mumbled. The operations officer said, "Sam. There's a flight tomorrow. It's pretty full but I think they may be able to fit you in."

"Put me on the manifest. I've already had my breakfast."

"What?" he said.

Sam laughed, "Local joke, never mind." He went to the club and ordered a scotch and soda."

Fernando said, "Captain, isn't it a little early for you?"

"Yeah, I guess so, Fernando, but this is a special occasion." He sat there for three hours nursing drinks. But then decided to go back to his room and continue his drowning. He stopped at the package store and bought a forty ounce jug of Johnny Walker Red and took it back to his room.

Two hours later, he was feeling no pain. He had already said goodbye to Jeri and Janie the day before and wanted to leave it at that. Jeri had started writing him a check for the piano lessons. He stopped her and said, "Part of the benefits. Make sure you get her a teacher and keep up the lessons. I'll call from time to time, about Janie, of course, to check." She had given him a goodbye kiss. Sam really wondered again if a man could love more than one woman at a time. There was no question in his mind that he loved her.

The knock on his door was not intense. He hoped it wasn't Jeri. "Hi Sam," Fiona said. "You're still here I see. Want some company?"

Sam was drunker than hed ever been in all the time he was at Lajes. "Sure, why not? Come on in," he was slurring badly.

When she saw how drunk he was, Fiona said, "Maybe I better go."

"Nah, I'm OK. I was bad before. Now, I'm under control."

"I just wanted to say that I'm sorry for how I treated you."

"How are your injuries? Recovered?"

"Pretty much, It took a while but I did a lot of thinking in the hospital. Do you think there's something there for us to start again? I've missed you."

"You'd never know it. Not a word, no letter, no message. Nothing. You know how bad communications are here. You had to make some kind of effort."

"You're right. I was dating a guy at Charleston but it died while I was in the hospital. It was pretty quick."

"I can understand him bailing."

"Why do you say that?" she asked with a touch of anger in her voice.

"You probably did to him what you did to me. No loyalty. Selfish."

"That's not fair, Sam."

"Sorry, but that's how I feel. So, tell me, why no message?"

"I don't know. Embarrassed, something like that."

"Not a fucking word. What did you expect me to do?" Sam recalled mostly the negative feelings not hearing anything and getting word from another stewardess that she was seeing someone else. But it wasn't pain.

"I would like to pick up again, Sam. Can we?" she said as she put her arms around him and kissed him. Sam wasn't so drunk that he was oblivious. It could have turned into a wild night but Sam started drinking again. They both got into bed and Sam reacted instinctively to her touch. It didn't take long for him to be so out of it that he soon fell asleep in bed. Fiona left early in the morning, but she had written down her address and phone number with a note.

Sam

I'm really sorry the way I behaved. I would like to keep in touch. Getting back together would mean a lot to me. Please call me when you get back to the States. I don't want to let our relationship die like this.

Much love

Fiona.

Sam intentionally didn't tell her anything about his life without her. He had been angry with her but no longer. He didn't want her to feel any of the same pain he once felt. He had little taste for being vengeful. When he awoke in the morning, he was badly hung over. He wanted to get some coffee and something to eat and then get to the terminal to check the flights. He remembered that he no longer had his car, which was down at the dock to be shipped to the States. He poured himself a tumbler of scotch and promptly fell asleep again with his clothes on.

Marty and Aaron McGee found him out of it. They tried to get him up but he was too gone. They both lifted him up, got him dressed and dragged him to Aaron's car. Marty got his B4 bag and his small bag and put them in the trunk. When they got to the terminal, they still couldn't wake him. Aaron handcuffed an attache case to his wrist and wrote a note. He got a piece of Scotch tape from ops and taped the note to the case They dragged him up the steps and sat him in an empty seat near the back of the plane and told the stewardess he was going to McGuire, and to please take care of him.

Arrival in the States

Sam rubbed his wrist where the handcuff was and walked into the reassignment office. He presented his orders to the clerk at the desk who told him to have a seat. Several minutes later, he was called into Major Bleifuss' office and sat down.

The major looked up at Sam after reading his orders. "When were you called to active duty, Captain?"

"I believe it was August 28, 1954, Major."

"That's what I thought. I just wanted to verify that. You know, you only have 89 days left on your duty tour?"

"I knew it was about three months, but wasn't aware of the days."

"I can't reassign you."

Sam perked up. "What do you mean?"

"I have to separate you. You have less than 90 days. Your tour is over."

Sam suddenly realized that being bumped one day put him in that situation. "I was supposed to return yesterday, Major. Would that have made a difference?"

"Yes. I could have reassigned you yesterday."

"That's not fair, Major. I got bumped yesterday by a courier. I was looking forward to going to McChord."

"I'm sorry, Captain. You win some, you lose some. I'm preparing your DD-214. In ten minutes, you'll be a civilian with considerable severance pay."

"There's nothing you can do? You can't make a small error?"

"I see on your record that you were tendered a regular commission. That offer is still valid If you were to accept that, I can reassign you. But that means another tour, at least 4 years more."

"That doesn't work for me." Sam got up and paced a few times back and forth. "Doesn't make sense, Major, to commit to four years just to see the west coast. How do I get to Brooklyn from here?" Sam asked sadly.

"There's a bus to the Port Authority terminal in New York City. Can you make it from there?"

"I should hope so."

"Is this your address of record? We need to know where to send your personal belongings from Lajes and to notify you when your car arrives. Right now, everything is aimed at McChord. We have to shortstop everything."

"That's it. My parent's house. That address works."

"OK. Give me a few minutes to get your paperwork done."

About ten minutes later, Major Bleifuss came out of his office. "Here's your DD-214, a card for your wallet and a check for your severance and unused leave pay. Good luck. Any plans?"

"You're not serious, Major. This was sudden and a surprise. I haven't had time to even digest it, yet."

"You'll work it out, I'm sure. Good luck, Mr. Golden." He emphasized the Mr., smiled and stuck out his hand. Sam, a bit shell-shocked, shook it and left. The last thing he needed now was to be doted upon by his mother. His mind was already making plans. He hoped he could get into graduate school for September and find something to get him out of the house this summer.

Sam wasted no time. He went to the NY State employment office two days later and they offered him a very well paying job as a meteorologist in Lagos, Nigeria which he immediately turned down. They sent him to TWA at Idlewild airport. The manager of the weather station hired him almost instantly. He was happy. That would keep him occupied and pay rent on an apartment, at least until graduate school in September.

Summer of 1965 Past is Prologue

Sam was poring over some work he was doing to prepare a paper for presentation. He was stuck. There was a flaw in his proof and he couldn't find it. Bach's English suites were flowing out of the radio and were distracting him. As he went to turn it off, the host announced a young people's competition and concert at the 92nd Street YMHA with a group of teenage pianists competing on Saturday afternoon. The list of performers meant nothing to him until he heard the name Jane Buczynski .

He stopped, a little stunned. "Holy shit." he mumbled and called the Y. Then he called home. "Hey hon. There's a concert at the 92nd St. Y on Saturday. One of the performers is a girl, a six year old, I gave her first piano lessons in the Azores. She'd be about thirteen now. I'd really like to go."

"Saturday's bad for me. Sam. I've got two clients in the afternoon. But why don't you go?"

"You sure you don't mind?"

"Course not, *Liebchen*. Should be interesting to see one of your proteges in action after all this time."

"I'd hardly call her a protege but I did get her started."

"Go. The babysitter will cover."

When Saturday came, Sam had difficulty keeping his calm. He didn't want to show his feelings. He was excited, but at the same time he was anxious. It wasn't hearing or seeing Janie that caused his attack of nerves. That was gratification enough. It was the possibility of seeing Jeri, seven years after their goodbye. He had fought the temptation all these years to find and call her.

He said goodbye to his kids, kissed Susan and drove to Manhattan. He was lucky to find a parking space a block away and bought a ticket as close as he could get to the stage, on the keyboard side. He decided to go backstage after the performance and not before. He scanned the audience looking for Jeri but didn't see her before the lights were dimmed.

There were five contestants. Janie came out third. Sam was stunned by the beautiful young woman she had become even at thirteen. He had been anticipating seeing the six year old, which was recorded in his consciousness. She had obviously inherited the best of both her parents. She played two Rachmaninoff preludes and showed even more talent than Sam had recognized. He was anxious waiting for the last two contestants to finish. During the last performer, a fourteen year old boy, he made his way to the back of the stage and the waiting area. While they were waiting for the winners to be announced, Janie was first to spot Sam and her eyes lit up. She ran to him and gave him a prolonged hug. Sam looked up and saw Jeri, beautiful as ever, walking toward them.

"'Who told you about this?" Janie asked.

"Heard it on the radio. I wouldn't have missed it for the world. You were great. Where are you studying?"

"Daddy's stationed in Texas. Van Cliburn took me on as a student, three years ago."

"Wow. Nothing but the best. I'm sure he's very proud of you. I certainly am."

"You really think I was good?"

Just then, they announced Jane Buczynski as the winner of the competition and were signaling her to come out and get her prize. When she went out, Jeri looked at Sam, walked up to him and after an uncomfortable delay, they embraced, a long silent one. "How are things, Jeri?"

"Great, Sam. Mal and I are fine. I missed you. When you left, I laid things right on the line. I had no choice. You were right. He had no idea how angry I was."

"I'm glad. I think about you often and resisted trying to find you."

"Same with me. What we had was a great memory and I'll never forget but it's past. "How are you?"

"I convinced Susan to come to the States and married her. Got my PhD, now teaching at Rutgers. Two sons. Very happy." He took out a business card and gave it to her. "If you think we can be friends with sweet memories and without pain, call me. Seeing you now, I think I can deal with it. I would also love to follow Janie's progress."

She looked at the card. "Let me think about it. If you don't hear from me, you'll know why?" He nodded. Janie came running back with her certificate and an envelope, smiling.

"Look, Mom." Jeri and Sam looked at the certificate. Jeri opened the envelope and looked at the check.

"This'll certainly help," she said. Looking at Sam, "And thanks for everything from Janie and me. You'll never know what it all meant."

Sam fought the tears welling up. "I"ve got to leave. Janie, keep it up. You've got the stuff and I'm very proud of you. Keep me posted. Your mother has my address."

Janie hugged him. "I'm so happy you came. I really missed you."

He gave Jeri a hug, looked at her, smiled and said, "My best regards to Mal."

"Will do. Bye Sam."

When he got home, he asked, "Busy afternoon?"

"Busy, but good. How was the concert?"

"It was great, Janie actually won. She's studying with Van Cliburn."

"How did that happen?"

"They're stationed in Texas and she auditioned. I knew she had talent and the temperament but I didn't have any idea how much. It'll be interesting to follow her career." Sam had never told Susan about Jeri and still felt uncomfortable about doing it now.

****

Several weeks later, Sam was reading the NY Times editorials when Susan came into the family room.

There's a call for you, Sam. Fiona Mandrel," His wife handed him the phone with a grin on her face.

He held his hand over the mouthpiece. "Fiona? If you're joking it's not funny." He had told her about Fiona before they got married so she recognized the name. Was this going to be one of those years where weird things happen? Janie and Jeri and now this? He removed his hand from the mouthpiece, "Hello."

"Hi Sam, Fiona, a voice from your past. Remember me?"

"Of course. How on earth did you find me? I can't believe this."

"I couldn't at first, but there was once an envelope in your room, a letter from your sister. I remembered her married name. She apparently still lives in the same place. I looked her up and called her. She gave me your number. How are you? Was that your wife that answered?"

"It was. We got married in '59. Two kids, boys," he volunteered. "What made you call?"

"I don't know. Just thought about you and thought it would be interesting to talk to you. I live in St. Louis. I'm getting married next month."

"Congratulations. What did you do after I left Lajes? I got discharged at McGuire and went back to graduate school."

"I thought you were reassigned to McChord. I called the weather station there looking for you."

"I was, but never got there. You remember I told you I got bumped from my flight. By getting bumped I wound up with only 89 days left. So with less than 90 days, they wouldn't reassign me. I was discharged on the spot. It was unexpected and disappointing. I hadn't made any civilian plans. I really wanted to see the far east on Uncle Sam's dollar. But such is life. It worked out all right. What did you do?"

I ... went to St. Louis after my discharge. Didn't want to go home for many reasons, some you're aware of."

"Why St. Louis?"

"I had a girlfriend there who offered me a place to stay until I could get myself … adjusted to civilian life and settled." Her answers were hesitant. Sam felt she wasn't telling him the truth or at least not telling him everything.

"When did you get out?" he asked.

"A few months after I saw you last in Lajes."

"Why'd you get out so soon? I thought you had another year and a half to go."

She hesitated again, "Had enough. I was ready to leave. I asked for a medical discharge and they gave it to me. My back was kicking up." Her discomfort was evident to Sam. She suddenly seemed to be anxious to cut the conversation short. "Anyway, it was good talking to you and let me give you my number in case you ever feel like reminiscing."

Sam wrote the number down. "Great to talk to you, Fiona. I wish you the best on your wedding. Take care."

"What was that all about?" Susan was listening to the conversation.

"Very strange. I had the feeling she wanted to say more but the fact that I was married stopped her."

"I should hope so." Susan gave a sarcastic smile.

"No, I don't think it was to try to rekindle a relationship. She's getting married next month. I don't know. It wasn't a random call. Of that I'm sure. But let's drop it. The past is past. Maybe she'll call again and tell me what she called for in the first place. I could call her back. Meanwhile, with Janie and now Fiona, this has been a weird year."

"You better not call her back." Her answer made him grin. She was too secure to be the jealous type.

"Where are we going for dinner?"

"Let's eat Italian for old time's sake."

"It won't be the same, you know that. It's not Rapallo or Portofino."

"Let's do it anyway, Liebchen." she said, giving him a hug. Sam was sure after seven years of marriage that he had done the right thing. Susan had given him the support he needed to get his PhD, besides working to help support them while he was in school. After he began teaching, she got certified as a therapist and found clients easily. She did not have to work at a bar.

Her father was beside himself with her marriage to a Jew. She cut him off and had nothing to do with him for the seven years she had been in the U.S. and was happier for it. At first she was worried that he might do something drastic to Sam. He was still a Nazi. But he must have accepted the result and was content that she had broken their relationship completely, which saved him embarrassment. She was sure he had retired from the wehrmacht by now so he had less explaining to do. She was able to think of her mother and brother with happy memories instead of reminding her of her hatred. She missed her mother and was sorry she did not get to see her grandchildren.

"Take the kids? Or baby sitter?" he asked.

"Baby sitter. I'll call."

Epilogue 1987 - Elizabeth

Sam was in his office at the university grading exam papers when he got a phone call from home.

"*Liebchen*, you got a call from someone that says his wife is looking for her birth father."

"What? Seriously?"

"I'm not kidding. We played geography. Mother's name was Fiona Weldon, maiden name Mandrel. Ring a bell?" she said dryly. "He asked if you were ever in the air force."

"My God. Fiona, again, after all this time? You're not serious? Let me call him. What's his name and number?" He wrote it down and called. "This is Sam Golden. May I speak to David Rosenbaum?"

"This is David. Glad you called back, Sam. My wife has been looking for her birth father. She was adopted and recently found out who her mother was, but discovered that she died. Her name was Fiona Mandrel. My wife, after a hectic search using a detective agency, was able to see the adoption papers without the names blacked out. One Sam Golden, Captain USAF is named as the father."

"Wow. That's wild. When was your wife born?"

"February 1959. Does that make sense to you?"

Sam did arithmetic from his last drunken night with Fiona. "It certainly does and explains some things. This is wild. But why is she so determined to find her birth father?"

"Why don't I put her on the phone. You can ask her yourself. She's was so uptight when I found you, she insisted I do the talking."

Sam waited a few minutes and then "Hello, Sam. This is Elizabeth Rosenbaum, call me Liz."

"Hi, Liz. This is as weird and unexpected for me as it is for you. I'm curious. Why are you so anxious to find your birth father? From what

I've read, most adopted children are content to accept their adopted parents and leave it at that."

"My birth mother. as David told you, was Fiona Mandrel. I was placed for adoption in St Louis. The religion of the father was listed as Hebrew. Missouri law stipulated that if either birth parent is Jewish, the placement has to be with a Jewish family. So I was adopted by Maurice and Sarah Cohen, who are very much alive, I should add."

"But why look for your birth father so intensely?"

"I have two children, a boy and a girl. As far as I know, they are the only blood relatives I have. For some reason, it drove to me look for my birth parents. I became obsessed. I was raised by a Jewish family and I'm married to a Jewish guy. I found my mother but found out she died at 42 of cancer and that she wasn't Jewish."

"Did that bother you?"

"Only because I was raised Jewish. You know Jewish law says the child carries the faith of the mother. I was looking for my Jewish roots. And that's my father. Do you think you might be my father?" she asked dolefully.

"I certainly could be." Sam answered, his mind trying to recall everything. "The timing is right." Sam explained their relationship and described, with some embarrassment, the last time he saw Fiona. He remembered being too drunk to care if he used a condom. But if she was pregnant, she never told him. He also told Liz about the odd phone call from Fiona about 20 years earlier. His sense then was that she wanted to talk more but changed her mind. "Maybe she wanted to tell me the real reason she got discharged in 1958 which in retrospect, I guess, she wanted to tell me she was pregnant and had you, but couldn't get herself to do it."

"Then there's a good chance you are my father. Are you Jewish, as the adoption papers claimed?"

"Both sides of the family. I don't practice the religion much. Occasional Yom Kippur service. My sons were both Bar Mitzvah but that's the end of it."

"You mean I have two brothers?"

"If I'm your father, you sure do, Julian and Edward."

"Wow. Can you send pictures? I'll send you some." They exchanged addresses.

Sam added, "You know, they have these DNA tests now. We should probably have one to confirm things. But first let's look at each other's pictures. In fact, I have photos of your mother. Do you have any?"

"You do? My God, That's a miracle. I have no idea what she looked like. But do it right away," she asked. "Please. It means a lot to me."

"I can imagine. I'll send what I have tomorrow morning. I have them home." Sam's phone line was blinking. "I have to hang up, Liz, I have another call coming in. But I'll keep in touch. It was quite a surprise finding out about you. I still have to digest it."

"Promise you'll send pictures right away?"

"I Promise, Liz."

"Bye, Sam. This was amazing. I still can't believe it."

THE END

Author's Comments

This story is based on many true experiences and events, some of which have been presented exactly as I remember them. Others are based on real events but have been fictionalized. For the reader it will be difficult to know which is which. I wager that the readers speculation about what is true will be wrong for the most part. And I will not reveal the truth.

Major Albert (Al) Paul Gsell Jr. was my real commander at Lajes. He served in World War II, Korea and Vietnam and retired as a full Colonel. He was a real gentleman and one of the best bosses I ever worked for military or civilian. I found him years later via the internet and kept in touch with him until his death in 2010.

The characters are based on real people or composites although some of their actions have been subjected to dramatic license to make for a better story.

Much has changed about the island of Terceira since the 1950s. It has become a tourist mecca mostly for Europeans. The dingy looking, depressing air terminal from those days, is now a beautiful airport. The primitive beach at Praia da Vittoria where I came very close to drowning, has evolved into a mooring area for yachts. Since the stroke in 1968 of Portuguese dictator Antonio Salazar and the subsequent military overthrow of his oppressive regime in 1974 the economy of Portugal as well as that of the Azores has been socialized and has improved dramatically.

American transport airplanes rarely stop over at Terceira these days but one thing has not changed. The miserable weather during most of the winter is still miserable.

Other Books By The Author

Corviglia, Murder in the Alps

The crown prince of Iran has been kidnapped on the ski slopes of St. Moritz and a young girl has been murdered. Henry Cain, a detective living in St. Moritz has to find the prince, hidden high in the mountains, and bring him back alive to the Shah to earn a huge payout. And then to find the murderer, a promise he made to the girl's mother. Years later, the murderer, having escaped, seeks revenge endangering Henry and his family. Confronted face to face by the furious killer, Henry is moments from death.

The Kieran Adventure Series

(For young readers, 10 and older)

Kieran Cummerford a young teenager discovers a weird window in his father's workshop, a portal to another universe. He risks going through the portal without telling his father leading to dangerous consequences. In Book 2, the Cummerfords are visited Rajilad a refugee from another universe. A genius scientist, she is fleeing from her director. In Book 3, Rajilad stabilizes the portals with controls and creates a time warp device allowing time travel in any of the universes. Kieran and a group of young adventurers visit a UFO sighting in the past and almost lose one of their numbers who is sucked up to the UFO. In Book 4, another portal appears and they are visited by two huge 7 foot robots from a universe where humans are extinct and the universe is inhabited by very advanced robots. The robots go back in time to find out why humans disappeared.

Book 1 – Kieran and the Weird Window

Book 2 – Kieran and the Visitor From Pimglammam

Book 3 – Kieran and Rajilad's Time Warp

Book 4 – Kieran and the Robots.

Solomon's Dozen

(Adult Fiction) Solomon Nassau, a 70+ widow, depressed from the loss of his wife comes out of it, decides to be pro-active and, inspired by the opera and legend of Don Giovanni, emulates the Don's womanizing creating his own legend. A dozen of his adventures are reported in salacious detail by the author who tracks him down and interviews him.

Moffett's Wife

Marcella Moffett's son, Michele, is accused of murdering his business partner and convicted. Knowing he is innocent she sets about to find his killer herself, after the authorities close the case. She devises an unusual but very dangerous plan and with the help of her sister and a brilliant friend of her son, discovers not only the killer but also a huge plot to steal millions from his company. Marcella also exposes the judicial corruption which led to Michele's conviction.

The Super

Monte Leonard, a gentle giant of a man in his 50s with a history of drug addiction, alcoholism, sex offense, the mob and prison becomes the superintendent of an apartment building. The story involves his relationships with tenants, his boss and girl friends. He is in love with an alcoholic who comes close to destroying him because he can't live with an addict. His life is a mess because he can't shake his past. No matter what he does, his past haunts him. He is accused of rape by his girl friend, arrested for murder and generally harassed by the police. His life is a fight to live a normal quiet life.

The Amerada Affair

NSA Manager Sarah Tepper discovers a computer account that she can't get into. No one in the agency knows anything about it and there is apparently no owner of the account. In trying to access it, it results in a strange murder. With assistance from the NYPD and an Italian cyber expert, she makes progress. But as she gets closer to finding out what's happening, she realizes that her life is in danger.

About the Author

Alan Wallach is a scientifically trained, former computer consultant who is now a prize winning author. He lives with his wife in Englewood New Jersey where he writes every day, broken up only by cooking, early morning basketball and practicing the piano, which has always been his first love.

Winner of the Lorenzo Nash prize for middle school readers with his four book Kieran Adventure Series, he will begin Book 5, which he intends as a full length novel for young readers.

You can find him at www.alanwallach.com or email him at alanwallach@gmail.com. He would like to hear from readers.

Made in the USA
Middletown, DE
13 February 2024

49028686R00144